Getting Old Is
the Best Revenge

Rita Lakin

A DELL BOOK

GETTING OLD IS THE BEST REVENGE
A Dell Book / April 2006

Published by Bantam Dell
A Division of Random House, Inc.
New York, New York

Map and ornament illustrations by Laura Hartman Maestro

Book design by Karin Batten

ISBN 978-0-440-24259-8

Printed in the United States of America
Published simultaneously in Canada

www.bantamdell.com

10 9 8 7 6

This book belongs to
Gavin and Howard,
my sons, who have blessed me
with their loyalty and their love

"Senior citizens. People say they don't know how to drive. You think it's so easy to maneuver a car on the sidewalk?"
> —*Jack Rothman, 78, Los Angeles, a new stand-up comic*

"Comedy is tragedy plus time. These funny people have a lifetime of things to say."
> —*Judy Carter, teacher of stand-up comedy for seniors*

"I'm very earthy and I sing earthy songs."
> —*Estelle Reiner, 91 (wife of Carl, mother of Rob), discussing her late-in-life cabaret career in an interview in* Time *magazine, December 2005*

Building Q-Quinsana

IDA 319 GLADDY 317 SOPHIE 314

TESSIE 216

CASEY & BARBI 118

mailboxes & elevator

DENNY 119 IRV & MILLIE 114

ENYA 219 EVVIE 217 BELLA 216 HY & LOLA 214

MARY 314

mailboxes & elevator

Building P-Petunia
Lanai Gardens

Sol Spankowitz lives in Phase Three.
Jack Langford lives in Phase Six.

Gladdy's Glossary

Yiddish (meaning Jewish) came into being between the ninth and twelfth centuries in Germany as an adaptation of German dialect to the special uses of Jewish religious life.

In the early twentieth century, Yiddish was spoken by eleven million Jews in Eastern Europe and the United States. Its use declined radically. However, lately there has been a renewed interest in embracing Yiddish once again as a connection to Jewish culture.

bubkes	nothing, worthless
fakackta	dirty
gevalt	cry of distress
kvell	glow with pride
kvetch	whine, complain
maven	know-it-all
mensch	a person of wealth and dignity
meshugas	craziness
meshugeneh	crazy
pupiks	navel, belly button; a term of teasing endearment
putz	penis

rugallah	pastry
schlemiel	a loser
schmaltz	grease or fat
shmuck	penis
shpilkes	on pins and needles
shtups	push, shove; vulgarism for sexual intercourse
tchotchkes	little nothings
vantz	bedbug; (slang) a nobody
yenta	busybody

Getting Old Is
the Best Revenge

1

Death by Double Bogey

Margaret Dery Sampson, sixty-four, always said the seventeenth hole would be the death of her, and she was right.

Let's not mince words. Margaret cheated at golf. After all, being wealthy (inherited, not earned) meant being entitled. It meant always getting what she wanted. And what she wanted was to break the women's record for the course. She had a feeling today would be the day.

Wrong.

She was with her usual perfectly coiffed and outfitted foursome—rich women who played every Friday at the exclusive West Palm Beach Waterside Country Club. It was a beautiful, perfect Florida day. The lawns glistened in the sunlight. The weather was not too muggy. Margaret was playing brilliantly. All was right in her world.

One of Margaret's techniques for enjoying the game was to golf only with women who played less skillfully than she did and were easily intimidated.

She knew her caddy saw through her, but she didn't care. He was the caddy everyone wanted, so she paid triple in order to get him at her convenience. He was worth it. The money bought his loyalty. When things went wrong, she blamed him.

So here was the dreaded seventeenth hole and all she needed was a bogey. Unfortunately, here too was a troublesome serpentine water hazard. She routinely selected her best balls for this hole, but that never helped. Invariably she'd hook the ball before it cleared the water, and it would land in the trees. Today was no different. With angry, imperious strides, she marched into the foliage, leaving behind her the timid catcalls of the gals. "Meggie's done it again!"

As her caddy began to follow, she waved him off.

Yes, *Margaret thought,* I'll get out of it! *No way would she take a penalty.*

To her dismay, she discovered her ball wedged hopelessly in a clump of decaying turf. Without hesitation, she kneeled to pick it up.

"Naughty, naughty," a strong baritone voice chastised.

Startled, Margaret turned her head to find a pair of snappy argyle socks at her eye level. She stood slowly, preparing her defense. When she saw who the other golfer was, her expression turned to happy surprise.

"Well, look who's here. I didn't know you be-
longed to our club."

Abruptly, he grabbed her, pulling her against
him with one hand as he expertly shoved a hypo-
dermic needle into a vein with the other. Moments
later, Margaret stopped struggling and sank down
onto the dark and mossy rough.

Her last, dying thought was that she should
have used the three iron instead of a wood.

One parting shot was irresistible to the killer.
"Sorry I ruined your day, Meggie, but you shouldn't
toy with a man's game."

2

I'm Still Here

N ever Trust Anyone *Under* Seventy-five! We
Take Care of Our Own." That's the motto of
our brand-spanking-new Gladdy Gold Detective
Agency. Because, if I've learned anything from the
traumatic last two months, it's that once you are
"old" you become invisible.

It opened my eyes to the fact that senior citizens had no representatives in the crime department. They were sitting ducks. No one cared. Who
could they turn to when in trouble? Who was old
enough to understand their problems? Me. If not
me, who? If not now, when? *Tempus* was certainly
*fugit*ing. I was their only hope.

It all began when I realized someone was mur-
dering the elderly widows of Lanai Gardens, Phase
Two, Oakland Park Boulevard, Fort Lauderdale.
Right in my own backyard. I did go to the police,

and although Detective Morgan Langford was young and adorable, he treated me like I was faded wallpaper. He didn't believe me. There was no motive. The women were all over seventy-five, so naturally they must have died of old age. Besides, who'd want to kill old ladies? he asked me. The general attitude? We're all on the checkout line anyway.

Well. I showed him with the help of the girls: my sister Evvie and my friends Ida, Sophie, and Bella. I use the term "girls" loosely. They're so old, they think they invented Medicare.

I proved there was a killer. And guess what? I identified the killer. And guess what else? Along with the somewhat decrepit senior residents of all six phases of our condo complex, we actually captured said killer.

It woke us up. No more sitting around waiting for the day we leave this mortal coil and go wherever it is we go from here. We're not dead yet and there's lots more living to do. That's why I started our detective agency. Boy, did it get the juices running again. We can't wait to get up in the morning and see what new adventure awaits us. Hey, we're the new "Old."

My experience for calling myself a P.I.? I read mysteries. I've read hundreds of them. With Carl Hiaasen and Edna Buchanan as my Florida gurus, how can I fail? Though, hopefully, I won't run into any of Carl's creepy alligators.

We made the headlines in the *Broward Jewish Journal* and got on local TV, and now the phones won't stop ringing. If you missed us the first time around—well, I haven't got the strength right now to tell you the whole story. But if you happen to be in Fort Lauderdale, ask anybody to direct you to Lanai Gardens, and drop by for a Danish and a cup of coffee. I'll be glad to fill you in. That is, if I'm not napping.

By the by, I picked up a boyfriend along the way. The very sexy, very tall Jack Langford. Not bad for a gal who sees her eighties looming ahead. But oh, when the girls found out—what aggravation...

Well, enough gossip. So, say hello again to Gladdy Gold, now the oldest living private eye in Florida—or anywhere else, for that matter.

3

Nothing Has Changed.
Everything Has Changed.

It's eight A.M. and my girls will be stirring. I walk outside my apartment and do my warm-ups. Evvie, perky and raring to go as usual, pops out of her apartment door across the courtyard, one floor down. I see her glance very quickly at my door and just as quickly avert her eyes, and I know what she's thinking. Is my new boyfriend, Jack Langford, in there? Falling in love has complicated my life. But not to worry, I will tell all. I won't leave out a single juicy detail.

I call out to her, "Morning, Ev. How goes?"

"Same old, same old," she calls back to me.

Thanks, Evvie, for not asking the question I know you're dying to ask.

Some sisters can look at one another and it's like staring in a mirror. Not the two of us. I've got Dad's looks, with straight brown (now gray), boring hair. I inherited his ways of thinking, too—logical and conservative and bookish—and his temperament—easygoing.

Evvie takes after our dramatic, excitable, emotional mother, as do her fiery red curls. She was always addressed as "my pretty one." Thanks a lot, Mom. I was pretty, too. So just because you were always mad at Dad, you ignored me?

I traveled down here from New York because Evvie's husband, Joe, was leaving her and she needed my support. I never intended to stay, being a dyed-in-the-wool New Yorker. But I needed a change of pace. I'd allowed myself to wallow in the tragedy of my life much too long. I could not shake the horrific circumstances of my husband's death and I was sick of my own self-pity. Even my daughter, Emily, told me to go, though it was very hard leaving her and my grandchildren.

I was sure I'd miss New York, but I never looked back. Instead, I became a stuck-in-the-swamp retiree, taking care of a bunch of gals in their second childhood who insist they need me. They drive me crazy sometimes, but I do love them.

Speaking of the gals, here comes Ida, sprinting down the walkway behind me. She has this way of shooting out of her apartment like a rocket, her tight, skinny body ramrod-straight, her stiff gray bun bobbing.

"Is *he* here?" she snaps in that snippy tone of hers. No subtlety with Ida. She has no problem staring at my door as if she has X-ray eyes.

I always ignore the question. But that doesn't stop the asking.

Next, Bella, our dear, oldest member, with her wispy silvery hair always elegantly coiffed, barely squeezes open her door to make sure Evvie is already on the landing, then tiptoes out. Taking little mincing steps, she walks behind Evvie. Bella's my only ally. But she joins the Jewish Greek chorus anyway. Smiling at me sweetly, she calls in her little, wavering voice, "Where *is* he, that darling *mensch* of yours?"

Sophie is always last. In the old days, pre-private-eye business, she had to be bandbox perfect before she'd let one exquisitely shod tootsie step out her door. Now she's so afraid of being left out of any new development, she's less careful. There might be only one eyebrow penciled in, or one cheek rouged. Her hair, this month's color, Wild Strawberry Blonde, is flying every which way. But she will make it to exercise on time.

With hands on hips, Sophie takes her turn to confront me. "So where's Jack? Did he sleep over last night?"

Sleep over? I feel like I'm fifteen again and all my teenage friends are jealous because I have a boyfriend and they don't. I met Jack at the grand opening of a new mystery bookstore while waiting to have my car fixed. I took one look at him and tried not to drool. Wow! Tall and elegant, waves of salt and pepper in his gray hair. Eyes that you could sink into and never come back. And he admitted he'd lusted after me years ago when he saw me at a

New Year's Eve party in Lanai Gardens. Instant fireworks!

When I got home I was too chicken to tell the girls that some good-looking guy had picked me up. A man who lived in Phase Six! I knew how they'd *kvetch* and I didn't want to hear it. Now that they know, boy, have they been laying on the guilt trip. Not that I don't have enough guilt of my own.

Yet, how can I be mad at them? Their men are gone. Just about all the men around here are gone. We lost three more last year, and three more lonely widows joined the rest of us.

On the other hand, what am I supposed to do? For the first time in many years, I find myself feeling something for a man. And yet, I'm still torn. How can I love again, even now?

"Nice day," I say pointedly.

"Let's get the show on the road," says Evvie, trying to move us along.

Sophie grumbles. "I still don't know why we have to exercise. All we'll do is die healthier."

"I like jogging," says Bella helpfully. "It's nice to hear heavy breathing again."

And so we begin our daily fifteen-minute version of exercise. We head downstairs, walk around the apartment building once or twice, each at her own speed. It's not much, but, as my darling Francie used to say, something is better than nothing. It was she who encouraged us to exercise to keep healthy. She was my best friend. Francie died two months ago and I still cry for missing her.

Today, like every day, the girls and I walk. We talk. We rest. We walk and talk some more. And nowadays there are only two topics that hold the girls in thrall: Jack, and our new private-eye biz.

"You're not doing too badly for a start-up company," Jack told me. "It's looking good." He was kissing me long and hard at the time he said that, so all I could do was mumble my agreement. Gee, is this man sexy...but I digress.

Business. Last month we found a lost pocketbook for a hysterical senior in Wilton. We retraced her steps and found it where she left it, hanging with all the other purses in the handbag department at Kmart.

We solved the mystery of the elderly cousin from Sunrise who disappeared. Turns out the relatives had a fight and she spitefully didn't tell them she was going to the Bahamas for the weekend. Like that. And more of the same. It's really nice helping people, but I'm waiting for a case that gets the heart racing.

We have a business meeting every morning after exercise and swimming. Need I say, it's what the girls live for. So, naturally, they try to rush through the exercise part.

"Is it time to quit yet?" Ida asks, puffing away, her flip-flops flapping.

"Yeah, *oy*, am I exhausted." This from Sophie, who has hardly flexed a muscle.

"Me, too," Bella, the jogging *maven*, adds as she sways daintily along.

The girls begin their cool-down exercises.

Sophie halfheartedly bends. She complains, "If God wanted us to touch our toes, he would have put them near our *pupiks*." Two bends, she's done.

Four sets of eyes look up at me hopefully.

"Swimming first," I remind them.

"Do we have to?" Pouting, Sophie repeats this every time.

But they disperse, hurrying back to their apartments to get into their bathing suits.

So here they are, my girls. My business associates. I already have nicknames for them—my private eye-ettes: my sister, Evvie Markowitz, a regular female Sherlock Holmes; Ida Franz, Miss Stubborn, great for in-your-face confrontation; Bella Fox, the Shadow, dressed always in pale beige or grays, hardly anyone ever notices her. Perfect for surveillance. And last, but certainly a major player, Sophie Meyerbeer, our Master of Disguise. She lives for color coordination.

I dread today's meeting. Jack said he was dropping by with a present for me.

That should make the fur fly.

4

More Swimming

And here we are at the pool. And there they are, the other early morning so-called swimming enthusiasts. Their lounge chairs parked in their usual spots on the grassy perimeter of the pool, guarding their tiny turfs jealously.

Plump Tessie Hoffman, the only real swimmer among us, is energetically doing her laps.

Enya Slovak, our concentration camp survivor, has her nose buried in the inevitable book.

The Canadian snowbirds are gathered together in their familiar clique. They are doing what they love most, lapping up the sun and reading their hometown newspapers and comparing the weather. Thirty degrees in Manitoba, fifteen in Montreal. They chuckle smugly.

We have new tenants, Casey Wright and Barbi Stevens. Bella shudders, still unable to believe anyone would want to live in an apartment where there'd been a murder, but the price was so low these gals found it irresistible. They've only recently moved in and it's nice to have young people around. They're cousins, originally from San Francisco. Barbi must be in her twenties, Casey in her thirties. They don't look the least bit alike. Casey is kind of chunky and wears her dark, curly hair very short. Barbi is a tall, skinny blonde, and very cute. Casey seems to live in blue jeans, but Barbi loves frilly sundresses. They told us that they had a small business of their own and handed us all cards. All the cards said was "GOSSIP? Call Casey & Barbi. We know everything!" along with a phone number to call for an appointment. One of these days I must ask them what their business is about.

Next up are our beloved eighty-year-old Bobbsey twins, Hyman and Lola Binder (aka Hy and Lo), bobbing up and down in the shallow water, holding on to one another like chubby teenagers in love.

Hy sees us and greets us with his usual inane comment. "Ta-da, enter the murder *mavens*. Caught any killers lately?"

Evvie glares at him. "You're just jealous."

Mary Mueller now joins us at the pool every morning. She's living alone since her husband, John, left her. It caused quite a stir, I can tell you, when he was "outed" (a new modern term we've learned). He had met a guy in a Miami gay bar and fallen in love. Boy, that was a first in Lanai Gardens. But Mary is holding up nicely, I'm glad to say.

Dropping our towels, we kick off our sandals and step carefully into the pool. The girls walk back and forth across the shallow end, splashing a lot. I do two laps and I'm done. And I'm out. Such is swimming exercise.

Pretty Barbi addresses Evvie. "So, what movie are you seeing this week? I can hardly wait for the review."

Evvie, the in-house critic for our weekly free newspaper, is on a mystery kick since we've gotten into the P.I. biz. Last week she did a hilarious review of *Hannibal*. Evvie wrote: "The monster who likes to eat people is back again. Maybe he should do a cookbook." She sounded deadly serious; I couldn't stop laughing. This week she'll be reviewing a French mystery. Who knows what she'll do with that.

"Wait and see," she chirps. "But I promise it'll be gory."

"Hey, girls, didja hear this one?" And Hy is at us like *schmaltz* on chopped liver. God help us, he's learned a new joke off his e-mail. It will be offensive as usual.

"So, Becky and Sam are having an affair in the old age home. Every night for three years, Becky sneaks into Sam's room and she takes off her clothes and climbs up on top of him. They lay there like two wooden boards for a couple of minutes, then she gets off and goes back to her room. And that's that. One night Becky doesn't show up. Not the next night either. Sam is upset. He finally tails her and, waddaya know, she's about to sneak into

Moishe's room. Sam stops her in the hall. He's really hurt. 'So, what's Moishe got that I ain't got?' Becky smirks and says, 'Palsy!' "

Hy grins at us, thrilled with himself. Affronted as usual, the girls turn their backs on him and paddle away. I look down and concentrate on my crossword puzzle.

"What? What'd I do? What?"

"Schlemiel!" Ida hisses under her breath.

"Hey, did you read this?" Tessie asks. She's now drying off on her chaise, her nose deep in today's *Miami Herald*. She half reads, half condenses: " 'Mrs. Margaret Dery Sampson, sixty-four, of West Palm Beach, died early yesterday morning on the seventeenth hole at the Waterside Country Club where she was golfing with three friends. Mrs. Sampson, "Meg" as she was known to all who loved her, died suddenly of a massive heart attack.' "

The group reacts with shocked surprise. The heiress is well-known. Our group has followed her colorful rich-girl antics for years. She married into the famous Dery shipbuilding dynasty. It was one of Florida's most extravagant weddings.

Reading the society news around the pool is a daily ritual. I only half listen. I am stuck on 33-across.

Tessie continues. " 'Mrs. Sampson, an active member of Florida society, was known for her charitable works. She was an avid sportswoman and a bridge enthusiast. Widowed three years ago, she is survived by her second husband, Richard Sampson.' "

"What a pity," says Evvie. "You'd think with all that exercising she'd be in perfect health."

"Never mind that. Think of all that money she didn't get to spend," Ida adds.

"But she left a nice, rich widower," says Sophie. She picks up a tube of sunblock off the ledge of the pool and slathers her face and shoulders. "Maybe he'd like to meet a nice, poor widow. Like me."

Ida takes the sunblock from her as Sophie turns to let Ida do her back. "Dream on."

Sophie twists around. "What? I'm not good enough for him?" She pushes Ida's hand away. "You're making me into a greaseball."

Ida slaps the tube back into her hand. "Do it yourself. As if a rich guy like that would even look at a nobody like you."

Sophie hands the tube to Evvie. "And you know what? If he's old and ugly I wouldn't want him anyway."

Evvie applies cream to Sophie's back. "What's old, anyway? Look at us."

This gets my attention. "Bernard Baruch, the famous statesman, said, 'Old is always fifteen years older than you are.' "

"Hello?" It is a wobbly little voice, and the Canadians, who still have all their hearing, are the first to glance up.

"Over here." The voice manages to rise a decibel or two.

Now everyone responds. An elderly wisp of a woman stands at the pool gate, seeming almost too fragile to hold on to her metal walker. Her back is hunched slightly, and she looks as if a strong wind would carry her away. She's dressed completely in black, including the kerchief on her head. She must be sweltering in that outfit. "I'm looking for Gladdy Gold."

All eyes automatically turn to me as I put down my puzzle and walk toward her. "I'm Gladdy."

Needless to say, the girls climb out of the pool and line up behind me, my little ducklings all in a row.

"Your neighbors told me where I could find you."

"They would," Ida mutters into my back. "Ask them when we go to the toilet. All our neighbors know that, too. *Yentas!*"

I ignore Ida. "What can I do for you?"

"I am looking for a detective," the woman says, and then adds worriedly, "if the price is right."

In a flash, Hy is at our side, dragging one of the plastic pool chairs. "Here, missus, have a seat," he offers, helping the woman into the chair. He positions himself right next to her. An instant later, here comes Lola, gluing herself onto her husband as she leans in.

Everyone around the pool shifts slightly to the left. My unofficial staff. Unwanted. Uncalled-for. The other inhabitants of Phase Two, determined to get into the act whenever they can. Tessie, ever so casually, moves her chaise a little closer. Mary puts down her crocheting. Barbi and Casey openly stare. Even the Canadians have folded their newspapers. All gape and listen intently.

The little woman puffs out her chest and grips the arms of the chair. She shouts, "I'm eighty-two years old and I don't need this *agita* in my life! My old man, maybe he's cheating on me! And I want to know who the *puttana* is!"

Ahhh...I hear a collective sigh of recognition behind me. A problem they can all relate to after years of watching Oprah, Sally, Geraldo, and the rest.

"Hah!" says Hy with great delight. "The old man is dipping his wick somewheres else!"

The woman stares up at him. "What did this fool say?"

"Hy! Butt out," I say.

He shrugs, feigning hurt. "I'm trying to lend a hand here."

"Maybe he's lonely," Lola contributes.

"Maybe he's not with a *woman*," says Mary darkly. She's still pretty traumatized over John.

I have to nip this group intrusion in the bud. Now.

"Shall we go to my office?" I say to the woman in black. Helping her out of the patio chair, I reposition her behind her walker and firmly move her out the pool gate.

As we leave, my girls scamper to keep up. I hear another sigh in the background. This one of disappointment. Followed by a buzz of complaints from the neighbors left behind and pointedly being left out.

Tessie whines, "Didn't I ruin my best bathing costume chasing after our murderer? Where's the gratitude?"

"Wait a while," says Hy complacently. "She'll figure out she can't do without us."

"Right," adds Mary. "She owes us. Big time."

I tell you, it's not easy being a star.

5

The Case of the Little Old
Lady from Plantation

We are in my dining room, which I suppose I
can now officially call my conference room.
My minuscule kitchen, because it has a phone, is
the office. Such are our business quarters.

The girls were so excited I could hardly contain
them. This may be our first case with some zip to it.
The lady in black, who has introduced herself as
Mrs. Angelina Siciliano from Plantation, also
seemed about to burst a blood vessel.

Obviously whatever's been bothering her has
been building up for quite a while. I sent the girls
home to get out of their wet bathing suits. And I
excused myself to put on dry clothes and left Mrs.
Siciliano drinking chamomile tea. It would calm
her down. I hoped.

The girls were back in a flash. I've never seen
them change clothes so fast. Bella, always

fastidious, is in one of her usual beige tailored pantsuits with tan sneakers. Evvie, always the optimist, wears a favorite pair of bright aqua capri pants with a matching Hawaiian-style shirt. Ida, she of the morose personality, wears a dark-colored plain sundress—always with sensible flat shoes. Sophie, ah Sophie, that queen of color coordination, is swathed totally in lavender. Lavender polyester slacks, lavender blouse, lavender sandals, and, the crowning touch (pun intended), a lavender ribbon in her hair.

I opted for comfortable and am wearing my usual light cotton pants, T-shirt, and white sneakers.

The girls swarm around Mrs. Siciliano, chattering in her ears.

I delegate. "Evvie, please take notes. Sophie, get the cups and plates. Ida, bring another chair to the table. Bella, stop hovering. Thanks."

We are all finally seated and sipping tea. I face our visitor and introduce the girls to her.

She looks puzzled. "You're all detectives?"

"Yes," the girls say in unison.

"They're my associates," I tell her.

"Just find out who my husband is humping!"

First, they are scandalized by Mrs. Siciliano's frankness, but they get over that fast. Then they all jump in.

Ida: "How do you know he's doing it?"

Sophie: "Do you have proof?"

Bella: "Did you catch him in the sack?"

Evvie to Bella (shocked): "Bella! Shame on you."

"How can I catch him? Look at me. In this

walker?" The woman glares indignantly at Bella. "If my five brothers were still alive, they'd find him with that *puttana* and string him up by the *coglioni!*"

Bella throws Evvie a dirty look. "And you think I talk dirty!"

Evvie says, "What's it mean?"

Bella shrugs. "Who knows, but it sounds terrible."

Mrs. Siciliano slaps her teacup down. Hard. "You want proof, I'll give you proof. My husband, Elio, he plays poker with the men from St. Anthony's Benevolent Society every night after dinner. Forty years he comes home when the clock strikes ten. Now, one night he's twenty minutes late. Then forty. Once, even an hour."

"That doesn't sound so bad," Sophie comments. "Maybe he has to clean up the cigarette butts or something."

"Sure. He always has an excuse. Dom's car broke down. He had to drive him. Dom is a mechanic. His car don't dare break down. Vinny had a headache. He had to drive him, too. Fifty years I know Vinny. He never had a headache in his life. Sal's aunt Costanza died. He was too broke up to drive. Sal *hated* his aunt Costanza. Now I question everything. Is he really playing bocce on Saturday? Is he really sitting home with the ball game on TV when I go to mass?"

I interject as delicately as I can, "Has your husband a habit of, well, seeing other women?"

Angelina smacks her old, black cracked leather

pocketbook hard on the table. "Never! He wouldn't dare!"

"Then why do you think he's doing it now?"

I hear the scrape of their chairs as the girls lean in closer, fascinated by this most unusual personality.

"I'll tell you why. Because every time he's late he comes home smelling from Johnson's talcum powder, that's how I know!"

Sophie scrunches up her forehead, which tells me she's puzzled. "Maybe he's diapering a baby somewhere?"

Angelina glares at her. "That's like perfume! A woman has her own smell. I use a little vanilla extract, myself. My cousin Josephine, before she got rich, she put a dab of virgin olive oil behind her ear. But this one! *She* uses talc! That's how I know!"

I pour her another cup of tea, but Angelina remains agitated. "If I only was seventy again, I'd go catch them myself."

I'm still trying to calm her. God forbid she has a stroke in my apartment. "A little history, please. How long have you and Mr. Siciliano been married?"

"Fifty years. We have six children," she adds proudly.

"How old is Mr. Siciliano?"

"Eighty-five."

Evvie is in awe. "And he still *shtups*?"

"*Shtups*?" Angelina grimaces, confused.

"Yeah, like you said—humps," Sophie translates.

I ask one more question. "If we do find out that Mr. Siciliano is having an affair, what do you intend to do about it?"

The old woman raises herself up from her chair and hangs on to the table for support. "What do you think?! *Mia famiglia* is from Sicily. You heard of Sicily? When I catch that *bastardo,* he's *kaput!*"

Angelina sits down again and sips her tea, apparently feeling much better now that she got it all off her chest. "Now let's talk about a senior discount."

6

The Meeting Is Called to Order

I'm still not sure we should take this case," I say to the girls as they swarm about my kitchen. A few minutes ago, it was the office; now it's the cafeteria. They're busy organizing their contributions to a communal lunch.

We put Mrs. Siciliano in a taxi an hour ago and we're still debating as the five of us squeeze in and out of that tiny space preparing and carrying food.

Evvie's smart. She's staying out of the crush by standing in the hallway, looking in. "But she gave you her word that she won't knock him off."

Ida huffs as she walks past, carrying her casserole dish into the dining room. "And you believe her? She may be eighty-two, but I wouldn't like to meet her in a dark alley. She scares the hell out of me. And that black outfit! She dresses like he's dead already."

"*Oy,*" cries Bella as if she is in agony.

"What now? What's taking you so long?" demands Sophie impatiently. Bella has been in and out of the kitchen a dozen times, and still no food.

She stands in front of the stove pathetically looking at the boiling water. "You wanna know how often I eat hard-boiled eggs?" she asks poignantly. "Every time I make soft-boiled."

From the hallway Evvie shakes her head. "I told you a million times. You can't leave a stove when you're old."

"Get out of my way," Ida snaps, pushing past Evvie on her way back into the kitchen for another plate.

"Let's eat," says Sophie, now placing napkins on the table, adding her two cents. "I'm starving!"

"All right already," I say. "Grab your food, and everybody out of the kitchen." I shake my head at the disaster they've left me. The counter is littered with paper bags, plastic wrap, and odd remnants of food; the sink is a mess from all the chopping and slicing and peeling.

We're going to have to get a real office soon, or I'll go wacko.

Finally all the lunch contributions are on the dining room table. Since everyone brought over what they had left in their refrigerators, we are having smorgasbord.

Evvie passes me her chopped liver. "I say take the case. It was an empty threat."

Sophie serves her cottage cheese and vegetable

salad. "I say it was a full threat. We catch him doing it, he's a yunich."

Evvie corrects her. "That's eunuch."

Sophie makes a downward-slashing gesture. "Yeah. Bye-bye, balls."

Bella serves her now hard-boiled eggs. "She looks like she goes to church a lot, so she has to forgive him."

Ida sneers into her strawberry Jell-O mold. "Yeah, sure, first she'll do a couple of Hail Marys, following which she'll put a knife in his heart. Then she'll cut off his *schmuck*."

"Right," Bella chimes in. "And then Jesus will forgive her for icing him."

I must pause to mention that ever since we started the business, the only things the girls read or watch on TV are mysteries, so they've picked up a lot of jargon.

I contribute my onion bagels and cream cheese. "I think we owe it to the husband to confront him if we catch him in the act. It might save his life."

Bella giggles. "Or at least his *coglioni*."

I suggest we get down to our business meeting. Sophie immediately waves her hand wildly in the air. "I thought of a name for us."

Ida moans. "We already agreed on a name. And not one word about T-shirts."

Sophie ignores her. "What about 'Glad's Girls'?"

"Forget it," says Evvie.

Ida moans. "Why does she always have to name everything?"

Sophie folds her arms across her chest. " 'Cause I always named things ever since I was a little girl. I named all my dollies and my turtles and my toys and my socks and my sneakers.... There was Susie and Selma and Shirley and Sidonia, my dollies. And Tony and Tootsie, my turtles, and—"

Ida presses her hand across Sophie's mouth. "Stop already."

Sophie defiantly burbles through Ida's hand. "And goo-goo..."

"Enough!" I say. Sometimes I feel like a traffic cop. Or a kindergarten teacher.

Bella raises her hand. "Since I'm on the advertising committee, I wish to make a suggestion. We put Gladdy's picture on bus stop benches. She's prettier than those ugly old bail bondsmen."

"But with what name?" Sophie insists. "I don't like the one we have."

"What's wrong with 'Gladdy Gold and Associates Detective Agency'?" I say, peeved.

Sophie yawns melodramatically. "Borrring..."

Evvie, secretary and treasurer, pipes up. "And where are we supposed to get that kind of money for billboards?"

"Also," says Bella, reading from her notes—she has obviously come prepared for this meeting—"I think we need to be armed and dangerous. We need a salt shaker and a jerk."

We look at her, dumbfounded.

Ida glares icily at her. "Don't you mean pepper spray?"

"Didn't I say that? I thought I said that. I know I said that."

"And what the heck is a jerk?" Evvie asks.

"You know," Bella says, gesturing, "that funny-looking thing that looks like a rock in a black sock. Cops hit guys with 'em all the time. In the movies . . ." she finishes lamely.

Evvie says with disgust, "I think she means a sap."

"Knock, knock," a male voice calls from the screen door.

Bella rushes across the room to unlatch it. "Come on in, Jack, and join the festivities."

Jack Langford enters. My heart goes flippity-flop at the sight of him; I can't help it. Who says men in their seventies can't look sexy? He looks delicious to me. The girls, on the other hand, do not melt under his charm. They stiffen and you can feel the icicles forming.

He is holding a cardboard box and five small bunches of posies. He winks at me as he puts the box down on the table and starts handing the flowers out to the girls.

"Bribery will get you nowhere," Ida mutters under her breath. Jack, of course, hears her and smiles.

Fasten your seat belts. Here we go.

7

The Fly in the Ointment

Bella is all aflutter when Jack comes around. She's the only one of the girls happy to have a man on the premises again. For years she was friends with his lovely wife, Faye, and always saw Jack as a decent husband. She quickly clears a space for him at the table and brings in another place setting. "Sit, Jack. Have a bite," she offers.

Watch the body language. Ida, our resident man-hater, backs out of the dining area and as far into the living room as she can without actually falling out the window. A bitter marriage long ago supposedly made her this sour, but I have a feeling there's more to it than that.

Sophie fidgets and moves around aimlessly. She no longer knows how to behave in front of a man. She knows she's too old to flirt, but how else do you behave with "them"?

Evvie stays close to me, unconsciously, as if protecting me from this threatening outsider in her life. The status quo is in danger. She doesn't want anything to change, and he is Change with a capital C.

I just stay away from the line of fire. Jack is a big boy. He can take care of himself.

"Just a cup of coffee, thanks." He smiles at Bella.

I can read his mind. He wants to come over and hug me, but he knows it will make me uncomfortable, so he shrugs.

"Thank you for the flowers," I say pointedly, glaring at the girls.

There is an immediate chorus of "yeah, thanks" from the rest. Ida's is so low you can't hear it, even though you can see her lips moving. Complaints get high volume; gratitude earns a mumble.

"So, what's new?" Jack asks.

I sit back and wait for the Greek chorus to begin.

Bella is first. "We have a new client. Mrs. Siciliano. From Plantation."

"Yeah," Sophie chimes in. "She wants us to catch her husband sleeping in somebody else's bed."

"Yeah, like Goldilocks." Bella giggles.

"Right," Ida adds with satisfaction, "so she can kill him." She looks at Jack and says, ever so sweetly, "Most men are such liars and cheaters, don't you think?"

"Well, that might be a little strong," he replies, trying to keep a straight face.

Evvie looks directly at me. "We're going on a stakeout tonight, so don't make other plans." That's her idea of being subtle.

Sophie is dancing around the table. "So, what's in the box? I can't stand the suspenders," says she who mauls the English language.

"It's for your office." Jack opens the carton as the girls gather around.

"What is it?" Sophie asks.

"An answering machine, so you won't miss any calls."

"Uh-oh, Jackie, you're in big trouble," Bella offers. "Gladdy hates progress."

"Hold it," I say. "It's not the progress. It's the loss of humanity. The day we substituted computer voices for real operators was the end of civilization as we knew it. And simplicity. One page in a type-writer was easier than having to be an engineer to learn a computer."

Bella ignores my soapbox speech. "She hates all new gadgets. You better just take it back right now."

"Yeah," adds Evvie. "Look at her phone. She still has a rotary."

Jack turns to me questioningly.

I sigh. "Next thing I'll 'need' to get two lines, and then we'll need a cell phone. And then maybe a fax machine and then maybe a photocopier. Not to mention a computer. A whole lot of new things to have to take care of."

Sophie agrees. "And learn. I've learned enough already for one lifetime."

Evvie jumps in. "Stuff just complicates your life."

"Besides," I say, indicating this impossibly small space, "where would I put it all?"

"But if you're running a business, you need business equipment," Jack argues.

"I guess," I say without enthusiasm.

"I promise I'll set it up for you so it will be very easy to use." He reaches down into the box and takes out another small package. He opens it and hands the contents out. "Business cards. Nice, huh?"

I examine them. They read:

Gladdy Gold and Associates
Senior Sleuths to the Senior Citizen

"Very nice," I say, not to be polite, but because they are. "Give me the invoices and I'll pay you back."

"It's a gift..."

I get testy. But I stop my mouth before I say another negative word. What? Am I crazy? Here's a man who says he loves me and I haven't the sense to say thank you when he gives me a gift? I smile and say, "Thanks, Jack, I really appreciate it."

His face lights up. I'm beginning to remember what having a man in one's life means. He reaches over and takes my hand.

There is a deafening silence in the room. Bella tries to fill it with some noise. "So, what's new, Jack?" she asks. "How is your adorable son?"

"Morrie's just fine," he answers.

Morrie is Morgan Langford, the policeman who became very involved in our lives before I met Jack.

"I'll bet he's very busy with all those assaults and batteries," Sophie comments.

Jack tells her, "Guess so. Crime is a twenty-four/seven kind of business."

I look at Jack, who is looking at me, and the girls are looking at us staring at one another. Finally Evvie takes the hint. "Come on, girls. Let's leave the lovebirds alone."

One by one they wrap what's left of their lunch contributions and file out without a word. Naturally, I feel guilty and call after them. "Take a nap. We're going to be out late tonight."

They mumble their OKs but don't look back.

I close the door and turn to Jack. With a slight edge of sarcasm, I say, "Alone at last."

He comes over to me and pulls me into his arms and kisses me soundly. It feels wonderful.

"I should apologize for them—"

He stops me with another kiss. "Nonsense. I think they're cute. Mean, but cute. They're protecting their territory."

I shake my head in wonder. "Don't you just love coming over here?"

"It's a shade better than a root canal."

I start clearing the table.

"Ida gives new meaning to 'if looks could kill,'" he adds. "I can almost feel the bagel cutter piercing my heart. Hey, gorgeous, before I forget. Guess who wants to have dinner with us on Friday night?"

"George Clooney, I hope."

"No such luck. Will you settle for Morrie? He actually has a night off."

I fake a sigh. "Too bad. But why would your son want to spend a 'date night' with two old fuddy-duddies?"

"He's between girlfriends."

Jack helps me carry everything into the kitchen. "What hit this place?" he asks.

"Just the girls organizing lunch. And talking at the same time."

"They really got to you today, didn't they? I mean, more than usual, with my being here." Jack pitches right in and starts to load the dishwasher. "By the way," he says, "Ms. Don't Like Progress, how come you have a dishwasher? How come we don't have to wash every little dish by hand?"

I swat him with a towel. "It came with the apartment, as you very well know, since you have the same model.

"The girls make me feel like I'm a naughty teenager and they're my disapproving parents. And they watch me to make sure I behave." I hand him the rest of the dishes.

"It's too late. They already assume you're not behaving."

"Not Ida. She's in denial."

"Then let's get married and I'll make an honest woman of you."

"Jack. You promised."

"I haven't asked you in one whole week."

"It won't solve the problem."

"Then let's just live together."

I pretend to look horrified. "What, live in sin?"

"Move to my place. Since it's the same model, you'll feel instantly comfortable."

"And deal with the jealous widows of Phase Six?"

"Let's move to Chicago. Or better yet, Alaska."

"I can't. They need me."

"I need you, too."

"They need me more." This is a game we play over and over. Like my dear best friend, Francie, and I used to do, I think sadly. God, how I miss her. Oh, how she would approve of Jack.

The kitchen is now spotless. "You're good around a house," I say.

"So keep me. I'm available."

"Don't start again."

I hang the dish towel up to dry. He hugs me again. " 'So, waddaya wanna do, Marty?' " he whispers in my ear, replaying the famous line from the old movie.

"I don't know. Wadda you wanna do?" I play back.

"I want to make love to you, as if you didn't know."

"They're watching out their windows. If we don't go out, they'll know. Oh, God, listen to me. I'm blathering."

"If we do go out, they'll figure we went to my place. And they'll still *know*. Besides, they don't *know*, since you are too terrified of them to actually *do* anything. Therefore they don't really know anything."

"Yeah, but they *think* they know."

Jack shakes his head in disbelief. "They're starting to make *me* dizzy, too."

By now we are both laughing.

"So far you're only lusting in your heart. And I'm taking a lot of cold showers. What are you doing?" he asks me as I walk toward the kitchen window.

"Nothing..."

He grins. "I can't believe it. You're at the window so they'll see you're still in an upright position."

I actually blush.

"Look," he says, "the only sensible thing is to just get the dirty deed over with. Then you'll have a right to feel guilty."

"I know I'm being ridiculous."

He is behind me now, nuzzling my neck. It feels wonderful.

"They'll see you," I whisper.

"Good."

"All right already. Let's make a date and just do it."

I feel his body shaking excitedly as he continues to kiss the back of my neck. "Pick a place," he says. "Any place."

"But not around here."

"Try to keep it within a hundred miles, OK? Take your time. Don't rush. Take five minutes, even ten."

"Let's get out of here." I turn, pull him around in front of me, and push him toward the front door. "Just make sure you get me back in time for the stakeout."

When we walk out onto the landing and start for the elevator, I can feel the eyes watching us.

8

Death by Bubbling Spa

Josephine Dano Martinson, sixty-one, practically lived at the Boca Springs Health Spa. And why shouldn't she? She certainly could afford it. She exercised with her trainer three times a week. Received a massage daily. Enjoyed weekly facials at the salon. The treatments pummeled her into youthfulness. She felt like she could live forever.

Alas, Josephine was wrong. Today was the last day of her life.

It was the end of her daily regimen and she was finally in her own private steam room, cold cucumbers relaxing her tired eyes, hot billows of steam cleansing her pores. She mentally reviewed the details of tonight's dinner party. The crème de la crème of Boca Raton society would be there to contribute to her favorite charity, the Boca Raton Opera. Of course they had to be entertained and coddled before their tight purses would open, so she was holding a "Las Vegas Night." Gambling with sexy croupiers in low-cut outfits for the men. A chance to show off new gowns for the women. And lots of gossip, of course. How she loved entertaining. And how she loved showing off her gorgeous husband. Of course she had hired the high-priced Los Ochos Cubanos band so that her Bobby could parade his fancy Latin steps. And make other women drool with envy. Wonderful...

"More steam, madam?" Her reverie was interrupted by a softly whispering voice.

"Turn it up, honey. You know I like it hot."

She could hear the hissing of the bricks as he poured more water on them. He? Was that a man's voice? In a women's spa? Instinctively she covered herself as best she could with her towel, sat up, and pulled off the cucumber slices.

At first she couldn't believe her eyes, then she grinned. "Hi, what the hell are you doing here, sweetie?"

He smiled back at her.

"Last time I saw you, we were both naked. Come for an encore?" She let the towel drop enticingly.

He replied by turning the steam up higher. It was getting unbearably hot. Then Josephine noticed he was dressed in a janitor's uniform, and that he wore gloves on his hands. Something was not right.

He walked out of the steam room and closed the door. She got up quickly, wincing from the heat of the tile floor, and grabbed the door handle. Incredibly, he was holding it shut from the outside!

"Hey, this isn't funny!" She dropped her hands from the burning handle. "Open the damn door!"

There was no response. She beat at the door with her fists, shouting for help. The heat was unbearable. Her feet were burning. She could hardly breathe. Terrified, she stared at him through the misted window, her eyes pleading. "Why?" she mouthed.

He smiled and sang to her. "Toyland, Toyland, little girl and boy land..."

She saw no mercy in his eyes. She knew she was done for. Her last, dying thought was Somebody had better call the caterers...

When Josephine finally crumpled to the scorching floor, the man opened the door. Her body tumbled out of the steam room. He bent down and felt her pulse, then walked out into the hallway, still whistling the same tune.

9

Stakeout

Picture this. It's eleven o'clock, way past my bedtime. I'm jammed inside my cramped Chevy wagon with my so-called associates, all of whom are trying to drive me crazy.

We're parked on an unlit, empty, gloomy street in Plantation, an area we never go to, in front of something called Salvatore's Bar and Grill. What do we old broads think we're doing, anyway? We're on our first stakeout! And I cannot believe how these girls are behaving.

Their idea of a stakeout: sharing the already cramped space with five ample bodies and a basket full of snacks, drinks, knitting supplies, cards, and blankets. In case they get hungry, thirsty, bored, or cold. I keep nodding off, but not them. They're all for this adventure.

Thanks to the revenge-driven Angelina Siciliano,

we're here stalking Elio Siciliano, an eighty-five-year-old potential philanderer. We are waiting for the alleged cheating husband to come out of the bar and head for some sordid late-night rendezvous.

Evvie is seated next to me in the front, of course. No one would dare try to take that sister privilege away from her.

The three others are miserable in the back, what with the supplies packed over, around, and under their legs. They keep shifting positions, annoying one another, in an attempt to get comfortable.

I told them they didn't all need to come tonight. Why did I waste my breath? As if they would take a chance on missing something. And I warned them that the car light would be off, so how could they knit or play cards?

That didn't stop them. They brought flashlights. Worried that the light might call attention to us? No problem. Sophie covered hers with a purple sock.

Bella is sitting between Sophie and Ida, who are using her lap as a table so they can play their favorite two-person card game, Spite and Malice. A game that calls for dirty tricks and the language of a longshoreman.

Evvie has taped the Sicilianos' home address next to the snapshot Angelina gave us of her husband up on the dashboard. She says that's how cops do it. However, Angelina gave us a fifty-year-old wedding photo. I must admit young Elio looks dashing with his black handlebar mustache and full head of hair. I especially like the twinkle in his eye as he gazes down on his pretty new wife. But it isn't much help to me.

Evvie's already scoped out where Elio's car is parked, based on the license plate number Angelina also provided.

With her oven-mitt-covered flashlight in hand, she is attempting to write her latest movie review for the Lanai Gardens' *Free Press* to pass the time. I am merely sitting there, simmering, as I hear crackling noises behind me, indicating food being unwrapped and knowing what a mess I'll find in my car tomorrow.

"How's this for a title?" she asks me. " 'Good Girl Goes *Très* Bad. Review of *He Loves Me, He Loves Me Not.*' "

"Pretty good," I say. Ever since our first case, the Kmart handbag rescue, Evvie has been dragging us to mystery movies only. The girls sit there scared witless, clutching one another, squeezing their eyes shut at the gory bits, yet secretly getting a charge out of all the excitement. Except that Bella now has nightmares and Ida never stops bitching about how much she hates those movies. Nothing deters Evvie. She sees it as necessary research for our new business.

Evvie continues to read her review aloud. " 'Another French movie, and you know how much this reviewer loves French movies . . .' "

"Yeah," Ida pipes up from the backseat, " 'cause they're so dirty."

"It's you, Ida dear, who has the dirty mind. The

French are sophisticated." She goes back to reading. "Anyway, 'remember that adorable Audrey Tautou from *Amélie*? She's in this movie, too, but watch out, no *petits pois* this time. Now there's blood on her *chapeau*...'"

"Are you sure you want *petits pois*?" I ask. "I think that means green peas."

Suddenly there is a commotion in the backseat.

"You block my ten and I'll smack you," Ida shouts at Sophie.

Sophie slams down the cards in Bella's lap, shouting as she does.

"Take that! And that! And that!"

"Oof," says Bella in reaction to Sophie's enthusiasm.

"Bitch!" says Ida.

"Nah, nah," says Sophie.

"I'll get you for that!" And Ida slams down her cards even harder on poor Bella's lap, ruining Sophie's run.

"Oof," says Bella again, her stomach really taking a beating. "Excuse me," she announces, "I have to go."

"I told you not to drink all that seltzer," Ida says.

"Well, you punching me didn't help."

"Can't you hold it in?" Sophie insists.

"No..."

"Now what do we do?" Ida asks.

Evvie turns to them. "Well, cops usually carry an empty bottle with them."

"A lot of good that would do us," Ida comments.

"I have to go. Now!" Bella is wiggling from side to side.

I look up and down the dark street. "Nothing's open around here except the bar," I tell her. "You'll have to go in there."

"No way," says Bella, scrunching lower in her seat.

"Take your mind off it," Sophie offers. "Have a bite of halvah."

Bella wiggles in the seat.

"I gotta go," she insists. "But I'm not walking into that place alone."

"I'll take her over there," says Sophie. "But what do I say if somebody asks me what we're doing around here?"

That stops us for a moment.

"Just act senile," says Ida. "That's what they think we are anyway."

"Good plan," says Evvie.

Sophie and Bella slowly get out of the car, looking around the empty streets fearfully. There isn't a soul to be seen anywhere. Evvie whispers out the window, "I'm going to lock the door after you."

"Just don't blow our cover," says Ida.

"I told you we needed a jerk," Bella whimpers as they head for the bar.

We wait, eyes glued on the bar door, *shpilkes*.

I turn the radio on to take our minds off what might be going on inside the bar. I get a news station. All ears perk up as we hear: "As reported earlier today, Josephine Dano Martinson, sixty-one, died tragically at the Boca Springs Health Spa where she was a member of long standing. She was found dead of heart failure, lying near her own private steam room."

We look at one another, surprised.

The announcer continues. "Mrs. Martinson, one of Florida's twenty-five wealthiest women, died on the day she was to host a fund-raiser for the Boca Raton Opera. She is survived by her second husband, Robert Martinson."

"Two dead rich women in less than a week," I say.

"Coincidence?" asks Evvie.

"Probably," I comment. "Maybe."

Ida says, "Too bad Sophie is missing this. Here's another rich widower she won't be able to get her hands on."

Suddenly the bar door bursts open and Sophie bolts out, practically dragging Bella with her. They are moving fast. I quickly unlock the car doors. Sophie shoves Bella into the backseat, knocking her on top of Ida, then jumps in after her. "Shut the lights, fast!"

"What?" spits Ida, as she caroms Bella back at Sophie. "What did you do?"

"Nothing. The card game's over. They're coming out."

"Did you get to go?" Evvie asks Bella worriedly.

"Yeah, but I was in such a rush I got my support hose all twisted."

All our eyes are now facing the bar entrance as

a group of tough-looking older guys pile out. They say their macho good-byes, playfully punching one another as they head for their cars.

"Quick," Ida says, smacking Evvie on the back. "Which one is Siciliano?"

"I can't tell yet," she says.

"That's what I keep telling you, they all look alike in the dark," Ida says maliciously.

"Don't look for the guy," I say. "Just watch his car."

"That's so smart," says Bella admiringly, as she gets her twisted hose straightened out.

Moments later Elio Siciliano climbs into his big black Chrysler. I try to get a good look at him, but all I see is a large, bulky guy with a semibald head of gray hair and bowed legs.

He starts up his motor, and I start mine.

The girls in the back lean over the front seats to stare out the windshield. They are fairly panting with excitement.

"Uh-oh," I say.

"What?" a chorus of four voices yelps.

"What if he's a fast driver and I can't keep up with him?" I've been doubting the sanity of this whole endeavor all evening.

"Never mind that," says Bella. "What if he catches us and has a machine gun?"

Luckily, Mr. Siciliano drives at a moderate speed. Eight blocks later he arrives at a modest light gray stucco cottage. I check the address. It's his. After he parks in his garage, I head for home. The stakeout is over.

Operation Elio is a bust.

So that's it. We wasted a whole evening and I have nothing to show for it but a car littered with garbage.

We arrive back at Lanai Gardens around midnight. The girls, still on a high, are already rewriting history, chatting about what they'll report around the pool tomorrow. Not me. I just want to crawl into bed with a pillow over my head and think about the possibility of moving to Alaska.

10

Attack of the Flying Aunts

I am awakened at four A.M. My pillow is damp; my sheets are in a tangle. I can't believe it. It's the Flying Aunts dream again.

Why can't I have one of those easy ones, like the losing-your-car-keys dream or the forgetting-where-you-live dream?

I hate this one. It's my mother and her three sisters, harpies, zooming kamikaze-like down at my poor father, screeching at him while he's strapped in an electric chair at the kitchen table. Like always, he's clutching the *New York Post* in one hand. But in his other hand? I always have to wait and see.

Evvie and I are also in this dream. As usual, I'm a shy eight and she's an adorable six. Tonight she tosses her curly red hair about and hits me with a giant jar of Gerber's baby spinach. Believe me, she's hit me with worse. A seltzer bottle last time. *Fakackta* dream. *Oy.* And her singing! *Jack and Jill went up the hill and Jack fell down* ... The Flying Aunts love it. They *kvell* how she's better than Judy Garland. And cuter, too. They never *kvell* over me.

Then, just before the screeching aunts can put the plug in the socket and electrocute Dad, he throws me the thing he clutches in his other hand. It's always a book. It's always a different book. Tonight it is an illustrated *Cinderella*. "Read," he says. "Read!"

The dream always ends with my mother's complaint: "He never remembers to take out the garbage."

I get up, make coffee, and ask myself, so what was that about, my childhood? Why now? Hey, that was sixty-seven years ago and *now* it's relevant? Give me a break. I need this like I need another hole in a bagel.

Mom was always talkative. And oh, so busy, and so was Evvie. Two curly redheads in perpetual motion, unlike the plain, straight-brown-haired, quiet, boring ones.

They went to the beauty parlor together and to Klein's department store on Union Square for every Saturday sale, while Dad's idea of excitement was to take me to the Plumbers and Steamfitters Union Hall down near the Battery.

All the guys hung out there. I was their mascot. They smoked cigars, chewed gum, and ate pistachios. They shot pool at the moth-eaten table in the back room. They listened to the Yankees games or the fights at Madison Square Garden on the big Philco radio. I thrived on secondhand smoke. I loved that place.

There was a small makeshift library where the guys left books to trade, mostly tattered male-action-adventure paperbacks. But for me, they raided their kids' bookshelves, handing their gifts to me shyly; their kids never read them anyway. *Black Beauty. The Wind in the Willows. The Red Pony.* I absorbed them all.

Dad was very careful to put the adult books on the highest shelf, where I couldn't reach them. The first book he ever bought for me was *The Wizard of Oz.* I always thought that was fitting. For me that was the beginning of my love of books, the most important thing in my young life.

My aunts picking on my dad, the girls picking on Jack when he came to visit. Is that what brought this dream on?

Cinderella. Me? Maybe Dad was telling me to keep sweeping the ashes until Prince Charming arrives so I can live happily ever after? Well? Yes and no on that one.

Jack and Jill fell down the hill? Jack fell and fell and fell ... Yeah, that's glaringly clear, too. He did fall, my first darling Jack, my husband, didn't he? Fell because of a bullet.

I sigh. I don't want to let my thoughts go there. Enough. Time to get up and work at my crossword puzzle until the sun comes up.

11

A Three-Letter Word

Someone else was up early. May Levine, seventy-two, content with living alone on the ground floor of Building J, Phase Five, always boasted that she'd made the right choice. She had easy access in and out of her apartment. No steps to climb. No waiting for the clunky elevator.

But this morning she would regret that choice.

She briskly massaged her face with Pond's cold cream. Her daughter in New Jersey should only listen to her. Doris, the big-shot tennis player, had skin like a crocodile, while her mother's face looked twenty years younger than the rest of her body. May's mother always told her, "May, save your face or your touchas—one or the other always goes." Easy decision. Nobody had seen her tush in years.

Time to get dressed. She dropped her nightie

and her old lime green chenille bathrobe onto the bed. She'd had it for forty years and it was still in good condition. You didn't grow up in New York on Delancey Street without learning how to save money. She stood for a moment looking at her naked body in the closet-door mirror. What a mess! Varicose veins everywhere, sagging stomach and tush, boobies that hung straight down. From osteoporosis, she'd lost about two inches in height already. Life wasn't fair. She'd been a beauty when she was young. Why did we have to get so ugly when we got old? She sighed. She whirled about, round and round, remembering the pretty young May she used to be.

Suddenly she froze. She thought she'd heard a noise. And then she saw something behind her reflected in the mirror. There was a man looking in her window! He had a mask on. Oh, God, she was going to be killed! Then she realized that his hand was pumping up and down along something pale and flabby.

May screamed. "Peeping Tom! Peeping Tom!"

It's noon and Evvie, who is always prompt, waits for me downstairs next to my car. I approach her with a nearly bursting bag of books. She, too, has a full bag. "What took you so long? I'm melting from the heat."

"Sorry," I say as I open my trunk and pile all of our accumulated reading materials inside.

A familiar gravelly voice calls out, "Yoo-hoo."

We turn to see Sol Spankowitz, from Phase Three, and his best and only friend, Irving Weiss, standing in the shade outside Irving's apartment, three doors down from where my car is parked.

Near them is Irving's wife, Millie, now in her third year of Alzheimer's, propped up in her wheelchair. Yolie—really Yolanda—the adorable young woman who is caring for Millie, croons Spanish lullabies softly in her ear, hoping to reach her somehow. Millie is going through a bad patch these days.

Sol wiggles his fingers playfully at Evvie. Evvie, who can't stand him, doesn't wiggle back.

Irving is small and thin, sweet and gentle. Sol is bulky and coarse and as sensitive as a slab of meat from his old butcher shop. The guys have been pals since they moved down here twenty years ago. Sol's wife, Clara, died three years ago.

The guys have the horse racing form open while they plot their daily bets.

We walk over to greet Millie, who no longer recognizes us. It breaks our hearts to see what has happened to our dear friend.

Sol winks. "Hello, you dreamboat," he says to Evvie, trying to sound suave. He flirts, but he does it poorly.

"Yeah, right, and why are you wearing two different color socks?" says Evvie, who can always find new ways to put him down.

Sol changes the subject quickly. "So, what're the five luscious lady P.I.'s up to these days?"

"None of your business," Evvie says unkindly.

"How is she doing?" I ask Irving. I always ask and always get the same answer.

"OK," he says. Irving is a man of very few words. And we know Millie is not OK; she never will be again. We know how much it takes out of him, always worrying about her, but he will never complain. Bless his heart.

We each give Millie a kiss, say *buenos días* to Yolie, and go back to the car.

Evvie punches my arm, laughing. "Don't you love the way Sol dresses?"

"Uh-huh, the pink flamingo shirt really works well with the blue shorts with little crawling alligators."

"And the mismatched socks look divine with the black wing-tip shoes." Then Evvie relents. "I do feel sorry for him. He seems so lonely under all that bad taste."

Now the girls arrive with their books and dump them into my trunk, as well. We have to wait a few moments for Sophie to finish the last few pages of one of her novels. Then, done, she sighs, closes the book, and tosses it in the trunk with the others. "That was so satisfying," she says.

Bella looks at her, puzzled. "Since when do you read the last page? You always read that first. So you know how it's going to end."

Ida sneers at her. "I never heard of anyone who reads the last page of a book first. Only you."

"What's so hard to understand? What if I die before the book ends? Then I'll never know what happened."

Ida throws up her hands, showing her disgust. "I give up. You're hopeless."

The books delivered, they take off for their mah-jongg game. Evvie leaves, as well, to polish her movie review. None of them ever wants to go to the library with me. And that's just fine. I enjoy this time on my own.

I am about to get into the car when Hy Binder sidles up and pokes his face next to mine.

"Hey, didja hear this one?" He never pauses to take a breath, so there's no stopping him. "How can a guy tell if his wife is dead?"

"I really don't need to know, Hy," I say.

"The sex is the same but the dishes pile up!" He guffaws.

Lola, standing off to one side, carrying her dry cleaning, calls out to him. "Tell her already."

"Yeah, didja hear? Peeping Tom in Phase Five!"

At the expression of surprise on my face, Hy grins. "Gotcha!"

My book bags are dragging my shoulders down as I lug them to the entrance of the Lauderdale Lakes library, one of my favorite places. It is a small brick building in a residential section. This branch is very bright and inviting. It is my weekly job to return all our finished books and to choose new ones.

In the good old days, three months ago, pre-P.I. biz, I was the only mystery reader. The girls adored romance novels, modern novels, and anything about Hollywood stars. But now it's only mysteries, except for Ida, of course, who always has to be different. The girls feel these are their textbooks on crime. Besides, they like being scared.

Roly-poly Conchetta Aguilar became my good friend years ago, after discovering that I had been a librarian, too. Her assistant, young Barney Schwartz, loves to hear the gossip and stories I tell about those wacky characters I live with. His favorite was always crazy Greta Kronk, who raided our Dumpsters at night and wrote odd poems and made sketches of everyone. Poor Greta, who no longer is with us.

The library is quiet right now, and we sit at one of the tables peacefully enjoying Conchetta's wonderful strong Cuban coffee as we gossip. "So, what's the latest word?" Barney asks, eager to relish a new story.

"You want a word? I'll give you a word. How about—*sex!*"

That was a surprise. For me, too. I didn't know I was going to say that.

"In your senior world? At your age?" tut-tuts the cheerful, thirtyish Conchetta. "Aha. The girls must still be spying on you."

"More than ever. Jack thinks it's amusing and I can't stop blushing."

"You're blushing right now," Barney says impishly.

And my cheeks feel warm enough for me to know I am. "Not only are the girls glued to *Sex and the City* reruns, they try out the smutty language on one another."

"I can just imagine." Conchetta grins as she refills my cup.

"Then there's our new case. An elderly Italian couple from Plantation. She's eighty-two and he's eighty-five and she thinks we're going to catch her husband in bed with some floozy."

"Delicious," says Barney, "considering that my folks are much younger and they haven't looked at one another in years. And neither one cares."

"I can relate to Gladdy. My mom and aunts are drooling over the actor Chayanne, after they saw that sexy dance movie about Cuba," says Conchetta. "I tell them Chayanne's a Puerto Rican, but they don't believe me. He played a Cuban so he must be one. Hollywood wouldn't lie."

"And to continue my sordid list," I say, "what about Hy Binder's nonstop dirty jokes? I wish everybody would just grow up."

"Must be something in the water at Lanai Gardens," Conchetta suggests slyly.

"Or maybe our local Publix supermarket is putting aphrodisiacs into everyone's hamburger patties," suggests Barney.

"And wait 'til you read Evvie's latest movie review, which comes out tomorrow."

"Wouldn't miss it," says Barney. "She can put an unusual spin on anything. Pauline Kael would have loved her."

"She dragged us all to see a terrifying French movie about sexual obsession."

"Now I really can't wait to read it," Barney says with a leer.

"But here's the topper. Just as I was about to drive off, I learned we have a Peeping Tom on the premises. What the hell is going on?"

We are still laughing when the front door opens to admit a vanload of talkative seniors from a nearby retirement home, carrying books to return and eager to get more.

Conchetta and Barney go back to work while I pick out new titles for my gang.

I have Carl Hiaasen's *Skinny Dip* in my hand when I suddenly get an idea. I drop it in my book bag and head for the newspapers section in an adjoining room.

On a hunch I look up the obituaries of those two rich women who died. Thinking about the twenty-five-wealthiest-women list losing two members less than a week apart gets me wondering.

I have the library table covered with newspapers, and I'm searching for articles about the dead heiresses, when Conchetta walks over and clucks at me. She takes my arm, pulling me out of my chair and over to a small machine. "You're going to join the twenty-first century whether you like it or not."

"Yeah. Kicking and screaming. You're as bad as Jack."

"It's been a while since you retired from library work. Let me introduce you to microfiche."

And within moments I am happily knob-turning, scanning article after article about the two women. Finally I lean back, sated.

"Now, was that so hard to take?"

"OK. OK, I loved it, but don't you dare tell Jack I said that."

"Scout's honor. What did you learn?"

"More coincidences. Both widowed from very wealthy husbands a few years ago and both remarried fairly soon after. Also, these society gals are in the papers and magazines whatever they do. Charities. Vacations. Parties. Family statistics—births, deaths, et cetera. When they sneeze it makes the news."

"But?"

"There's hardly anything written about their latest husbands. No big write-ups about the nuptials. No fancy wedding photos. Mr. Sampson was in plumbing. Mr. Martinson was in the entertainment business. Was. But are they still? *Nada*. Isn't that odd? As if there were a news blackout covering the second-time-around hubbies."

"And what do you make of all that?"

"Nothing yet."

I look at my watch. "Gotta go or, God forbid, I'll be late for the early-bird special at Nona's."

Conchetta walks with me to the checkout counter and stamps my books. "You might need a textbook," she says as she reaches under the counter. "I picked this out for you a few minutes ago."

She surreptitiously hands me a copy of the *Kama Sutra*.

12

The Men in My Life

I'm about to leave my apartment on my way to meet Jack and Morrie for our Friday night dinner date, when the phone rings. One of the girls? A possible client? I could let it ring. I now have an answering machine, thanks to Jack's persuasiveness. "It's so simple an idiot could work it" was what he said to convince me. I didn't know whether to smack him or kiss him. I did a little of both.

I grab the phone before the machine picks up. Old habits die hard.

It's our client calling. "Hi, Mrs. Siciliano."

"Any news?"

"Not yet. I told you I'd get in touch with you as soon as something developed."

"Don't you think I know that?" Mrs. Siciliano humphs.

I think to myself, This Angelina is one tough

cookie. Of course I don't use her first name when I talk to her. She's not much into familiarity.

"I just called to tell you you're off duty for a while. My cousin died, and me and Elio are leaving for the wake and the funeral. We'll be gone a coupla days. So if you stake him out, you're staking for nothing."

"Thanks for letting me know. I'm sorry about your loss—" I start to say.

But she's already hung up.

Morrie has been entertaining us with stories from the recently built police station on Oakland Park Boulevard as he, Jack, and I share sushi in a charming Japanese restaurant in Margate.

"So we drag him into the station—the guy's just robbed his own neighborhood bank, where everybody knows him, and all he wants to talk about is redecorating our building. 'Who picked out this pissant wall color? A blind guy?' he demands to know, this Martha Stewart of stupid thieves. Maybe he'd like us to decorate the walls with the hundred-dollar bills we found stashed all over his body?"

I look from father to son. Morrie is sitting across from me. Now I know what Jack looked like when he was in his thirties. When he married Faye and had this lovely son. Lucky Morrie—if he continues to take after his dad, he'll be just as attractive a man at Jack's age.

Jack is laughing at this wry account. Over the

years Morrie must have shared a lot of war stories with him.

"Hey, Dad," he says, "tell her about the time you captured that crazy doper who locked his pals in a basement for a week when he was high because he thought they were aliens from outer space."

Jack starts to fidget. I see him making hand motions at Morrie under the table, but Morrie isn't picking up on them.

Morrie continues. "When Dad caught up with that nutcase, he ran to hide in a shower, turned it on full blast, and the only way Dad could cuff him was to get in the shower with him."

He swats his father playfully. "And what about that extortionist you had to chase driving up Fifth Avenue opposite the one-way traffic?"

"Morrie, eat your miso soup, it's getting cold," Jack says, obviously trying to stop him.

"Hold on," I say. "What's this? You were a cop?"

"Of course he was," says the proud son. "One of the best detectives the NYPD ever had."

"I thought you told me you had a desk job in Administration."

"I did, for my last ten years," Jack says, embarrassed.

"You said all you did was take information."

"Yes, that, too."

Morrie chimes in, "Yeah, in a lot of sweaty interrogation rooms."

"Jack, why didn't you tell me you were a detective?"

"Well," he says uncomfortably, "you had just become a successful private eye, and I didn't want to steal your thunder."

"I can't believe you lied to me."

"Not a lie, a slight exaggeration. It's not easy telling people you're a cop. Do you have any idea what they do when they find out? There's always one joker who's going to ask, 'How many people did you beat up today?' "

Morrie joins in. "Or 'Does it give you a thrill to carry a gun?' That's what all the gals want to know."

"It makes you gun-shy," Jack says, "and excuse the pun."

I give Jack a look that says we're going to talk more about this "slight exaggeration" later. He smiles and shrugs.

Morrie easily leans over the table and gives me a friendly peck on the forehead. "I've been very self-involved here. Your turn. What's the Gladdy Gold Detective Agency been up to?"

"Oh, nothing much." I dip my dragon roll into the soy sauce, dropping half the rice off my chopsticks as I do.

"Don't be modest. I saw you on TV. You're a celebrity now. Cases must be flooding in."

"Well, the girls and I are on a stakeout. Cheating hubby, you know how that is."

"Stakeouts are a drag. All that sitting and waiting."

"Yeah," I say, one tough comrade to another. "How do you handle the boredom?"

"I do a lot of thinking. Try not to crave the coffee I want but don't dare drink. Go over notes of the case. Think about all the things I'm doing wrong in my love life."

We all smile at that.

"I, on the other hand, can do no thinking. I'm stuck listening to the girls shriek at one another as they play cards in the dark. As they rustle sandwich bags and continuously eat. As they *kvetch* about everything."

Jack says, "Having company makes it less boring."

"Boring, they're not. They're adorable, but you don't want to spend too much time locked in very tight places with them."

Our main courses have arrived. My tofu sukiyaki smells delicious.

As we dig in, I ask Morrie, "What's happening with those two cases, the wealthy society ladies in West Palm Beach and Boca? You hear anything new about them? I know it's not in your jurisdiction . . ."

He looks puzzled. "You mean the woman who died on the golf course?"

"And," I add, "the one who died of heart failure in the steam room at the spa."

Suddenly, I am winging it. Up to this minute I hadn't given a thought to mentioning these events. But as I listen to their crime stories, my library research resonates in me. "All that money? Sure sounds like a motive to me."

"You're reaching," Jack says mildly.

"Don't you think their precincts investigated?" This from Morrie.

"And I'll bet both husbands had perfect alibis."

"From what I've heard—they did. But they didn't need alibis."

"I think it was murder." Even as I say the word, something icy creeps into my heart.

They both stare at me.

"I mean, in all the books and all the movies, the husband is always the prime suspect."

I can't stop my mouth. It just won't listen to my head. "Sure, death by sports and leisure. Maybe the next one will be a 'heart attack' in a hot-air balloon."

Two sets of chopsticks are put down. Two sets of eyes show astonishment.

Why can't I stop myself? I babble on.

"You don't like the husbands? Maybe there's a serial killer who is after very rich women. Someone who had a very deprived childhood." In my embarrassment, I'm trying for a light tone. But I sound like an idiot.

At Morrie's raised eyebrow, I continue my imitation of a lemming jumping off a cliff. "Maybe some other very rich ladies want to get on the twenty-five-wealthiest roll and they're knocking off these women so they'll move up on the list."

Morrie says, "What don't you understand about 'natural causes'?"

"You'll change your tune when the next heiress bites the dust. Pardon me for mixing my metaphors."

The two of them now talk over my head, pretending to ignore me.

Morrie asks Jack, "What would you do about such insubordination if she were in *your* precinct?"

"I'd probably demote her to Traffic," he answers. "And tell her to stop reading so many books and watching so many movies."

"Stop talking about me as if I weren't here." I need to get off the hot seat. "Enough about me. So, Jack, tell me. How did a nice Jewish boy like you decide to become a cop?" I pour myself some jasmine tea. I need the distraction. I could kick myself for getting on to this subject.

Jack's obviously told this story many times. "As the old ads used to say, I was a ninety-pound weakling and I was getting smacked around a lot. We grew up in a tough neighborhood in Brooklyn where there were three sets of immigrants—Jews, Italians, and Irish. And since Jews always seem to be the 'chosen' people, I was chosen to get beaten up by whichever gang was roaming the streets that day.

"So I joined a gym, buffed up, and met some guys who were cops. Italians, Irish, *and* Jews. They taught me how to fight back. They became my mentors and I followed in their footsteps. I had found my career."

"And, naturally, I followed in my dad's footsteps," adds Morrie.

"Now if you'd marry me, we'd have three detectives in the family."

I shouldn't say it but I do. "Jack, just don't tell
me you were in Homicide."

He looks at me for a long moment and says in a
flat tone, "Then I won't tell you."

The two men stare at me curiously.

Why did I bring it up? Why? I lower my eyes
and clutch my fingers around my chopsticks. I
never talk about that. Never.

13

Dancing Books

I squint at the clock in the very early light. Six A.M. Dream wake-up time again. Don't these dreams of mine ever give me a break and come at a decent hour?

I'm supposed to analyze you, Mr. Dream? Wait. First I've got to deal with Mr. Coffee.

This one usually makes me smile. Get this: Imagine an MGM extravaganza. In Technicolor, with the Glenn Miller band playing "Moonlight Serenade." A glamorous Busby Berkeley Hollywood set all in white and gold. With a double staircase and glittering chandeliers. Here they come, the Dancing Books. Perched atop sexy legs, like the old Chesterfield TV ads, tap-dancing their way down to center stage, then into the audience where I sit enraptured, front row center. Each book kisses me gently on my forehead as it imparts its story to my mind and heart. *Little Women. Marjorie Morningstar. Catch-22. Madame Bovary. To Kill a Mockingbird. Bonjour Tristesse. The Catcher in the Rye. Breakfast at Tiffany's. East of Eden.*

On and on they come.

I keep saying thank you, thank you, for loving me. I keep smiling until *The Reluctant Hero in Modern Fiction* jumps off the stage and hits me in the head.

And as usual, that's when I wake up.

Thanks, Jack. You always ruin this happy dream. I'm sorry. I didn't mean that, my darling. I must explain that I'm referring to the first Jack, Jack Milton Gold, the love of my life, the man I married when I was twenty. He of the glorious light brown curly hair and hazel eyes and infectious smile and love of everything and everybody.

I met him in college five years after the end of World War II. Those were the happy days, that era of my most intense reading. I went to college and discovered I wasn't an alien from another planet after all. There were actually others like me.

He was getting his master's in literature; I, my B.A. in library science. We met in Chaucer, fell in love in Shakespeare, and decided to get married halfway through the Romantic poets.

Could anyone have been happier? Living in New York in the fifties, the home of everything artistic and exciting. We had our very own, very small three-room apartment near the Hudson River. Jack taught at Columbia University. I was a happy housewife, learning to cook and trying to study at the same time. Fanny Farmer in one hand, the Dewey decimal system in the other.

And then our beautiful baby, Emily, arrived.

I was blessed.

And then I was cursed.

The Reluctant Hero in Modern Fiction. That was the title of the textbook Jack wrote and used in his classes. And it always hit me in the head at the end of every Dancing Books dream.

Once, during one of our all-night study/love-making sessions, I asked him to tell me about his war. I remember him saying that, yes, war had been hell, but afterwards, if you survived, life went on with or without your participation. "You have two choices," he told me. "You can wallow in what you can't change or you can fall in love with the miracle of every single day."

Jack Gold was my hero. He chose to fall in love with me and with life.

When the fairy tales I read as a child told me I'd find a hero to love, they were right. They also promised I'd live happily ever after. I didn't know "ever after" was only eleven more years.

I distract myself from dredging up the past by rereading a few pages from an old favorite, *Gone with the Wind.* (Is that a boring title, or what? I guess all the good biblical titles had been taken.)

Is it eight A.M. already? I see the girls out my window gathering for our morning workout and I close the book.

Like Scarlett, I'll think about the bad stuff tomorrow.

14

A New Job

It's eleven A.M. and the mail has arrived. Front doors open, people stroll over. For many, this is the big event of the day.

Evvie is already at the mailboxes. It's also the day her weekly Lanai Gardens *Free Press* is delivered, and she's graciously handing them out to her admirers. There's something for everyone in this newspaper my sister started years ago because, as she said, she desperately missed the *Daily News* and the *New York Post*. She covers everything from Hadassah meetings, clubhouse events, and religious services to garage sales. Everybody reads her reviews of plays, movies, lectures, and concerts, written in her own highly individualistic style.

Sophie is down early, a minor miracle. The pile of *Bingo Bugle*s is there and she can't wait to see the photos of this week's big winners from all over the country. Sophie's flavor today is lemon and she's dressed head to toe in that confection.

I open my mailbox to find letters from my grandchildren in New York. Bless them, they write me every week, with a little urging from my daughter, Emily. I look around to make sure Ida isn't here. She never gets mail from her family. It breaks her heart, and I don't like to read mine in front of her. This week's offerings are drawings. Elizabeth, the oldest, sent ballet sketches. Erin drew her beloved horses. Pat sent cartoons he's created, and Lindsay, the budding photographer, sent funny photos of her menagerie of dogs and cats. I put the mail in my pocket to reread and enjoy again later.

I hear a smattering of laughter and I turn to see a group clustered around one of the picnic tables. Tessie is holding court. I walk over to see what's got everyone's interest. Tessie is reading Evvie's latest review aloud. She's laughing so hard her massive chins and arms are jiggling. Her audience is rapt.

Our two newest tenants, the cute cousins Casey and Barbi, are enjoying the entertainment. They look like they are just about to leave to play tennis, and they are adorable in their tennis togs. It's nice to see young faces around here.

Even Denny Ryan, our maintenance man, has stopped sweeping the palm fronds to listen. Denny has finally recovered from the harrowing escape he had two months ago. He's back to working on his garden, and he has a new interest: the adorable Yolanda, who takes such good care of our Millie.

So far, the two of them have only exchanged shy smiles, but we hope they'll soon get further along in their relationship.

When Tessie sees me she starts over. I want to tell her not to bother, since Evvie makes me read everything before she sends it in, but Tessie starts emoting.

" 'Knishes or Knocks? Good Girl Goes Très Bad by Evvie Markowitz. Review of the French movie *He Loves Me, He Loves Me Not.*' "

Evvie, pretending to stroll, is watching people read her paper, occasionally smiling at a thumbs-up sent in her direction. Hearing Tessie, she turns. She waves toward us in her most grandiose manner, graciously bowing, like the true *artiste* she is.

Tessie waves back. As she continues to read, Evvie lip-syncs along with her.

" 'Another French movie, and you know how this reviewer loves French movies.' We sure do know, Evvie." There is a happy nodding and murmuring at that.

" 'We loved her in *Amélie,* but I warn you, you're not gonna love Audrey Tautou here as she stalks a doctor, a handsome cardiologist who she loves. Wink, wink, a cardiologist, a doctor of the heart. So how come he doesn't love her back, she's so sweet? But then again, he's married, so maybe that's why. At first it doesn't look like she's stalking, she looks like a girl in love. But believe me, she is stalking, because later in the movie everything turns all around and what was one thing five minutes ago is now something else. But we don't care; she's gorgeous whether she's good or bad, until she starts destroying her friend's apartment and then rips up her wedding dress. She gets weirder and weirder and we start to think maybe she should have gone for a psychiatrist instead of a cardiologist. It was a confusing movie but I'm sure I explained it perfectly.' " Tessie grins as she finishes the review. " 'So, Knishes or Knocks? I give it two knishes. Loved Audrey but the story was not much.' "

Tessie bows and her audience applauds. Evvie comes over to shake hands with all her admirers.

Ida and Bella show up finally and our group moves off to another of the picnic tables on the grass. We are gathering to plan our errands for the day.

"So how was your date last night?" Bella jumps right in.

"Great," I say noncommittally.

"So how was the food?" asks Sophie, still reading the *Bugle*. "You really ate raw fish?"

"Yes," I say.

"So how's Morrie?" asks Ida.

I love the way they always take turns. I wonder if they draw straws beforehand to see who goes first.

They never take the hint. They know I won't tell them anything, but they still ask. "Fine."

"Feh," complains Bella, "she's worse with words than that stingy Irving." She gives me a gentle poke. "It wouldn't kill you to share."

"Hey, listen to this," Sophie says, excitedly waving the newspaper. "They're having a drawing in the *Bugle* for a free luxury bingo cruise for two! And it ends this week."

"Big deal," says Ida. "You really think you have a chance in hell of winning?" She continues to browse through her mail. "All ads," she says with disgust. She hides her disappointment.

"Well, it couldn't hurt to try. I'm buying five dollars' worth. Anyone want to throw in a buck?"

Bella dips daintily into her purse, pulls out a dollar bill, and offers it over to Sophie. "Count me in, partner."

There are no other takers. "You'll be sorry," Sophie warns. "When I win, I get to pick my companion, so you better start being extra nice to me."

"What do you mean—when *you* win? What about me? I put my money in. Can't I be the companion?" Bella says.

Sophie ignores her.

"I miss bingo," Bella complains. "Now that we stay out late on our stakeouts, I'm too tired to play the next day."

"Me, too," adds Sophie.

"I never win, so I don't miss it," says Ida, the perpetual voice of negativity.

A group of women walk toward us, looking very determined. Those who are still hanging around the mailboxes stay to see what this is about.

Hy and Lola, standing on their balcony on the

second floor, are leaning over the railing scanning the action. Mr. and Mrs. King of the Roost!

"Well, look who's here," says Tessie, sunning herself on her bench while eating potato chips. She's always eating something. She waves to one of the women. "Hey, Sarah, what's up?"

There is an exchange of greetings between those who know these members of Phase Five.

May Levine is the spokesperson. "We've come to see Gladdy." The four women walk up to our picnic table. "We want to hire you."

Hy leans far over the railing. "Hey, Glad, I told you about the peeper. She's the one who got peeped." He struts up and down the balcony, proud of himself.

May looks at me, surprised. "You already know?"

Hy isn't finished. "Of course she knows. I told her. I know everything that goes on around here. Sometimes before it even happens."

May scowls, turns her back on Hy, and looks at us.

Evvie asks, "Did you recognize the guy?"

"No," May says, hands on hips, "but if I ever see that limp *putz* again I'd know it!"

Bella covers her ears as everyone else laughs.

"The coward was wearing a mask!" number two in the delegation, Sarah, contributes.

"A Superman mask," says number three, Edna.

"Did he wear a cape?" Casey wants to know. Her cousin Barbi adds, "With a big yellow *S* on it?" Apparently this is more interesting than getting to the tennis court.

May says, "I don't know, all I saw were his eyes through the mask. And the *putz*."

More giggles.

Practical me asks if she called the police.

May says, "Of course I did. Did I expect they would do anything? No. They laughed! And embarrassed me because they wanted me to translate *putz*."

"This is a job for Super*woman*," Sophie announces dramatically, pointing at me.

Sarah announces, "We, the women of Phase Five, want to hire you to find—"

"The *putz*!" Tessie screams out hysterically, spilling potato chip crumbs down her sizable bosom.

It's becoming a circus. But why am I surprised? I should have moved this meeting upstairs. Too late. Hail, hail, the gang's all here.

Hy joins in again from above. "Let's get all the guys around here to drop their pants!"

Lola smacks him on the head. "You'd like that, wouldn't you, you letch! Showing off your equipment. We don't know that he's even from around here!"

"First," says occasionally practical Evvie, "let's talk about the fee."

The four ladies of Phase Five look shocked.

"What fee?" asks Sarah.

"You do this for money?" asks May. "I never heard of such a thing."

Evvie raises an eyebrow. "You got a problem with that? What do you think—we're a nonprofit organization?"

May says, "This affects all the phases. Let everybody chip in."

"Hey," says Edna petulantly, "next time it could be you! If you live on the ground floor."

"Yeah," says Sarah. "What about doing it *pro bony?*" Obviously they, too, watch the jargon-filled lawyer and cop shows.

"How about *pro boner?*" Tessie screams with laughter.

"That's *pro bono,*" Evvie corrects, hiding a grin.

"Just go and catch him," demands May Levine, hands on hips.

"*Oy,*" moans Bella, "more night work."

Well, I guess I have a new client. *Pro boner.*

15

A Funeral in Boca

I still don't get it," Evvie complains. "Why are we schlepping up to Boca? And why did I need to wear dark colors and stockings?"

She hasn't stopped questioning me since we started our drive up the AIA to Boca Raton.

"Can't you just enjoy a nice ride along the coast and not make a big deal about it?"

"No," she says. "I had a *nice* rummy tiles game set up for today that you made me cancel. Besides, enquiring minds want to know. And furthermore, why did we have to lie to the girls? Why couldn't they come along?"

"I gave them an assignment, didn't I? I asked them to go door-to-door in the other phases to find out if anybody would like to report on a Peeping Tom incident."

I think about Evvie when she was a kid. Always

asking "Why?" No matter how many times I'd answer, there was another *why*. Even though I was only two years older, big sister was supposed to know everything.

"And besides," I say, "aren't you glad to have a day alone with me for a change?"

"Yeah, but I still would like to know why."

I smile. Good old dependable Ev. It used to drive me crazy when I was young, but now I really like her "enquiring mind."

Evvie pulls at her black cotton blouse, trying to blow air down her front. "Black makes you hotter and I'm sweating. Turn up the air."

"It's as 'up' as it goes."

"But why didn't you just tell them where we were headed?"

"All right already. It's because we're going to a funeral. And you know how they behave at cemeteries. Bella won't walk on the grave markers, Ida hates anything to do with death—"

"Wait a minute. Somebody died?"

"If one is attending a funeral, one might say that. But relax, it's nobody we know."

"Then why are we going?"

I sigh and turn off my Andrea Bocelli tape. Boy, do I love that guy's voice. "I intended to use the time on the trip to fill you in, but no—you have to know everything all at once. I'm filling you in now."

"Well, if you had just said so ..."

"Shh, listen. When I had dinner the other night with Jack and Morrie, I opened my big mouth and said I thought those two women, the one in Boca and the one in West Palm Beach, were murdered."

"You're kidding."

"Don't comment. Those two women were both wealthy, both died unexpectedly of heart attacks. Less than a week apart? Too convenient."

She looks at me for a long moment. "You believe that?"

"I've no idea. It just popped out of my mouth. I really made a fool of myself, spinning theories like there might be a serial killer who hated rich women, or someone was killing them to work their way up the twenty-five-richest list."

Evvie ponders that for a moment. "Like Alec Guinness in *Kind Hearts and Coronets*?" Evvie relates everything to movies she's seen.

"I mean, it's possible, isn't it?" I ask her. "How come unexpected heart attacks? They weren't that old. They had plenty of dough to spend on keeping healthy. My money's on the ones who will be getting their money. Like their husbands."

Evvie's look is shrewd. "You can't just be happy finding cheating husbands and lost purses?"

I don't answer.

"You already solved a big murder in our condo. Wasn't that enough? Now you think everyone with heart attacks is murdered?" She looks at me intently. "Glad, what are you doing?"

For a long moment I don't speak. My sister knows me better than I ever give her credit for. Evvie waits.

"I don't know."

Evvie reaches over and pats my shoulder. I see tears form in her eyes. "You can't save the world," she says.

"All I want is closure."

"It won't bring him back."

"Please change the subject." I'm sorry now that I let this come up. What's the use? Even after forty years the pain is still fresh.

For a while we concentrate on scenery. We are afforded quick views of the beach between the fancy high-rise condos along the road.

"Wonder what those babies must cost," Evvie says to break the tension.

"A lot."

After a few moments, I look at Evvie. She's too quiet. "What?"

"Just remembering some stuff."

"What?"

"When our kids were little. And Emily used to come to my house after school."

"Until I got home from my job at the library."

"Yeah."

"Our kids got along real well." She laughs. "When they weren't beating one another up."

"And when Emily wasn't crying over losing her father."

"That, too. She was very brave. She didn't inflict her sadness on the rest of us."

"No, she saved it for when I got home and the two of us cried together."

Evvie leans her head against my shoulder for a moment. "Those were hard days."

"Yes, but thanks to you, there were so many wonderful ones. You organized the birthday parties. You took them to zoos and movies and parks. You gave my daughter joy in her childhood. I owe you big."

Evvie is never good at taking compliments. "You would have done it for me."

We are quiet for a while.

"The nightmares are coming back," I say softly.

Evvie throws me a worried look. "About Jack?"

I nod. "Funny, both men in my life named Jack. And it's the new Jack putting pressure on me to marry him that's bringing up the memories of my old Jack."

"Are you seriously thinking of marrying him?"

"That's just it. I don't know. I really feel as if I could love that man. He's such a terrific person. Yet, I'm afraid."

"You dated over the years. What's the difference now?"

"I never was serious about the others. Now I am."

"But you're afraid you'll lose him, too?"

"Yes. And I can't give up my loyalty to my husband."

"Glad. He'd want you to be happy."

"I know, but my mind won't accept it."

"But we've got it good, us girls. Why would you want to change that? Isn't it enough? Do you really need a man in your life at this age?"

"Hey, what side are you on? First you encourage me to marry and then you're making a case for staying with you and the girls."

"I only want what's best for you. And I'm not sure which it is." Evvie warms to her subject. "Maybe I'm just being selfish and I don't want to lose you.

"I mean, I know how it was when you first got here. You had your Brainiacs Club—you and all your smart college-grad pals. Francie and Millie and Conchetta and Sandra and Joan. You and your *New York Times* crossword puzzles and the political lecture series and plays you went to that we never understood."

"Things changed."

"They sure did. Francie's dead and Millie's got Alzheimer's and Joan and Sandra moved back up north. You still have Conchetta."

"Not very often. Between the library and her very big family, I hardly see her."

"My friends made room for you. I know they're not the smartest, but they all love you."

This is the first time Evvie has ever said these things, and I am touched.

"Hey, I love you all, too. You're all cute and sweet, even though sometimes you drive me crazy. I'd give you a hug, but I'd run the car off the road."

She grins. "I'll collect later."

I sigh. "I don't know, Ev, I don't honestly know what I want to do. I'll let you know when I decide."

"Yeah, you do that." Evvie smiles at me.

"You'll be the first to know." I reach for my water bottle. Evvie sips at her Diet Coke. For a few moments, we are both lost in our thoughts.

"Wanna laugh?" I say. "Guess what I just learned the other night? Jack was also a cop—a homicide detective like Morrie, not in some boring office job in 'Administration.' "

"No kidding. That's nice to know. Maybe he can protect us with that great big gun he must have."

I laugh. "Naughty, naughty. Shame on you."

Evvie pokes me in the shoulder and laughs.

I can tell she is trying to get past our past. She straightens in her seat and freshens her makeup using the sun-visor mirror.

"About this funeral . . . ?"

"It's for Josephine Dano Martinson, who died all alone in a steam room in her health spa."

"And we are going to accomplish . . . what?"

"I'm not sure. I just thought if we went there something might jump out at us."

"Yeah, a ghost."

"Very funny."

"*I* thought so."

"I mean, I thought of going to the golf course where Mrs. Sampson died or the spa where Mrs. Martinson died, but those are private places and we'd never get in. By now, whatever evidence there was is probably gone. Anyway, this funeral is outside. We can meander and not be noticed, so that's why we're going. Clear?"

"Clear as mud," Evvie says. Then she smiles. "Okay, lady detective, let's detect."

We pass the Deerfield Beach pier, so I know we are getting close.

"Look at the map; the Boca turnoff is pretty close now. Just find me the way to get to the cemetery."

We walk quickly up the slope of the Holy Order Catholic Cemetery. I can see that the funeral is already in progress. The priest is speaking of the deceased in low, seemingly heartfelt tones.

"Look at how they're dressed," Evvie whispers. "Like they're going to a cocktail party."

"Now you get to see how rich folks live."

"Look at all those gorgeous hats. And the fantastic wreaths! They must have bought out every flower shop in Boca Raton!"

"Pretty impressive."

"What's the plan?"

"Just hover in the background, try to listen to any conversations, and don't be obvious."

"I wonder which one is the husband."

"Look next to the priest," I suggest.

Evvie looks. "Nah, can't be. That guy is young. And what a build! But on the other side of the priest is a woman, so it must be him."

If that's Robert Martinson, he is a looker! He seems to be in his early forties, dressed in an elegant black summer-weight suit. Probably cost more than my car. He's got on a black straw

Panama hat tilted at a rakish angle that covers some of his almost platinum blond hair and most of his face. The "shades" cover more. If the face is like the rest of him—poor Josephine, having to leave that behind.

Evvie has moved from my side. She is now practically leaning into a couple who are talking quietly. I hiss at her. "Subtle!"

She waves her hand at me as if to say yeah, yeah.

I amble about, now nearing a couple whose backs are toward me. They are both dressed in black, and the woman is holding on to a walker. They seem to be arguing softly. I get close enough to hear the man say, "Leave her alone already. At least she died happy . . ."

Suddenly I start to back away, fast. I recognize those two backs, now both in profile. I can't believe my eyes. Angelina and Elio Siciliano!

I almost trip on a tombstone as I try to get Evvie's attention. She sees me but shakes her head, annoyed. She's busy. I finally get over to her and pull her by the arm.

"Move!"

A few people glance at us, annoyed, but I get her away from there as quickly as I can. Out of the corner of my eye I see Angelina now turning and glancing toward us.

I pull Evvie behind a tree. "Just get over to the nearest grave and pretend we're visiting it."

"All right, but don't break my arm."

"We need flowers." I'm looking every which way for something floral.

"I see a bunch," Evvie says.

"Grab them!"

Evvie quickly reaches down in front of one of the stones and removes a small vase of flowers. She hurries after me.

We are now out of sight of the Martinson funeral party, and we are both out of breath.

"What was that all about?"

"You'll never believe who's here. What's that mess?" I say, staring at the pathetic wilted stems in Evvie's hand.

"You said grab something. I didn't have time to go shopping."

"Mrs. Gold? Is that you? I can't believe my eyes."

I see Angelina Siciliano moving briskly toward us in spite of the walker and the uneven ground.

"Oh, boy," Evvie whispers, getting it now. "What do we do?"

"Wing it."

Angelina reaches us. We smile phony smiles.

"Mrs. Siciliano, what a surpise," I say, and believe me, I mean it.

"What are you girls doing here?"

"Oh," I say in my best winging-it voice, "just paying respects to our uncle."

Angelina, Evvie, and I automatically glance down at the stone beneath us. It reads "Sum Wang Ho" in both English and Chinese.

Evvie, thinking fast, says, "I told you we went

down the wrong aisle. This isn't Uncle Charlie!"
And seeing the expression on Angelina's face at the
sight of our bouquet, she says airily, "Isn't it a disgrace the way they leave flowers lying around in
this condition? Now, where is that trash basket?"

I jump in at high speed before Angelina has
time to wonder why we Jewish women have an
uncle in a Catholic cemetery, let alone one who's
Chinese. "This is your cousin's funeral?"

Evvie pipes up, piecing together the various
things Angelina has told us. "The one who put
olive oil behind her ears?"

Angelina dabs at her eyes. "My cousin
Josephine. What a tragedy. She is married to
Dominic Dano for twenty-five years. Such an angel, he was. Up from nothing, he makes a fortune
in sheet metal. When he dies he leaves her very
rich. Not that she ever shares a penny with her
relatives."

Evvie is about to say something. I tug at her
sleeve to stop her.

"Then what does she do? Does she sit around
and get old and die with the rest of the widows?
No. Rich old women get very stupid. She marries a
dancer. Robs the cradle. Who can make money
dancing? Not that he bothers to work after he marries her. She marries beneath her. A disgrace to *la
famiglia*. I hate to be catty about my own cousin,
but she was no beauty. All the spas in the world
didn't turn her into pretty." She shrugs. "*Faccia
brutt'*. Some tough life she had. Bridge games,

cocktail parties, cruises...Did she ever invite me? Hah!"

"Angelina, where did you go to?" someone shouts.

We turn to see Elio, standing on a knoll, squinting down at us. Evvie and I turn our heads away quickly.

Angelina waves impatiently. "The man never gives me a minute's peace."

"Better go, Mrs. Siciliano. We don't want him to see us."

"Right. Right." She smiles conspiratorially. "Talk to you after the next stakeout."

We watch her trudge back to him. I wait until they are out of sight, then I hug Evvie. "You were brilliant! 'Down the wrong aisle! Uncle Charlie! Where's the trash can?'"

She smiles modestly. "It was nothing."

"You deserve a raise."

"Hah! I'll settle for a salary." Evvie breaks out laughing. "I really think we owe Uncle Sum Wang Ho a better bouquet than this one."

16

Sophie Gets Lucky

It's Sophie's turn to host our weekly canasta game. It's pouring outside and the afternoon sky is black, a typical Florida rainstorm with crashing thunder and flashes of lightning. But not to worry, we are cozy inside. Sophie has dozens of lamps, all brightly lit. Then again, our hostess always has too many of everything. Too many pillows on the couch. Too many doilies, too many little *tchotchkes*, like her salt and pepper shaker collection and her miniature doggies collection. Our hostess, as usual, outdoes herself with the food, as well. Not only is there a sponge cake, but *rugallah*—not just chocolate, but raspberry and prune, too. And with coffee later, there will be pie, three different kinds—cherry, apple, and pineapple cheese. Everybody complains, it's too much! But that doesn't stop us from wolfing it all down.

The game is going as well as can be expected, and it's war. Two killer players, Evvie and Ida, determined to win at any cost. One indifferent player, me. One in there pitching, but seldom a winner, Sophie. And poor Bella. She hates to play. She has never understood this game and never will. She'd rather watch, even do dishes or scrub the toilet, anything but take the other players' abuse.

It's my turn to sit it out and I end up as referee.

"Gimme a deuce," Ida prays as she picks from the deck with her eyes closed. "Yesss," she hisses happily at Evvie. Evvie answers back with a high five.

"*Oy,* I've got *bubkes,*" Sophie moans through a mouthful of raisins.

"I just picked up a joker," Bella says cheerfully to her partner, Sophie.

"*Shah!*" says Sophie. "Keep it to yourself."

"Big deal," Ida comments. "She wouldn't know what to do with it anyway." She clenches her fists. "Why do we put up with her?"

"For the same reason we put up with you," Sophie says with venom.

I try to calm things down by talking a little business. "That was really good work you girls did yesterday, finding two other women who saw Peeping Toms."

Sophie says, "And we only got through Phases Four and Six. There could be more."

Evvie slaps down a card and says, "You know who really surprised me? Eileen O'Donnell in Four.

She's always the big complainer, but not a peep out of her about her peeper."

I suggest we start a chart, but no one is listening to me because Evvie cries out, "Everybody shut up. I'm going down." With that she flamboyantly starts unloading her hand.

"Way to go, partner," Ida congratulates her.

"Now watch out, Bella; they're down, so don't let them get the deck," Sophie warns her.

Bella shivers. "I don't know what to play."

"If you got a jack, play it. Their jacks are already in fifth position," Sophie reminds her.

Bella sighs. "Thank you."

"Why don't you just look in all our hands and save yourself the trouble!" Ida yelps.

Sophie gets huffy. "You two should talk. You cheaters!" She looks from Ida to Evvie.

"Sore loser," says Evvie indignantly.

"And you gloat when you win and that makes you a *sore winner!*" parries Sophie.

"Girls, girls," I say. Here we go. It's spinning out of control.

"How do we cheat?" Evvie demands to know, standing up, hands on hips.

Sophie mimics them with a vengeance. " 'Nu, have you seen *Hy* lately,' when you want Evvie to throw you a high card, and 'So, how's *Lo*,' when you want a low one."

Now, trying to hide my smile, even I can't resist. "Or suddenly you want to discuss *Queen* Elizabeth."

"Or *King* Hussein," adds Sophie.

Bella braves up enough to hum "*Three* Blind Mice."

" 'Tea for *two* . . .' " Sophie also hums maliciously.

Bella whispers, "Oh, boy, do I need *sex!*"

"You have one hell of a lot of nerve!" Evvie shouts.

Ida gets up and throws her cards against the wall. "That does it! I quit!"

The doorbell rings.

Saved by the bell. Everybody freezes, ashamed of their outbursts.

"Maybe it's time for pie," Sophie suggests as she goes to the door.

The girls get busy making space, removing the cards and setting out the cups and plates.

Sophie looks through the peephole. "Who is it?" she trills.

"Registered letter. I need you to sign," a voice answers.

Sophie leaps away as if she were shot.

"What's wrong?" Evvie asks, alarmed.

"Someone died! I don't want to know about it. Go away," she shouts at the door.

Sophie starts keening. Bella flops onto the couch, fanning herself.

We're aware of an envelope and a piece of paper being pushed under the door. "Just sign it and slip it back. OK?" the delivery man calls. Obviously he's dealt with hysterical old ladies before.

Sophie, Bella, and Ida stare at the envelope as if it were a rattlesnake.

Evvie, disgusted with the bunch of them, goes and picks it up. She signs the receipt and pushes it back under the door.

Sophie covers her eyes with both hands. "I never in my life got a registered letter."

Evvie tries to hand it to her. "Are you going to open it or should I?"

"You!"

Evvie takes the letter out of its envelope and reads. "Oh, boy!" She starts jumping up and down. "Oh, boyohboyohboy!" Now she starts to twirl, holding the letter high.

"What is it already?" Ida hits her on the arm.

"We won! We won the free trip on the bingo cruise!"

Now the girls are jumping up and down, singsonging "We won!" as Sophie pulls out of her panic attack.

"Let me see that!" She grabs the letter out of Evvie's hands.

There is a long, pregnant silence as the girls grin, now excitedly holding their breath.

Sophie's hands go to her hips. "Waddaya mean, *we?*"

The grins disappear; grimaces replace them.

"Waddaya mean, 'waddaya mean, *we*'?" asks Bella plaintively as she nibbles nervously on her prune *rugallah*.

Evvie grabs the letter and waves it in Sophie's face. "We're all going!"

Sophie grabs it back. "Fine. Go buy tickets! I've got mine and I'm gonna take my own sweet time to pick a roommate! And it might not be any of you!"

Ida tries to grab the letter from her, but Sophie isn't going to fall for that again; she holds on tightly. Ida shrieks, "Since when aren't we partners?"

"Since now!"

I look at this heavy-breathing, fist-clenching, glaring foursome and I think, This is bad. Very bad.

17

Yet Another Stakeout

We're once again at Salvatore's Bar and Grill in Plantation. A very different mood permeates the old Chevy tonight. No card playing, no eating, no gossiping. Nothing but silence. No one is speaking to anyone since the free cruise raffle brouhaha. The girls are staring straight ahead out the windshield. All day long, it's been arguments and threats and words spoken that hurt to the very bone.

Sophie has made it clear she won't be picking a companion from this group unless the behavior improves. Bella has been vying for that favor, more than willing to beg if necessary, but the other girls demand that they remain a united front.

Evvie, with her long experience as secretary of the Condo Association, has spelled it out for us: We all get to go. Five tickets would cost five thousand dollars. But if we subtract Sophie's two free tickets, then we only have to pay for three tickets. So, if everyone chips in for the three thousand, it will only cost each of us six hundred dollars, a savings of four hundred each. And we can all afford that.

Everyone but Sophie agrees. I can't blame her for being sore. She's getting her ticket free; why should she chip in six hundred dollars? But since we've all shared any good fortune in the past, even I have to admit that Evvie's way is fair for all.

Not that I'm looking forward to a bingo tournament, but the travel part sounds like fun. All those pretty ports along the way to Cancún. I start to think back on all the places my husband and I planned to visit, places we never did get to see. But I stop myself and turn my attention back to the here and now, where we are at an impasse.

"Elio and the guys should be coming out pretty soon," I say, hoping to break the tension.

Nothing.

Bella, always in the middle in the backseat, squirms to get more comfortable.

"Stop that wiggling!" says Ida angrily.

Bella freezes.

"I was thinking," says Evvie, turning to look at the backseaters, "that we girls might take a bus trip to, say, Key West. That is, when Miss Penny-pincher is on her cruise, *alone.*"

Ida jumps right in. "I was thinking along the lines of Disney World. I hear they've added some new attractions."

Bella looks alarmed. "What are you talking

about? I want to go on the bingo cruise!" She turns to Sophie. "Are you sure my one dollar didn't give *me* the winning ticket?"

Sophie finally speaks. "No! It was my ticket!"

Now the rage bubbles over again.

"Either you chip in with the rest of us and we all share the expenses or you die alone!" Ida is shrieking.

"Damn straight!" says Evvie. "You can be on your deathbed yelling for help and *nobody* will come to you!"

"I might," Bella says timidly.

"No, you *won't*!" both Ida and Evvie shout at her.

"They're coming out," I announce.

All eyes swivel toward the men exiting the bar.

We watch in silence as Elio gets into his car and starts the engine. I turn on my ignition, as well.

As usual, Ida leans anxiously over my shoulder and Sophie leans over Evvie's.

Evvie pushes her back. "Get away from me, traitor!"

Sophie falls back deep into her seat, suffering.

I follow Elio, but he doesn't make the right turn at his home street. This time, he turns left.

"This is it! Don't lose him," Evvie says excitedly.

"Yeah, stay on his tail," Sophie adds.

"Shut up," Ida says to her. "As far as we're concerned, you no longer exist!"

Two blocks later, Elio pulls up in front of a

small pink stucco house with a dim light over the door. I drive past, then stop and park.

We all watch as Elio gets out of the car carrying a couple of bags with a logo we all know well—from good old Publix supermarket. He walks up to the front door, takes out a key, and lets himself in.

Bella gasps. "And two blocks from his own house." She shakes her head. "Shameless!"

"I knew it!" says Ida gleefully.

"Okay," I tell them, "here's the plan. We all go in a different direction and pick a window to look into. See what you can and then get back to the car, fast. Got it?"

"Am I allowed to go?" Sophie whimpers. No one answers her. I feel sorry for her by now, but I can't intercede. What, and get that gang on my back, as well?

Everyone spreads out toward a different window. Sophie follows timidly.

We don't recognize the hissing sound until it's too late. The night sprinklers come on. Instantly we are all drenched. We run back across the lawn as fast as our poor old legs will let us. The dog next door hears us and starts barking.

Breathlessly we throw ourselves back into the car and I careen off, the tires squealing.

We're sitting in the Flamingo Road Media Café, still damp. The towel I keep in my trunk to wipe windows is all we have to dry us off, and it barely does the job.

Keeping to the theme of the book, then the movie, and finally the beloved TV series about sex, greed, and revenge in steamy Florida, the bright orange walls of the café are covered with posters and memorabilia of said three media. The plates are painted with flamingos, the lamps are shaped like flamingos. Ditto, the glassware; everywhere one looks one sees pink.

We are shivering and drinking hot tea. Evvie, our movie *maven*, looks around admiringly. "Joan Crawford was great as the hussy with the heart of gold."

"I loved that gorgeous Mark Harmon, who was the hussy's lover in the TV show. Not Joan Crawford this time," says Bella, admiring his image in a photo.

Sophie sits at an adjoining table, soaked and miserable.

I wanted to go directly home, but they voted for hot tea and maybe a piece of Danish. All that stimulation calls for a nosh. Majority rules.

Ida has already complained three times that she's going to get pneumonia from the damn air-conditioning.

"So, after all that excitement," I ask, "did anybody see anything?"

A shaking of heads. The rooms were all dark. Bella raises her hand.

"I did."

"Well," says Evvie, "spit it out."

Bella preens at the attention she's getting. "The lights were on in a bedroom. Mr. Siciliano comes in carrying the groceries..." She pauses for effect. "And there's a lady sitting up in the bed..."

"Just waiting for him," says Ida with satisfaction. "We've got him!"

"Go on," Evvie urges. "What does she look like? Tell us everything!"

"They smile at one another. Then he takes out something from one of the bags and gives it to her."

"What is it?" Sophie, from her own table, can't stand the suspense.

"I don't know, but she ate it."

"Did he take off his clothes?" Evvie asks impatiently.

"I don't know. That's when the sprinklers hit."

"Damn," says Ida. "Just when we were getting to the good part."

"Think, Bella," I say. "I know you only had a few seconds, but make believe you're a camera. What do you see in your picture?"

She closes her eyes dramatically. "A bed. Lamps, a rug." She brightens. "The lady is wearing a very nice peach satin bed jacket!"

"How old is she?" Ida asks.

Bella shrugs. "I don't know. I couldn't see too good without my glasses."

"Think," says Evvie. "What else?"

Bella thinks hard. "There was something..."

Everyone is eagerly waiting.

"But I forget."

A series of groans.

I reassure her. "It'll come back; you know it always does."

"Yeah," says Ida, "but sometimes it takes *her* a *week* before her mind turns back on."

"Well," I say, "we can't force it."

"So," says Evvie, "what do we do now?"

"Tell Angelina," says Ida gleefully as she beckons the waitress in pink to refill her teacup. "And collect our blood money."

"I sure hope she doesn't have a gun," worries Bella as she blows at the surface of her tea to cool it off.

"I think we better meet with Elio first," I say. "Let's hear his side of the story."

"Yeah," says Ida. "I want to watch him squirm."

"Maybe he'll give up the floozy," suggests Evvie. "He has to promise never to see her again ... or else."

"Forget about it," Ida says with a toss of her head. "He's a dead man!"

"That's it! I've had it!" Sophie walks over to our table, hands on hips. "All right already, I give up. We share the cruise tickets!"

There is a chorus of hoorays.

Evvie pats the seat next to her. "Sophie, darling, welcome back to the living."

18

Code Name: Peeper

The clubhouse is jammed. I knew I was taking a chance letting the girls spread the word around Phase Two that we were having a meeting on the peeper situation and that anyone with information or possible solutions should attend.

I admit I have an ulterior motive. Some of our neighbors tend to be jealous of our small success, so I'm hoping that letting them share in the process might quiet down the catty comments. Such as "Hoo-ha, who do they think they are—such big shots now . . ." and a lot more of the same.

Every *yenta* has shown up. Every trouble-maker. The curious, the bored, and the concerned. The social butterflies consider this an event. Even the group around the pool, tired of sunbathing, grab towels and muumuus and follow us pied pipers inside. As the TV commentators say, it's a slow news day—apparently my neighbors can't find anything better to do.

Believe me, I don't expect results. In fact, I expect chaos. All I hope for is that it might convince them to be alert for any suspicious persons. And maybe cut out the rude remarks for a while.

My mind wanders while Evvie runs the meeting. I try to think of some subtle approach of confronting Elio Siciliano tomorrow. There has to be a way to prevent him from getting furious with us. I'm kidding myself. The man's family came from a place famous for sharp tempers and revenge. Wait 'til he hears what his wife has been up to. And I wish I could talk more with Angelina about her dead cousin, Josephine. My gut instinct tells me there is some connection between the deaths of those two rich ladies. But Lanai Gardens has its own problem at the moment.

Evvie, as recording secretary as well as moderator, is listing on the chalkboard the names of the women who have come forward. She's also noting the times of day the peeping occurred and which buildings were peeped. We're looking for a pattern.

May Levine, the woman who first brought this situation to our attention, reminds us her peeper showed up at four-thirty A.M.

Eileen O'Donnell from Phase Four speaks up: "My peeper came at six."

Jane Willis from Three informs us her incident was at ten P.M.

"*Oy,*" I hear Bella say behind me. "Why

couldn't they be at the same time? Why didn't he make it easier for us to catch him?"

"So what are we supposed to do?" Lola Binder asks. "Lots of us are asleep by eight. We never see anything." Hy congratulates her for speaking up.

"Yeah," says Mary Mueller, "and who gets up that early? I personally like to sleep 'til noon."

Everyone has a different opinion on what to do.

"Maybe we can hire a night guard," suggests sweet Barbi Bailey.

Her cousin Casey slaps her playfully on the back. "Right on, cous'." Barbi blushes.

Evvie shakes her head. "Six phases, thirty-six buildings. We'd need more than one guard. Where are we supposed to get that kind of money?"

Irving Weiss raises his hand about an inch high. He is seated with his wife, Millie, and Yolie Diaz. Millie is dozing.

"Yes, Irving," I say. "Do you have a suggestion?" We are always amazed when Irving volunteers words. They are few and far between, but when he speaks, he usually makes sense.

"Maybe go back to the police. You have enough victims to report. Now they have to believe you."

"Good idea," Evvie starts to say, but she is quickly interrupted by the "victims."

"I already tried that," says May. "Forget it."

"I'm not giving my name to any cops," says Eileen. "Then it will be all over the neighborhood. You promised us," she says, glaring at me. She turns to the whole group. "Everything said here stays here, you got it?"

There is much nodding around the room. And probably as many crossed fingers.

"Yeah," says May. "Gladdy Gold, you're a *private* detective."

"But Morrie Langford is a good guy," I say. "Remember how he helped us a few months ago?"

"All I remember," says Ida, "is Tessie tripping and falling down on him while he chased our killer."

There is much fond laughter at this memory.

Three sets of arms are crossed and tightened against their chests. "No cops, you heard her," says May.

"Well," says Tessie, standing up, "if the gals who got peeped don't want us neighbors to help them, let's not waste a nice day. I vote we go have lunch instead."

Tessie's mind is never far from her next meal. She's the only person I know who discusses the dinner menu in the middle of lunch.

"How selfish can you get," says May indignantly.

Some of the other women also stand, stretching, preparing to walk out. Others are chagrined. They aren't receiving enough good gossip from this meeting.

The three victims jump up angrily. "This is how you help?" says Jane.

Evvie, sensing mutiny about to erupt, says, "Everybody sit."

There is much grumbling and a shuffling of chairs, then everyone settles down again.

Our handyman, Denny Ryan, puts his hand up.

Evvie acknowledges him. "Denny, you have an idea?" This is a new Denny compared to the overly shy man he used to be. His close shave with murder has awakened him. Now he's making an effort to participate. And dress better. His new style is to wear a Marlins cap at a jaunty angle, and a clean T-shirt and fairly well fitting jeans. We suspect that's because of Denny's infatuation with Yolie, who glances shyly at him as often as he glances at her. In fact, he gives her a quick grin before standing up to speak.

"I don't sleep so much. I could walk around and see if I see anything..." He breaks off. That was a huge speech for Denny. Yolie claps her hands.

The group murmurs. Evvie says, "That's really kind of you, Denny, but it's too big a job for one person."

"Yeah, way too much ground to cover," says Ida.

"Right, maybe by the time you go around the corner of one building he just went the other way," adds Sophie.

"Thanks anyway," says Evvie.

Denny sits, a little disappointed.

"So what about a team taking turns?" Bella suggests.

"It's too cold to go out at night, or even in the early morning," says Ida, who can never find a temperature that pleases her. "We'll catch pneumonia." It's seventy-five degrees outside, but Ida is wearing a heavy sweater to combat the dreaded air-conditioning.

Mary says, "Not only that, we'll never get enough people to go out seven mornings and nights a week."

"Even if we did," Tessie adds, "some blabbermouth would talk about our schedule and if the *vantz* lives here, he'll know everything we're doing."

A chorus of yeahs follows.

"What about an alarm system? Someone on the first floor gets peeped, she bangs a big pot," says Lola.

"And then what, we all come running out? At night? In the dark?" says Ida. "And who would hear a pot, anyway?"

"Stupid idea," says someone in a back row.

"What a bunch of wusses," says May.

Hy Binder jumps up, waving his arms. Uh-oh, I think, here comes trouble. I knew he was too quiet.

"Just suppose," says Hy, "someone does run into the peeper. Then what? All we got left around here is a bunch of decrepit old broads. Excuse me"—he tips an imaginary hat to Barbi and Casey—"I didn't mean you. So some old dame is gonna beat him up and wrestle him to the ground? Are you crazy?"

The crowd boos. Hy is definitely a man you love to hate. He is always far to the right of politically incorrect.

"All we gotta do is grab the mask off his face," says May.

Evvie shakes a fist at him.

"Yeah. Right. He'll just stand still and say, 'Oh, please take my mask off. And maybe while you're at it, should I drop my pants so you can see if it looks familiar?'"

More boos, and now the group starts throwing peanuts and candy from their pocket stashes.

But Hy is on a roll. "And if Mr. Peepers runs after you, you won't be able to run away. Anybody can catch you, you infirms." He shouts this last part over the catcalls.

Hy charges up to the front of the room and takes over, pushing Evvie out of his way. "Quiet! I have the solution. It's so simple a moron could have thought of it."

Louder jeers erupt from the crowd.

"Yeah, moron, tell us all about it!" wheezes a smoker's voice from the left aisle.

Hy sure knows how to stir up a room the minute he opens up his mouth. All except for his brainwashed wife, Lola, who gazes up at him adoringly.

"Okay, *shlemiel*," says Ida. "What's the solution?"

Hy has to make a dramatic event out of everything. He dances around wiggling his butt, a favorite, but nauseating, antic of his. He waits until the chatter dies down and he has everyone's attention. He then announces at the top of his lungs, "Keep your friggin' shades down!"

The women are throwing anything available at him: tissues, beach towels, paperback books, stale celery sticks left over from the cooking class held here yesterday.

He shields his face with his hands. "What? What's your problem? It's cheap, don't cost nobody nothing. Don't even have to pay the hotshot P.I.'s a cent."

Ida goes after him with her sun umbrella, threatening to clobber him as he ducks behind a chair, still ranting. "The guy will never come back again if there's nothing for him to see, and frankly, why he'd want to look at you ugly old broads— Ouch!" he says as Ida whacks him across his precious rear.

Tessie comes forward and lifts Hy up. "Shut up, squirt," she says, and dumps him back into his seat.

He slinks down, terrified of big Tessie.

Everyone applauds.

The door is suddenly flung open. Sol Spankowitz from Phase Three hurries in, both hands carrying huge and obviously heavy grocery bags. "Hey, somebody said there was a party in the clubhouse, so I brought deli. Corned beef, pastrami, chopped liver, and lots of Dr. Brown's Cel-Ray tonic." He grins broadly. "And if this isn't enough, I'll run out for more."

For a moment all stare at the newcomer.

And then the rush begins to get at the food, the women laughing with delight. Those who don't rush Sol reach for their own hidden little brown bags and remove their snacks.

Tessie hugs Sol. "My savior," she says as she digs deep into his huge sack from Moishe's Deli.

"I guess the meeting is over," I tell the girls. It was just as well Sol broke up the meeting. We were getting nowhere fast.

19

Macho Man

It's time to take on Elio Siciliano. We are sitting in a coffee shop across the street from Siciliano & Sons Construction, looking out the rather dingy windows, spying on our prey. Our almost unanimous decision was to give Angelina's husband a chance to save his life. We'll tell him what we know about his alleged philandering before we report him to his scary wife.

It was not an easy vote, since no one except Evvie and I was willing to meet him face-to-face. Sophie wanted to send him a letter. Bella's idea was to leave a message on his answering machine. Ida, needless to say, would have had us go straight to Angelina so that vicious justice could be meted out. We outvoted her.

Sophie points out the window. "Those two guys must be Elio's sons. Mmm, what muscles."

"The muscles on the old man ain't bad either," says Evvie, though the direction of her gaze makes it clear that she's enjoying the testosterone types working with shirts off, sweat glistening on their chests.

"He must be some kind of hot stuff, still working at his age," Bella offers.

Evvie says, "I doubt he does any of the hard labor anymore. He looks like the kind of guy who'd die before he'd retire."

"Yeah, I bet he likes to come in just to boss his sons around," says Sophie.

Ida pipes in, "If I were married to a shrew like Angelina, I'd do anything to get out of that house."

Evvie gets up and goes to the next table to pick up another napkin. She wiggles her way back, singing, " 'Macho, macho, macho man.' "

"What's that?" Bella asks.

"A song from a very funny movie," says our entertainment *maven*.

"Well," I say, "have we stalled enough? Bad coffee, greasy doughnuts, and more bad coffee." No bagels in this industrial neighborhood.

I look at my "associates" shriveled up in their seats. Nobody moves.

"*OK*, I'll go it alone," I say.

"Yeah," agrees Sophie, "we don't want to gang up on him."

Evvie gets up. "I'll go with you, Glad."

As we leave, we hear behind us a whispered "Good luck." And then, "Another doughnut?"

And then, louder, "Look out for the cement mixer. You don't want to end up on a freeway."

Evvie and I cross the street. It's very hot today. How can these guys stand it?

When we reach Elio, all three men turn and look at us. "Mr. Siciliano?" I ask.

I get a chorus of three yeses. Definitely sons. Same big shoulders, though Elio's are bent. Same sharp, dark eyes, except that Elio's are watery.

"Mr. Elio Siciliano?" says Evvie.

Now the boys move off. This is of no interest to them. If we were blond, young, and cute, I'm sure they'd stay.

"Ladies. What can I do for you?" says Poppa.

"A private word?" I suggest, looking around at the rest of the men working close enough to overhear.

He leads us into the small shack that serves as his office. We sit down facing him on the only two rickety chairs behind a scarred brown desk. The tiny room smells heavily of cigar smoke. He stands in front of us, arms crossed. He doesn't bother to hide his impatience.

I've practiced what I'm going to tell him, as tactfully as possible, but now in front of Mr. Macho, I hesitate. Not so, stalwart Evvie. Where fools rush in, she's usually first.

"Your wife hired us," she blurts.

"What? You know my Angelina? She sent you here?"

He seems to loom over the desk at us. I tug at Evvie's skirt to shush her.

"What she means is—" I start to say, but Evvie's too fast for me.

"We're private detectives, and we were hired to find out if you're cheating on her."

Elio bursts out laughing. "OK, what's the joke here? I'm a busy man. It ain't April Fool's, so waddaya want?"

"Do you know a woman living at Forty-four Magnolia Court?" I ask. Thanks to Evvie there's no use pussyfooting around.

Now the humor disappears. He leans his arms on the desk and moves in too close for comfort. I can smell his cigar breath.

"What the hell is this about?"

Suddenly the room seems claustrophobic. Even fearless Evvie looks scared. I stand slowly.

"Mr. Siciliano?" My knees are shaking. "First, may I say, don't kill the messenger. We've come here to help you if you would just stay . . . calm."

"Spit it out!" He's yelling so loud that I imagine even the girls across the street can hear him, along with all the men on the site. Two male faces peer in the one grimy window. Elio waves them away.

"Your wife was worried about you—" I begin.

"My crazy wife never worries about anything but herself. Are you saying she hired you to spy on me? To find out if I was cheating on her! I'll wring her neck!"

Now he's got Evvie mad. "We were supposed to report to her what we found out," Evvie shouts.

"If we told her, she'd wring *your* neck...or worse. But we came to tell you first. To warn you."

"Listen, you old broads, who the hell do you think you are?"

With trembling hands, I take out our brand-new business cards and hand him one.

"Gladdy Gold and Associates Detective Agency?" he says incredulously. "You gotta be kidding!"

Evvie and I just stare at him. He glowers back at us. Through the window I can see the cement mixer outside, churning away. I shudder.

He slams his fist hard on the desk. Papers fly into the air. "All right!" Elio says. "You bring that jealous lunatic to Forty-four Magnolia Court at eight o'clock tonight! Now get outta here, I got work to do!"

He didn't need to say it twice. We ran.

20

Showdown on
Magnolia Court

Seven forty-five P.M. I am walking with Angelina Siciliano from her little gray house at 37 Petunia Drive to 44 Magnolia Court, two blocks away, where the big showdown is about to take place.

Angelina, dressed totally in black, is wielding her walker like a pair of skis, slaloming her way angrily from side to side, venom dripping from her moving, though soundless, lips. She refuses to speak to me. God knows what's going on in her head. When I came to get her, I "accidentally" leaned against her body. It didn't feel like she was packing a gun. I could only hope not.

Meanwhile, the girls are hiding in my Chevy, in the dark, in front of the place of assignation. I tried to get at least one of them to stay home so I'd have room to pick up Angelina. Their response to me? Not a chance. Or I could have left the girls standing on the sidewalk and driven the car around the corner to get Angelina. Their response? No way. Stand outside in the dark and get mugged? Some associates I have. So, walking it would have to be.

Earlier, after dropping the girls off at home, I had gone to Angelina's house to report on our terrifying visit with Elio. I explained that after her husband had heard that he had been caught, so to speak, in the house of another woman, he had demanded a meeting tonight. At that very same house.

If she hadn't been only four and a half feet tall, Angelina might have hit the ceiling at that news.

"Who asked you to tell him? I paid you to tell me."

I took a deep breath. "Well, it was a judgment call."

"Ya think I'm gonna pay you for that? It was none of your business to talk to him."

"But Mrs. Siciliano—your threats—" I began.

She cut me off and pounded at her heart. "Such *agita* you give me." She grabbed a washcloth and scrubbed viciously at an imaginary stain on the sink.

I should explain. She and I were in her spotless red 1950s-era kitchen. I subtly positioned my body in front of her knife rack in case she, too, wanted to kill the messenger. When she demanded to know the address, I told her. That made her even hotter.

"So that's who it is. Now it makes sense. I knew it. The queen of all fleshpots he goes to." She spit. "You're not gonna get me in the same room as that *puttana*."

She refused to tell me who it was.

"I shoulda guessed," she ranted. "Old dogs go back to old bitches. And he has the *coglioni* to tell me to meet him there!"

"He must have a reason."

"Yeah, to rub my nose in his filth. And in my own backyard! Do all my neighbors know?"

That was followed by a string of juicy curses. Since they were all in Italian I could only guess at the gist. But I heard what sounded like *minchia* and *sfacheen,* and plenty of *madonna*s.

"I'm not going!" Angelina glared at me, arms folded. "You can take a message to my husband, who soon will leave this world, and his whore: Drop dead!"

Finally, I stopped trying to convince her. I walked to the front door and opened it.

"Well, I'll be there tonight. I'll send you a written report. And a bill. Good afternoon!"

That did it. She lunged after me, clutching at my arm to hold herself up. "You better pick me up. I ain't going in there alone!"

Like my nosy associates—no way would she miss out on tonight.

The girls jump out of the Chevy the minute they spot us coming down the street.

Angelina ignores them. Just as well, since they've already had a taste of the Siciliano temper.

Spotting her husband's Chrysler in the driveway of the little pink house, Angelina neatly raises her walker and slams it onto the freshly washed and polished hood.

The front door bursts open. Elio runs out, enraged, fists clenched. I can hear strains of "Volare" coming from the door chimes. Cute idea, I think. Maybe I could get a set that plays "Hava Nagila."

"*Stu' gazz',*" he screams at her. "Lunatic!"

"*Minchia!*" she screams back. "May it shrivel up and fall off!"

He stands over her, strong hands itching to commit murder. Since she's so much shorter, her fists are dangerously close to his privates, which are directly within her reach.

By now my girls, sensing that violence is about to erupt any second, are backing off, moving closer to my car in case we need a quick getaway. In fact, Ida already has her hands on the door handle. Evvie is signaling—shall we run for it? I wave my hands to tell them to stay put.

At this moment I am seriously thinking I've gotten into the wrong line of work.

The door chimes sing out again as six middle-aged adults come rushing out.

Angelina screams at them. "You, too! Traitors! All of you! In the house of that *puttana!*"

"Shut your mouth, Angelina!" Elio growls.

The group on the steps shares the same opinion. They chorus a variation of: "Yeah, Mama, be quiet!"

I look at my girls and they look back, equally

surprised. Mama's children are in the *fleshpot* with Poppa?

Mrs. Take Charge takes charge once again. Evvie calls out over escalating voices, "Why don't we all go inside? You're drawing a crowd."

And sure enough, other front doors are opening. Windows are being raised. Cars are stopping.

We all retreat inside to the tune of the door chimes once again trilling "Volare."

The house is tiny. In fact, it's a replica of Angelina's place. I'm guessing the two houses were built at about the same time. The décor is very similar, too. I am beginning to get the feeling these two women shopped together at one time.

Elio looks at each of us and announces, "We are going into the bedroom now, and you will all show respect."

Barely able to sit up in her bed is an emaciated woman whose head is covered by a scarf. She is surrounded on all sides by medical equipment, and her arm is hooked up to a machine. There are pill bottles everywhere.

"Aha!" Bella shouts. "That's what I saw through the window and that's what I forgot! Medical equipment."

Ida swats her shoulder. "Now you remember?"

Bella shrugs. "I remember when I remember."

The Sicilianos stare at us. "You were looking in the window?" asks one of the guys we saw earlier today at the construction site.

Elio cuffs him. "Where're your manners? Introduce yourselves to the snoops—Gladdy Gold and Associates Detective Agency. This one's Frankie."

"Detectives?" says another of the men, the spitting image of his father. He introduces himself as Paulie. Come to think of it, all six children favor their father. Elio must have very strong genes.

"Who hired a detective, and why?" asks Joey. Then Sal and Louie and the one female, Josie, take their turns echoing his question and introducing themselves.

Elio wags a finger at Angelina. "That crazy one, your mother."

Angelina and the woman in bed stare intently at one another.

"What is it, Connie?" Angelina says. "What's wrong with you? You look like hell."

"Thank you very much. You look well."

"Never mind about me. What is it with you?"

"I got the cancer. What else?" Connie whispers.

"You're dying?" asks Angelina.

"Do I look like I could swim the Atlantic?"

"You look like you're dead already."

"You always did have a way with words, Angelina. It won't be much longer."

Elio addresses us. "Fifty years she stops talking to Connie. Sisters and best friends they were. Never apart. Back and forth from each other's house twice a day. Turns into hate. Over nothing."

"You got that right," Angelina says. "Over you. A whole lotta nothing."

"Don't start," he threatens.

"Fifty years!" says Ida, flabbergasted.

"Fifty years," echoes Bella. "You can last that long without seeing a relative?"

Connie manages to lift herself up slightly on the bed. She looks at Angelina, sadness in her eyes. "Right after the marriage. What did I do that you should hate me and shut me out?"

"And make all our lives totally screwed up," contributes Josie.

A roomful of mournful faces look to Angelina for some explanation. Cornered, she lashes out at Connie.

"Did I need you walking in and out of my house to check on me? Was I as good a cook as you—you, with the perfect marinara sauce? What about the sex? Did I want you inspecting my marriage bed to maybe see if I knew what to do? I was a new bride. I needed my privacy. And you two, always laughing together. As if you had secrets."

Elio is astounded. "You were jealous of your sister? Did I ever once compare you? Didn't I show you love? All these years you shut her out? For that?" He pauses. "Women!" he adds, as if that explains everything.

"Don't tell me you didn't have a crush on my Elio." Angelina throws at Connie.

"Sure, I found him attractive, but once he gave you a ring . . ."

"So, why didn't you get married? So I wouldn't have to worry anymore."

Connie manages a small shrug. "Every family has a spinster they can feel sorry for. I was it." She leans back on her pillow, exhausted from the effort. "Did I deserve to have to sneak around to visit your babies, my niece and my nephews?"

Elio says, "I brought our children together with their aunt years ago. It was the right thing to do."

"Traitor!" Angelina cries.

"Lunatic! You had no right to deprive them."

Elio turns to us snoops, frozen in place, mouths open in amazement, and pleads his case. He gestures toward Connie.

"My sister-in-law gets sick. She's all alone in the world. She asks me to help. Is it so terrible? I buy a few groceries, cook her a little broth sometimes. So I'm twenty minutes late getting home. Maybe thirty. Is that a federal crime? Can I tell *her* what's going on? No. She'd cut my head off."

He whirls toward Angelina. "You think I'm cheating on you? Did I ever cheat on you in fifty years?"

Angelina folds her arms and turns away with a lofty shrug.

Josie puts her arm around her dad. "I come over and help Auntie Connie take a bath."

"My job is to take out the garbage for her," adds Frankie.

"I drive my aunt to the doctor," says Joey, the youngest, proudly. Angelina looks at all the shining faces sending love toward Connie.

For a moment, there is silence. All eyes again are on Angelina. Her face contorts. Eyes narrow. Mouth a thin, tight line. Her hands clench and her body seems to lift from the very floor.

Suddenly there is a bloodcurdling wail.

Angelina covers her mouth, trying to hold back her hiccupping sobs. She abandons her walker and runs to the bed, scrambling to find a way through all the tubes and bedclothes to reach her sister.

"Connie," she blubbers, hugging her as hard as she can. "I'm an idiot! I shoulda had my head examined years ago."

Connie, using what little strength she has, hugs her back. "Angelina," she bawls, "I shoulda broke down the door and made you talk to me."

"I shoulda got down on my hands and knees and begged you to come back in my life!"

"All those years. What I went through. I had to hide in the back of the church for the baptisms and the confirmations. I had to miss every celebration. Christmas. Easter. We had to exchange gifts behind your back. I missed how we always went shopping together. The cooking together. But most of all I missed my sister."

"*Mamma mia,* I missed you every day."

"Me, too."

Now there's a lot of blubbering going on around the room. And hugging. Everyone talking at once.

I beckon the girls. Time to leave. Nobody notices us walk out.

When we reach the front yard, Ida, Evvie, Sophie, Bella, and I are also hugging and blubbering.

"Italians are so emotional," Bella says.

Death by Pirate

The yearly Orphans' Play Day, held by the exclusive Sarasota Springs Women's Club, was a major social charity event. This year the women had chosen Happyland Fantasy Park as their destination. This colorful amusement park was a great favorite of the orphans. The girls, from eight to twelve years old, excitedly walked in pairs, each line of six following its own individual leader.

Photographers clicked after them everywhere they went.

The Pink Poodle group was led by wealthy socialite Elizabeth Hoyle Johnson. At fifty-nine she was still considered a beauty. Her platinum blond hair was styled forever the day she had her first sight of Kim Novak in Hitchcock's film Vertigo. *She was dressed in a luscious pink backless sundress with matching straw hat and white strappy* sandals. Pink was her girls' color, so it was hers, as well. Her girls were all dressed in brand-new rayon dresses and matching ballerina slippers, a gift from the charity.

They were babbling happily away as they skipped from ride to ride, every spot a photo opportunity. Girls eating pink cotton candy. Girls screaming with pleasure as they rode the Fantasy Chip and Dip ride. Mrs. Johnson was a good sport: she went on the rides with them and pretended to be frightened, too. But she only went on the gentle ones. Her severe asthma kept her away from the more demanding rides.

Every once in a while the Pink Poodles met up with the other groups—the Purple Puppies and the Blue Bassets—and there was much happy chatter back and forth. Even the socialites were calling out to one another and having a good time. It was a day they could let down their hair and pretend to be young again.

When the Pink Poodles arrived at the Pirate Cave, they were so far ahead of the other groups they had even left the photographers behind.

Elizabeth, holding back her giggles, told the girls to be scared, very scared. "If the pirates get hold of you . . ." She made a strangling motion with her hands. The girls squealed and held on tightly to their buddies.

The empty gondolas pulled up on the rail tracks, and from around a corner came the operator of the ride. He was dressed in an elaborate pi-

rate costume. Elizabeth gasped. He had a parrot on his shoulder. She could feel her throat constrict. As long as she could remember, she'd had a phobia about birds. Years of therapy and it had never gone away. But she hid her fear. She didn't want to spoil the ride for her girls. They giggled as they tumbled into their seats and the mean-looking pirate pretended to be menacing. The girls squealed and laughed at his big mustache and huge gold hoop earrings and big black hat and black eye-patch. The noisy bright green parrot on his shoulder cackled, "Don't go in there, dearie ..."

Elizabeth was about to join the last two girls in their gondola, but the muscular pirate stopped her. For a moment she held her breath as the parrot leaned close to her. The pirate led her to a seat by herself in the next gondola back. A moment later she was disappearing into the pitch-black tunnel after the girls.

Deafening screams came from all sides of the cave and whizzing lights zigzagged every which way. Pirate dummies popped out to have vicious cutlass fights with each other, and bats seemed to swarm down all around them. The girls kept ducking their heads and laughing, gripping the edges of their gondolas.

They passed a huge, gleaming treasure chest squatting on the ground, its dazzling make-believe jewels piled high. And on the top, a skeleton wearing pearls around its neck was sitting and grinning at them. It was so close, the girls could have touched it, but they reared their bodies as far back as possible and screamed in terror as their gondola careened around a curve in the track into the next frightening pirate scenario.

At that moment Elizabeth Hoyle Johnson was pulled off her seat by the wicked-looking pirate.

He kicked the skeleton out of his way and pushed her down against the chest.

"What...why..." she stuttered. "What are you doing?"

To Elizabeth's surprise, the pirate yanked off his mustache and eye-patch. "Why, it's you," she said, upset. "What are you doing here? This is not a funny way to say hello..."

"Not hello, Beth. Good-bye. No more toys for you."

He released the parrot and on command it dived down at her, over and over again, screeching. Elizabeth clutched at her throat as an asthma attack came on full-strength. She was unable to breathe. Her hands groped for her purse, where her inhaler was kept. The satisfied pirate shoved the purse out of her reach. She looked into his eyes and saw no mercy there. The pirate waited as her eyes grew big, then closed. He felt her pulse and smiled.

When the little girls' gondolas exited the cave, they were surprised to find themselves alone. For a few minutes they sat, bewildered, as shadows darkened

*around them and clouds eclipsed the sun. Then one
of the littlest orphans gave in to her fright and began to cry.*

Where was Mrs. Johnson?

I put my Carl Hiaasen novel on my night table,
along with my reading glasses, prepared to fall
asleep. But sleep is not following its usual pattern. I
can't help thinking about Angelina and her family.
So I click on the TV for some late-night news to
distract me. What I see immediately knocks the
sleepiness right out of me.

The footage is of wealthy socialite Elizabeth
Hoyle Johnson at a charity function at Happyland
Fantasy Park in Sarasota Springs. She is beautifully
dressed all in pink and surrounded by a little group
of girls, also in pink, on their Orphans' Day outing.
The next footage shows a still, covered figure on a
stretcher, being carried out of some kind of cave.
The camera then shifts to a bench where several little girls sit crying, and an older woman, also crying, says, "Everything happened so fast. She was
on the ride with her girls and she never came out of
the cave. We knew she had severe asthma, which
must have weakened her heart, but..." Here she
breaks down. In the background I hear the children
chattering about the "mean pirate and his funny
parrot, who hosted the ride."

The newscaster gives a brief report about Mrs.
Johnson and her many charitable works, ending

with the same phrase that every reporter seems to use to sum up a woman's life, "She is survived by her husband, Thomas Johnson."

As the news shifts to the latest city council meeting, I turn the set off.

Number three. Why am I not surprised? I told them so, didn't I?

A Romantic Evening

Even though the salsa band in José Aragon's open-air tapas bar is very loud, even though the surf pounding the beach a few hundred feet away is near deafening, even though the rowdy group of young men just back from a successful fishing trip are seven beers to the wind, Jack and I are aware of nothing but one another.

Another sip of my Mai Tai, another sweet kiss, then I ask him again, "So, what's the surprise?"

"Not yet, oh impatient one. I'm working up to it. What's new on the P.I. front? Caught the peeper yet?"

"Still very elusive, that sly guy."

What is this big secret he is teasing me with? He keeps grinning, so he thinks I'm going to like it. It's certainly something *he* likes. I smile. Probably has to do with sex. That's a look I remember from way back. Oh, no. Is he going to propose again? Or want us to officially get engaged? He's driving me crazy. I wish he'd tell me already. I can't stand the suspense.

"Earth to Gladdy," he says.

"I'm here. Honest."

We munch some more of the cold papaya and pineapple chunks. And sip more of our drinks.

"How's your bridge tournament going?" I ask.

"Lucy and I are in second place. But we're closing fast."

"You better watch out for that Lucy. She's gunning for you."

"Nonsense, all she lives for is bridge."

"Yeah. Right."

We both laugh. Jack pulls me closer to him. We snuggle for a few moments, blissfully looking out across the barely lit beach toward the hammering surf. This is romantic. This is very romantic.

"Now?" I ask.

"Not yet."

"You're such a tease."

After another few moments of comfortable silence, I decide to tell Jack about my theory. I want his feedback. "There's been another one. Just a few days ago."

"Another what?"

"A very rich society lady who died suddenly and unexpectedly. I saw it on the news."

Then, incredulously, "You're not still on that?" he asks.

"Well, I just find the similarities meaningful. I don't really believe in coincidences."

"If I remember correctly, the similarities were that the women were very rich. Period."

"Three of them in less than three weeks? Just as I said it would happen."

He looks at me. "Now you're clairvoyant?"

"They were all middle-aged and seemingly in very good health. Three supposed heart attacks."

"And that's your similarity? Your mind works in mysterious ways, my dear Glad."

I punch him on the cheek gently. I sense he is getting annoyed at me. "You are trying to make me lose my train of thought."

"You're right. And you know what? Take this 'train' to Morrie's station and drive *him* crazy. That's what he gets paid for. This is one of the few nights we've been able to slip away, and now all we're talking about is business."

Why isn't he taking me seriously? This is important to me. Besides, he's the one who brought my business up. And I'm about to tell him so. But I think to myself, Not so fast. He wants his romantic woman, not this busybody private eye. Should that make me mad at him? This man loves me. I should shut up and enjoy the moment.

Jack pays the check. We cross the street, slip off our shoes, and stroll along the cool sand, arms entwined around each other. Mmm. It feels so good.

"Now," he says.

"Now what?" I've already forgotten.

"My surprise."

"Great, fire away," I tell him.

"My old friend, Paul Levitt, has a house in Key West. He's going off to New York on a five-day business trip. And we can have his condo. It's gorgeous. You'll love it. Right on the water. Incredible view. There's so much to see and do there. Hemingway's house, with its dozens of cats. Truman's southern White House. Nonstop Cuban music. The food. The romantic nights. The very, very romantic moonlit nights." He laughs and hugs me tight. "That's if we ever get out of the bedroom."

I stand there, shocked at my unbelievably mixed feelings. Why am I not instantly happy about this? After all, we've been talking about getting away for months.

"Wow!" I say. "When?"

"I don't know. He'll get back to me as soon as his trip is firmed up."

"Jack. The girls and I are leaving on our bingo cruise in one week. Are you sure it won't conflict?"

He is just too happy to be concerned. "It will work out. Not to worry, darling."

I am worried. Ridiculously, I am reminded of words in a Jimmy Durante song of more than fifty years ago. "Did you ever get the feeling that you wanted to go and you wanted to stay . . . ?" That's me, and I don't like that "me."

23

Girls on the Job

"Try to look inconspicuous," says Evvie as the girls crowd in on one another.

"Look relaxed," I add, though I should talk. I'm nervous. We have purposely picked the end of the day. Happyland closes in an hour. Our reasoning is that there will be fewer visitors around to witness what we will be trying to do. The downside is, we will also stand out more because of the smaller number of people.

If we're spotted, we're in big trouble. If Jack knew what I was doing, he'd think I was mad. But there is no point in talking to Morrie unless we can find some proof of what I believe.

I told the girls to dress casually so they wouldn't stand out. Of course, Sophie's idea of casual is a bright purple pair of capri pants with a matching beribboned top, purple heels—and guess what color sun umbrella?

"Do you see it yet?" I ask anxiously. We're trying to find the Pirate Cave ride where poor Mrs. Johnson was found dead, lying across what I have since learned was a treasure chest.

"This is gonna be a waste of our time," says Ida, baking in the hot sun and jumping from shady spot to shady spot.

"I hope not. Maybe we'll get lucky and hit upon something."

"The police probably didn't or it would have been in the paper," Sophie says.

I disagree. "Just the opposite. If they did, they wouldn't give that information away, and besides, they weren't looking."

"Yeah," says Evvie, "and what's with a pirate and a parrot anyway?"

A couple of men are coming in our direction carrying ladders and toolboxes.

"Duck!" says Evvie.

We move as fast as we can and hide behind an empty hot dog stand.

"We'd better locate the Pirate Cave, fast," says Evvie.

"Maybe we should spread out a bit," I say, thinking five nervous women are going to call too much attention to ourselves. "A couple of you go on some rides," I suggest.

Bella eagerly waves her hand in the air. "I'll volunteer."

"Anybody else?"

No one answers. "Well," I say, "we'll be going into a dark cave. Who doesn't want to do that?"

Ida immediately says, "I hate dark places."

"I love them," says Sophie, shivering with expectation.

Bella jumps up and down. "Let's hit the merry-go-round first," she says, linking her arm through Ida's.

Ida snarls, "I'm going to hate this."

They head toward the rides, Bella pulling Ida like an excitable two-year-old with a reluctant nanny. I hear Bella as they turn a corner. "What about that ride that turns you upside down?"

Poor Ida, I think.

"There it is!" Evvie points across a patch of grass to a dark cavelike structure.

Yellow police tape surrounds the entrance. So, the ride is closed, and no one is nearby. A break for us.

We quickly climb the stairs and follow the tracks inside. We turn on the flashlights Evvie was smart enough to suggest we bring.

"How can you walk in those shoes?" Evvie asks Sophie.

"Don't you worry about me, I'm an expert. I can walk anywhere on heels."

"The chest!" Evvie cries. We've reached the section with the illuminated treasure chest. There's a skeleton lying near it. And across the chest is more yellow tape, indicating where the body was found.

We are silent for a moment as we think about poor Mrs. Johnson.

"Look around," I say in a low voice. I think how strange it is that her body wasn't found in one of the gondolas. Why would she have gotten out?

"What should we look for?" Evvie asks.

"I have no idea. Something that doesn't seem to fit."

"Help," says Sophie, "I'm caught." Sure enough, her heel is caught in the train track. Evvie and I pull at it as Sophie *kvetches* about not hurting her expensive shoe. After much tugging we get her free.

"You ruined my favorite shoes," Sophie says, exactly as we knew she would.

"I told you to wear sneakers," Evvie says, annoyed.

"And I told you I'm not a sneaker kind of girl."

We begin searching. Evvie is carefully examining the ground. Sophie, seating herself next to the skeleton, is having a picnic going through all the "jewels" in the chest. She pushes the yellow tape out of her way so she can dig farther down.

"*Oy*, if only this stuff were real," she says longingly, twirling the skeleton's long rope of pearls.

I examine the chest itself. A lot of graffiti has been scratched along the sides.

"Eeek," Sophie screeches. "Get over here!"

We scramble next to the chest beside her. She raises a diamond ring up high for us to see.

"What?" asks Evvie.

"This is real. Really real! My God, this thing's worth a fortune!"

Evvie and I look at it. It certainly looks real, but then again so do the pearls and gold jewelry.

"Are you sure?" I ask.

"You ask a woman whose son Jerome is the best jeweler in Park Slope, Brooklyn?"

"So?" Evvie says, unimpressed. "What has that got to do with you?"

"He taught me everything. This is a two-carat emerald-cut diamond with four flanking baguettes. I'd bet anything on it!" She puts it on the edge of a finger and waves it up and down. "Finders keepers!"

Evvie snatches it off her hand. "Don't be ridiculous. This could be evidence of a possible murder."

Now I'm getting excited. Did Elizabeth Johnson drop the ring? Unlikely. A ring like that wouldn't fall off. Did the killer try to take it, then drop it? Not probable. Mrs. Johnson was left for dead. Or maybe she wasn't dead yet. Is it possible she took that ring off to leave a clue? But what? I imagine her lying there, almost helpless, reaching out—what could she reach? I look at the skeleton, its bony hand dangling inside the chest. I shine my flashlight along the surface and I pray I'm right. Sure enough, I find two letters faintly carved into the brown paint.

"Look at this," I say, pointing to the scratching. "I bet she didn't die right away. I bet she took her ring off and used the diamond to carve a message."

"*HL*," Evvie says, squinting to read it. "That's not the beginning of a word. Maybe she only had time for initials."

"My God," I say. "I think we finally found some real evidence. Do you know what this could mean?"

Evvie gets it; Sophie looks puzzled.

"She knew her killer!" I explain. "She knew the name of the man who killed her!"

"Let's get out of here!" Evvie carefully slips the ring into the little change purse in her bag. "Let's get to a phone and call Morrie!"

Sophie sulks. "Well, that ring should be my reward for finding it."

"Wait." Evvie stops. "Maybe we should leave it here and tell Morrie where to find it. After all, the cave is a crime scene now."

"I was thinking about that," I say. "We should call Morrie now and then come back and stay here until he arrives."

"If we had a cell phone," Sophie says, "but you..."

"Don't start. Besides, we wouldn't get reception in here anyway."

"Maybe staying isn't such a good idea," says Evvie. "I don't want us to get caught in this creepy place."

"We can't leave the ring here. Anything could happen and it might be lost forever. What if someone else finds it? Okay. We take it with us. Besides, I'm sure experts will be able to tell that it's hers."

"Yeah," adds Sophie, "then we can tell them to go look at the chest." She high-fives us. "Boy, are we good."

We move off fast, Sophie moaning, "Wait for me," as she tiptoes carefully on her preposterous high heels.

We find Ida throwing up in the bushes while Bella is high up above her, shaking her seat backward and forward, laughing hysterically, on something terrifying called "The Black Ride of Death!"

24

Morrie and Me

I'm surprised to see Morrie standing in a rather badly neglected lot on Oakland Park Boulevard, not ten minutes from the police station. It's taken him three days to get back to me since I gave him the ring we found. He called me this morning on his cell phone, informing me that he was very busy but he could give me a few minutes if I could meet him at this address.

Something awful must have happened here. Yellow tape surrounds what used to be a Greek diner, now long abandoned. Police cars are leaving, as are an ambulance and a few other, unmarked vehicles.

I can't resist. As I step out of my car I ask, "What's going on?"

"You don't want to know," Morrie says, still jotting down details in his notepad. Then he glances over at me and laughs. "Knowing you, Ms. Curiosity, of course you do. You want all the gory details of this crime scene. Kids broke into the deserted diner to have themselves a party—drugs, booze, knives—"

I hold my hands up. "Stop. Got the picture."

"Hungry?" he asks.

"A little. Why? Are you inviting me to lunch?"

"Well, here's this diner." He points at the pathetic remains behind us. "We could order some blackened moussaka."

"Or hundred-day-old pita? I think I'll pass."

"Wanna share mine?"

With that he sits down on a bus stop bench, takes out a sandwich, and offers me half. "Chicken salad, with my own secret dressing." His long legs stretch practically out to the curb.

I sit down next to him and accept the sandwich. "Boy, you cops sure know how to live big."

He tears his napkin in half and hands me a tattered portion. He takes out his water bottle, I take out mine. Ignoring the incongruity of our backdrop, we sit contentedly chewing and drinking for a few moments.

"Am I on the clock yet?" I ask. I'm excited. I know this time I've given Morrie a real lead. I lean forward in anticipation.

"Ready when you are, sweetheart," Morrie says in his best Bogart imitation.

"What did you find out in Sarasota Springs?"

"I had to make up some far-fetched story about a robbery bust and a tipster who said he heard a very expensive diamond ring in the take had been found in the Pirate Cave at Happyland. And, being such a genius, I put one and one together and remembered that a Mrs. Johnson from their precinct had died on that ride. I didn't dare tell them the tip came from my father's nosy soon-to-be bride, who should never have been in that cave at all, investigating a case that isn't a case, in a city where she doesn't live."

"Ignore the bride thing, that remains to be seen," I say quickly.

"What does?" Morrie asks, feigning innocence, knowing my blushing always gives me away. He's finished with his half of the sandwich and tosses the wrapper in a nearby trash barrel.

"Let's stick to the facts," I say in my most hard-boiled tone. "Did they track the ring to Mrs. Johnson?"

"Yes, it was definitely hers."

"I knew it!" I want to jump up and down with joy. "And what did they say about the initials on the chest?"

"I didn't tell them any of that. The story was improbable as it was. I stopped while I was ahead."

"But the HL on the treasure chest was a clue! It proves she was murdered and that she knew the killer." I am so upset, I can hardly speak.

"Gladdy, be reasonable. I went out on a limb for you to get the ring to that precinct. I could not justify having more information about the cave. And besides, there is no way to tell for sure whether the diamond had etched out any letters. She could have dropped the ring accidentally when she fell."

"That ring didn't just fall off her finger. The initials are evidence, and now the cops don't know about it. It would at least make them investigate the possibility of there being a murder!" Having finished my sandwich, I squash my napkin with a vengeance.

"And maybe it wouldn't. Probably someone else at some other time carved those initials." He tries to take my hands and hold them to comfort me. I don't let him.

"Forensics could tell us all that."

He grins. "Forensics, huh?"

Yeah, Morrie. This old broad has heard about forensics. Every twelve-year-old who watches TV knows, too.

"And how did the guys in her precinct explain her body being out of the gondola?"

"They probably assumed she was walking along the track and had a heart attack and fell down and landed on the treasure chest. That's also when her ring dropped off her finger."

"Morrie! That doesn't make any sense. Why would she walk on the track? She was in the gondola. She would have just slumped in her seat."

"Maybe they thought she was in pain and got out to go for help and she fell over. You're asking me to second-guess what others might think."

"Ridiculous. If she was in pain, she would have stayed put 'til the car rolled back outside and she could call for help, or at least end up outside so someone would see her."

Morrie is getting annoyed. I am furious. He will not take me seriously. If this came from some young rookie cop—a male—he'd listen.

"Gladdy, listen to me. I did what you asked. I made enquiries at each precinct. If there had been any kind of anomaly, the medical examiner would have picked it up. From my understanding, Margaret Sampson was only a few feet away from her golfing partners. Josephine Martinson was alone in her private spa; the staff at the front desk would have known if anyone went in there. Elizabeth Johnson was with a whole group of children when she died. No one saw anything. There was nothing to see."

I feel so discouraged.

"Look," Morrie concludes, "this isn't in my jurisdiction. I have a caseload of my own that keeps me busy twenty-four/seven. Even if I believed these cockeyed ideas of yours, there's nothing I can do. I was only trying to protect you."

I attempt to calm down. I turn my back on him so I won't say the angry things that are bubbling up in me.

"Gladdy, do you hear what you're saying? You think there's a killer husband in Boca, a killer husband in Sarasota, and another one in West Palm Beach."

I wheel around. "Yes. And they could be connected."

I am stopped by the arrival of a tiny, bent-over

senior, probably in her late eighties, carrying a sun parasol. She sits down gingerly next to us. We wiggle about to give her room. "You waiting long for the bus?" she asks.

We inform her we aren't waiting, but no bus had been by for quite a while.

I pull Morrie back to our discussion. "What if they all know HL? And hired him for the job?"

"I thought you said Mrs. Johnson knew who it was by the initials you insist she carved."

"I don't know how to explain that, but in some way they were all connected to the same..." I pause. The woman is definitely listening in. "The same contractor for the job to be done."

"Boy, what a coincidence that would be."

"That's my point. I don't think it's a coincidence. These men either knew each other or had some link and exchanged information on this... contractor, or they met somewhere and worked it out and hired the same...contractor. Can't you at least check bank accounts to see if there are similar large withdrawals in each of their accounts?"

"Gladdy, come on..."

Just then the bus arrives. The woman pulls herself up by holding on to the side of the bench, closes her umbrella, and begins to climb the steps. She turns to Morrie. "You should listen to your mother, young man, and stay away from building contractors. They'll steal you blind."

When the bus pulls away, Morrie unfurls that long, slim body. "Gotta go. I hear you and the girls are going on a bingo cruise. Just have a good time and forget about all these imagined conspiracies."

He tries to give me a quick hug, which I do not return. He heads for his car. Then he turns and winks at me. "Hey, Gladdy, when are you going to make an honest man of my dad?"

Exasperated, I wave him away. He gets into his car. In frustration I take a swipe at the photo on the bench of an ugly bail bondsman in his equally ugly ad.

Morrie's car pulls up alongside me. This time he looks serious.

"What?" I say to him. "You're going to apologize and say how wrong you are?"

He pauses, then in a low voice he says, "I wasn't sure I should tell you. I Googled you..."

"What is this Google nonsense, anyway?"

"It's a way to find out information on the computer about everything and everybody."

I laugh nervously. "So what big secret did you find?"

"I know what happened to your husband. You might want to tell Dad." He gives me a wan smile and drives off.

I stare at him, dumbfounded.

25

The Hero in Fiction

Four a.m. I open my eyes and peer at the clock. Why do I always do that? I know it's still dark and I should be sleeping. I turn over and I turn over again. Close my eyes and give myself an order to dream of something else. Fat chance. I'm back in that accursed alley again. I pull myself into a sitting position. Not this dream again. I keep thinking there must be a statute of limitations on how many times I get to relive this one.

I put on my bathrobe because I feel chilled. This nightmare comes with a caveat: Red sky at morning, sailors take warning.

It usually hits me on anniversaries. Thanks a lot, Morrie. You and your darn Google. This is the dream I don't share with anyone. Not even with Evvie or the girls. Not even with my own daughter, Emily.

No point trying to push it away. It just pushes back. So I close my eyes and experience it as quickly as I can bear. *Gevalt,* big-time.

I'm standing in a dark street. No, I wasn't there when it happened. But I've had to relive the real nightmare so often, it seems as if I were. Does that make sense? No, nothing makes sense. That it happened at all will never make sense.

My dream and my reality always take place not far from Columbia University. Near Riverside Drive and 124th Street.

I see an alley with a coffee shop on the corner. A shortcut during the day, treacherous at night. This night, my husband, Jack, works late at his office. He's finishing the last polish on the newest edition of his textbook. Now he heads home. It's New Year's Eve and our daughter Emily's eleventh birthday. He carries her present, always a book. (Like my father, always a book.) Jack and I invariably chose for Emily's birthdays the novels we most enjoyed at her age. His present is *Captain Horatio Hornblower.* That night mine was to be *For Whom the Bell Tolls.*

Jack hears a scream. From that dark alley.

I hear it, too. In my dream, I'm there.

"Don't go," I cry out, knowing what lies ahead.

He rushes into the blackness. There is a student. Her book bag has spilled over. There is a man. I can't see his face.

I try to run to help Jack, but the street has

turned to quicksand and my legs keep treading; I cannot move.

I hear Jack shout a warning at the girl: "Run, Patty!" It's one of his own students. An eighteen-year-old girl. She runs and then a shot rings out.

And that's when I always wake up.

Enough of that. Don't cry for me, Argentina.

You can grieve until you are an empty shell of yourself. Like Enya Slovak, who survived the concentration camps and sleeps in a bedroom with photos of her murdered husband and children on the dresser and will never smile again for the rest of her life. I once told her that I really believed her family wouldn't want her to keep suffering. She said, "What do you know?" If she lived a million years, her torment wouldn't match what they went through.

I chose my husband's way. To smile at each miracle of a day.

But in my dreams I do what Enya does. I cry.

I never gave Emily *For Whom the Bell Tolls*. And the police never found Jack's killer.

26

Getting Ready to Go

My first stop is at Bella's, where her entire wardrobe lies across her bed awaiting our opinions. The girls are already there. I survey the matching ensembles. Light peaches and neutral beiges and whiter-than-whites. Liquid lavenders and lemony yellows, all the pastels blending into the pastel bedspread in her pastel bedroom. It's a wonder when she gets her light-skinned little body into bed at night that she doesn't disappear altogether.

Her hands fluttering, she whimpers, "I don't know what to take."

"Take it all," says grandiose Sophie. "Ya never know what you'll need."

"No," says Ida, stamping her foot, beyond irritated by now. "How many times do I have to tell you? The staterooms are tiny. Not only do we store all our clothing in our rooms, according to the ship's brochure, we also have to keep our suitcases there, too."

"Big deal," says Sophie, fluffing out a long sea-green chiffon evening gown and holding it against Bella for effect. "*We* have no problem, since there're only *two* of us in *our* room." She puts her arm around her roommate, who leans into her lovingly.

Ida grimaces, forming her hands into claws, ready to strangle her, but Evvie holds her back. Sophie will not stop rubbing it in that she had the winning ticket and that the other three of us will have to share a smaller room. At the same time, she is still sore that she was forced to share in paying for all our tickets.

I decide to leave them at it. Each bedroom will play out its own packing drama; now that I've seen one, I've seen enough.

The telephone is ringing when I get my door open. It's Angelina Siciliano calling to ask if I got her check. I say yes and thank her. I wait for her to express some gratitude for what we did for her, but that isn't going to happen.

I ask how things are, and now there is a lilt in her voice. Her sister, Connie, has moved into their house, and "Guess what?" Angelina says. "Elio is taking me on a second honeymoon. All the kids will take care of their aunt while we're gone."

I feel good about what she is telling me, and I congratulate her on this happy turn of events. But with murder still on my mind, no matter how hard I try to get it off, I can't resist this opportunity to ask questions about her late cousin Josephine. "Did she ever mention knowing someone with the initials HL? A friend? Someone who worked for her? Would you think for a moment... ?"

"Are you kidding?" Angelina stops me, says sarcastically, "HL? JK? XYZ? How would I know? Once she got rich, she forgot she ever had a *famiglia*. You think she'd invite us to her ritzy parties? Or how about a swim at her fancy country club? Hah! We were like chewing gum under her shoes. She never let us meet anyone she knew. The disgraceful way some people act to other members of their family."

This from the woman who didn't speak to her own sister for fifty years?

The moment I hang up, the phone rings again. This time it's Jack. "Can you meet me right now?" From the anxious tone in his voice, I don't ask questions. He tells me where, and after a brief hair comb and a dab of lipstick, I am out the door.

With great trepidation I walk quickly over to Phase Four. Jack said he'd leave Phase Six and meet me halfway. I don't pay attention to the many scattered palm fronds the wind blew off the trees. Or that I have to hold my sweater close to me, because that wind is blowing hard. I am aware only that something serious is on his mind.

Did Morrie decide not to wait for me and tell Jack what he found out about my husband?

He's already standing next to the prearranged park bench. Before I can even catch my breath, Jack blurts it out. He knows we are leaving on the cruise next Sunday afternoon. And now he informs me he has the use of his friend's house in Key West that very same week.

I can hardly hide my relief. Morrie didn't tell him.

He puts his arms around me. "I know I shouldn't ask you to give up the cruise. But I want you to be with me."

"I'm so sorry," I say.

"The girls would be disappointed," he says softly.

"Yes, they would."

"But it's such a great offer. I don't want to lose it."

"I see ..." I feel my throat tightening and I can hardly swallow.

We hear someone coming down the path and we sit down demurely next to one another on the bench.

Jack hesitates. "You could tell them something came up and you have to make other plans ..."

"They'll have a fit."

Jack gets up, paces. "Do you really want to go on that cruise? Truth?"

"No."

He comes back to me and stares into my eyes. "Glad, we're not kids anymore. If you don't do what you really want to do at this stage of your life, when will you?"

"Don't...you aren't being fair...It's more complicated than that."

"Okay, they'll be mad for a while, but they love you and want you to be happy. They'll understand...They'll get over it."

"I don't think they will."

"Now, that's silly."

"Please don't ask me to choose."

"I guess that's what I am doing."

"I won't be able to choose you this time." I bow my head. This is awful. How can I explain how I feel? My back is to the wall and I can't deal with the pressure. I want to beg him to back off. For now.

Jack doesn't move. "Honey, I'm trying to understand, but I can't. What's this really about?"

I see the expression on his face. "It's only a cruise!" he says. "They'll be back in a week. What's the big deal?"

I need to say something. "They won't be able to manage things alone," I blurt. "I'm their designated driver!"

He looks at me as if I've lost my mind. He tries to laugh. "These aren't kids, Glad. These are grown-ups."

"That's what you think," I say weakly. "Please. There'll be other weeks, other places we can go."

"And you'll find another excuse. You've been putting me off for a long time," he says petulantly.

I want to reach out and touch him, but the distance is too far. There is coldness facing me for the first time.

"I guess I'm tired of being reasonable. Either you want me—or you don't."

"Honey, I promise when I get back..."

"Do you know how long we've been planning to take a trip? How many times you've found an excuse not to go?"

"Jack, please, next time..."

But he's walking away from me. I can't believe it. I want him to come back. This is just a difference of opinion, isn't it? I feel tears welling up. An icy voice inside says, You've lost him. Now you don't have to tell him.

The bench has that same ugly bail bondsman ad I saw the day I met with Morrie. I feel like that mean face is following me everywhere. Like some kind of evil totem.

27

Gossip

Are you sure this is the address?" I ask Ida.

"Positive." She looks again at the piece of paper in her hand. "Barbi wrote it down for me."

I pull into the minimall on University Avenue.

Sophie bounces up and down in the seat behind me. "I know where we are. There's Moishe's Deli."

And indeed it is. A place where we've eaten many times. The address we want is two doors away. For a moment we stare at the window. It's totally covered with some kind of pale gray paint, so no one can see through it. I remember the last time we were in this mall, that location was a shoe store.

We get out of the car and move closer. "Look there." Bella points.

In the right-hand corner of the window is a small, printed sign:

GOSSIP by Appointment Only

and a phone number.

"This is where Casey and Barbi work?" Evvie tries in vain to see through the paint. "Weird."

Bella ventures a guess. "Maybe they'll be dressed as gypsies and have a crystal ball."

A few days ago Ida ran into Barbi in the laundry room. They got to talking and Ida mentioned our case. And how frustrated I was, unable to get enough facts. Barbi suggested that she and her cousin might be able to help. And here we are, because after that dismal meeting with Morrie, I can't think of anything else to do.

I put my hand on the doorknob. "I hope we aren't wasting our time."

Bella is happy. "No matter what, it won't be a total nothing. We can always go next door for a nosh."

The door is locked. I see a doorbell and ring it.

Casey opens the door. Barbi is right behind her.

"Welcome," Barbi says.

Sophie gasps. I hope the rest of my troupe can keep from reacting. What I am immediately aware of is the way the cousins are dressed, and what this huge open space behind them looks like.

"We're running a little behind. Would you mind waiting a few minutes?" Casey leads us to a round white table and chairs. "We've set out a *petite* refreshment for you. I hope you like chai and scones with orange marmalade."

We sit down like obedient children. The girls are flummoxed. Even I am in awe.

The cousins leave us and move across this huge, seemingly empty room, where they sit at two computers.

The girls start whispering all at once.

"What's chai?" Bella asks.

"Why is everything white? It looks like an operating room in a hospital." Sophie wastes no time digging into a scone.

"It's only tea." Bella winces as she tries a few tentative sips. "It's spicy and too sweet."

Ida is astounded. "Do you believe those outfits?"

Casey is wearing a man's navy blue pinstriped suit, matching tie, and brown leather oxfords. Barbi is wearing what I see a lot of young girls wearing today: layers of unmatched tops with a long flowery skirt and straw sandals. Whatever happened to the jeans and sundresses? Their backs are to us. They are busily typing.

Bella asks, "Why is she wearing a man's suit?"

Evvie gives me a look. "Are you thinking what I'm thinking?"

I nod and look around the room. Three of the walls have low, attached white shelves. Most of the space is covered with machines. The only furnishings in the entire room are our table and chairs and two black desks with two matching rolling chairs that the women are seated on.

Evvie is glancing in the same direction. "I know those are computers," she says, pointing to the women working. "And that's a fax machine and a copier and a lot of phones. I don't know what the rest of that stuff is. This looks like state-of-the-art high tech."

"Have you ever in your life seen a business office," I say, "with not one single piece of paper anywhere?"

Except for the diplomas hanging on the wall above our table. They inform us that both women graduated with MBAs from USC in California. Both have degrees in law and computer science.

"You girls doing okay?" Casey says to us from across the huge room.

"Just fine," I answer.

So this is the future. All machines. No paper. Everything on computers. No books. I was right to fear technology. It will completely take over our lives, and this sterile environment is what it will look like. God help us.

Barbi and Casey wheel back to us, sliding over on the two black chairs.

I hear Ida stifle a cough as she stares and indicates to me her ring finger. I follow her stare. Barbi and Casey are wearing rings they don't wear around the condo. Wedding rings—identical gold bands with silver edges.

The two "cousins" seem not to notice. Casey takes charge. "What can we do for you? Ida suggested the other day that you might need access to information. That's what we do." She points to the banks of machines. "Whatever you want to know, HAL will tell you."

Evvie claps her hands in delight. "*2001: A Space Odyssey*. Stanley Kubrick."

The women smile. "Exactly," says Barbi.

Well, in for a penny, in for a pound, as the old saw says. I'm here. I might as well jump in and see what they have. "You know I'm trying to investigate some murders."

They nod and listen intently. My girls, of course, can't take their eyes off our hosts.

"I've been to the library and microfiched." All of a sudden I'm talking their language? What a hoot.

"Names?" Casey interrupts me and whizzes back across the white tile floor on her movable chair. She starts hitting the keys of a computer.

I nearly jump, taken aback. I manage to stutter out, "Margaret Sampson, Josephine Martinson, Elizabeth Johnson."

Barbi snaps out at me, "Cities?"

I have to think for a moment. Casey and Barbi are in superspeed mode, but my old gray cells need warming up. "West Palm Beach, Boca Raton..."

Evvie helps me out. "Sarasota Springs."

Barbi slides away to another machine. And we see two sets of hands typing and typing and typing. "What do you want to know?"

Now I get up and move closer to the two typing virtuosos. They remind me of a concert I went to in Carnegie Hall once with two amazing pianists dueling one another musically.

Naturally the girls all follow.

"I know some information about the women, their upbringing, their first husbands, their families' histories, their charity work. But what I thought interesting is that there wasn't very much about their second husbands. I assume Mrs. Johnson was remarried, too. I didn't have a chance to look her up."

The typists are typing away. It is fascinating watching their fingers.

"Okay," says Casey, swinging around to look at us. "What do you want to know about the second husbands?"

"Everything," says Evvie, fascinated by it all.

"You want to know everything about them since the day they were born? Parents? Entire family tree? Schools? Playmates? Hobbies? Higher education? Careers? Former relationships? Bank accounts? What kind of cars they drive? Where they buy their clothes? Clubs they belong to? Magazines they subscribe to? Legal difficulties? Were they ever in jail?"

"Whoa," I say. "Can we narrow it down? Specifically to their marriages to the women I named?"

Casey starts up again. Her hands never stop moving as she speaks. "Margaret Dery married Richard Sampson, June 10, 2001. They went to Bermuda for the wedding. Private ceremony, St. Paul's church rectory. Sampson was born in San Diego, California, April 5, 1960. Background? Parents owned a small mom-and-pop grocery..."

"Hold on," Evvie interrupts, counting on her fingers. "That makes him—"

Casey interrupts her. "Aha. I see you want the math, got an instant calculator. He's forty-five years old. Mrs. Sampson is sixty-four."

Was. Poor Mrs. Sampson will never see sixty-five. Twenty years difference. Now I'm intrigued. "Anything on his business background?"

The fingers keep tapping. "Sampson's last known business address five years ago was with Pipes Are Us, a plumbing establishment in West Palm Beach."

Barbi chimes in as her fingers keep clicking away. "Josephine Dano married Robert Martinson of Little Rock, Arkansas, August 17, 2002. She is sixty-one, Robert is thirty-seven. His last place of occupation, The Dance Palace in Miami Beach."

And I think about that gorgeous thirty-seven-year-old mourning at her graveside. Hmm.

"What about the lady in the cave?" Since Sophie found that ring, she feels Elizabeth's case should have first priority.

Casey types more. "Elizabeth Hoyle married Thomas Johnson, formerly of Baton Rouge, Louisiana."

"Cut to the chase. So how old are they?" Sophie sees where we're going and she's impatient.

Type, type, type. "She's fifty-nine, he's forty-two."

Evvie can be as rat-tat-tat as the cousins. "His line of work?"

"He was a nurse at the Sarasota Golden Years

Assisted Living Home. That was four years ago. No other work references since then."

I'm excited. "This is a real link. At last. All the women married younger men. Younger men. No money. If ever there was a great motive for murder."

"Happy we could be of help," says Casey.

Ida has obviously been pondering this for a while. "Are you blackmailers?" she blurts. "I mean, what do you do with all this information?"

"I beg your pardon," says Barbi. "We are lawyers, not crooks. We specialize in legal research."

"How can you know all this stuff?" Now Evvie jumps on the bandwagon.

"Anyone can get these facts. Don't let the name 'Gossip' fool you. That's for PR. Every single piece of information about you that is recorded somewhere can be accessed. By anyone. At any time."

Ida jumps in again. "So, if that's so, what does anyone need you for?"

"Good question," Casey says, not the least bit insulted. "We sell to law firms, magazines, writers, law enforcement, private parties—yes, and private detectives like yourself—who don't have the time or personnel to do all this research. Much of what we do takes a lot of digging. What you wanted was easy to access."

I glare at the girls. "I apologize for my friends' rudeness."

"No apology needed. A lot of people don't understand what we do."

I take a breath. Now that I've seen what they

do, the price must be exorbitant. Their machinery alone must cost a fortune. "About what we owe you . . . ?"

Barbi tells us they charge five hundred dollars an hour. Now there is a collective gasp of horror. Evvie manages to whisper, "Any senior rate?"

"Yeah," Ida says, still hostile. "We were only here about twenty minutes and I'm not counting the tea."

Barbi and Casey laugh. "No charge to our good neighbors. This first consult is free," says Barbi.

There's a group sigh of relief. We start to leave. They walk us to the door.

"Thanks for all your help," I say.

As I begin to step outside, Barbi asks, "What about prenups?"

"What about what?" Ida asks, confused.

"Most wealthy people draw up irrevocable premarital agreements called prenuptials. Especially when they marry someone with fewer assets than they have. Documents that can't be broken."

With shoulders slumped, I turn around and walk back inside. I am getting a sinking feeling in the pit of my stomach. "Can you check that out?"

Barbi is back at the console in a flash. I listen to the tap-tapping with dread this time. More tap-tapping. The girls move in closer. Casey is at the other console. Those two sure are compatible. I think the tapping will never end. But it does and the two turn to us, frowning.

Barbi starts. "Margaret Sampson's prenup agreement with her husband, Richard, gives him the house in West Palm Beach, the yacht, and a huge monthly stipend for the rest of his life should they divorce."

I am getting a picture and I don't like it. I urge her on. I want all the bad news over fast. "Josephine Martinson?"

Casey reads, "Prenup gives Robert the beach house in Key West, the estate in North Carolina..."

"Stop," I say. "Spare me the details. I suppose the Johnsons have one, also."

Tap-tap-tap. "Yup," says Barbi. "Basically the same. These women have been more than fair, settling amounts over a million with each of them if they ever divorce. Very lucky guys."

I pace. This is not what I expected. I whirl around. "They must have separate wills."

And they do in each case. Barbi shrugs, looking at her screen. "They are written up in different ways, but basically the husbands inherit it all when each woman dies."

"That's it," Evvie says. "They were greedy. They wanted everything. So they killed them."

"Greedy is right," adds Sophie. "I sure would have been happy with what they had already."

Something doesn't sit right. "Why now?" I ask. "Margaret's been married five years. Josephine, four." I look to Barbi—she scans her screen. "Seven years married for Elizabeth Johnson."

"Why didn't any of them kill their wives

before? Or just get a divorce? Suddenly all three men, living in different cities, get greedy at the same time? Doesn't make sense."

Unlucky me, I'm thinking. I just lost my motive. And my prime suspects. Older rich women, young husbands. I thought I had a slam dunk. Miss Marple would have been proud of me. But these husbands are rich enough without killing their wives. Why risk it? And if it's not the husbands, who's left? Nobody. And even worse, then Morrie is right. They weren't murders, after all. I have no case.

When we get outside, the girls want to eat at Moishe's. All that information has made them hungry. They're looking forward to some really good gossip of their own about Casey and Barbi. Not me. I've lost my appetite.

28

Bon Voyage

"Twelve minutes more." Bella announces the time yet again. She hasn't stopped looking at her watch since we got to the clubhouse this morning. She's terrified about being late, even though I told her we had all day to board the ship.

Phase Two gave us a bon voyage party. Naturally we are eating the Sunday brunch staples of bagels, cream cheese and lox, and egg salad and orange juice. We'll be sorry later when our thirst kicks in from the salty lox.

The girls are all dressed up. Everyone had to buy a special going-to-the-ship outfit. Very nautical. Blues and whites and white canvas deck sneakers. The obligatory sunglasses. Blue sailor caps. I am the only one dressed as I usually am. Sol Spankowitz is snapping photos for posterity.

It's Bella's turn to open her farewell gift, and just like all the others, it's Dramamine.

Evvie, who put herself in charge of getting information for us, exclaims, "But the brochure says with those modern stabilizers, you never even know you're on a boat."

Ida worries. "I sure hope that's true, since I've only been in the water in a rowboat thirty years ago and I did get seasick."

"Well, I'm not worried," Sophie announces. "My darling Stanley took me everywhere on cruises. Miami Beach. Key West. Everywhere. I never get sick. Let those winds blow as hard as they want."

Sophie is referring to this third day of high winds we've been having. No one dares mention the H word. Hurricane season isn't due for a month yet.

"I got another joke for you," says Hy. The rest of us groan. "What has seventy-five balls and makes women smile? Bingo!" He playfully gooses his giggling wife, Lola.

"What about the Peeping Tom?" May asks.

"It'll keep 'til we get back," Evvie answers.

My mind is not on these festivities. I keep looking toward the door, but there is no sign of Jack and we have to leave in about ten minutes. I can't believe he hasn't called me, and I stubbornly refuse to call him. Our first fight and neither of us will give in. I guess I thought he was perfect, but he's not. But then again, neither am I.

Sol sidles up to Evvie and hands her a small bouquet of daisies. "Bonnie voyagee," he says, mutilating the phrase. "Maybe when you come back, a little date?"

"Thanks, but no thanks," Evvie says, looking pointedly at Sol. "I'm allergic."

"I'm not," says Tessie, who is standing next to them, chomping on a huge egg salad sandwich on a kaiser roll. Evvie shoves the flowers at her. Tessie grabs them, spilling egg salad all over her ample front as she does. She actually blushes. "Thanks, Sol," she says. "How nice of you."

Sol looks confused. "Don't mention it."

"Don't forget to send postcards," Mary Mueller says.

"Bring me back something. Anything," says Barney. He and Conchetta came from the library to join in the send-off.

"Five minutes more," Bella says, getting more antsy by the minute.

I'm still staring at the door. He's not coming. Should I call him? I can't just leave this way, with both of us angry.

When we hear the loud honking of horns, everybody is on the move. We are followed along the pool path back to our parking area, where two drivers wait for us. Denny Ryan has his old Ford Fairlane at the ready and Casey Wright waits by her small lavender VW. They've volunteered to drive us down to the pier. When I reach her car, Casey winks at me. She now shares a secret with my team of private eyes. Much as I'm not looking forward to this cruise, I am looking forward to putting my imaginary murder case behind me. I feel like such a failure.

Our luggage is already stacked in the two open trunks. Bright Day-Glo identification tags proclaim that we are on the *Heavenly* cruise ship and have our names and stateroom numbers written on them.

Evvie obsessively counts each one to make sure nothing has been left behind.

There is much hugging and calls of "Bon voyage" and "Have fun" and "Win a lot of money" as we pile into the vehicles. I am still looking everywhere for Jack.

The girls are giggling and punching one another in excitement, and all I feel is gloom.

29

All Aboard

Such excitement. And chaos. Mobs of people boarding the ship. Suitcases stacked everywhere. The girls are holding on to one another, thrilled and petrified at the same time as they look up and up at their ship. The *Heavenly* is awesome. It is gleaming white and incredibly huge. Evvie, clutching our information packet, tells us the ship is ten stories high. We walk up the gangway and the ship's publicity picture-taking starts. Say cheese. Over and over again.

The interior main deck is gorgeous. Evvie is reading as we stare. " 'The ship weighs sixty thousand tons. It carries two thousand guests and nine hundred staff. The atrium is the *Heavenly*'s famous white, brass, and glass centerpiece. Our *Heavenly* personnel stand ready to help plan your day-onshore tours and offer information on just about anything else you might need to know.' "

We stand inside the atrium looking at the spectacular adjoining staircases and glass elevators. The girls are oohing and aahing.

Two huge placards read *Welcome Bingo Tournament Players!* and *Welcome Bridge Tournament Players!*

"That's us," Sophie says, pointing to the bingo notice. It informs us that registration opens tomorrow morning at eight.

Finding our rooms is a challenge. If we take the wrong elevator we'll end up in the wrong section. I foresee much confusion and lost girls in the near future. As if reading my mind, Bella says to all, "Don't you dare leave me alone. Ever!"

Sophie hugs her. "We would never do that to you, sweetums."

Evvie is reading aloud from her ship's instruction sheet. " 'Rooms are found by looking for odd or even numbers. Only two elevators will take you to the front and to the back of your stateroom path. Learn where they are.' "

Sophie takes a turn and proclaims the ship's slogan from its daily newspaper: " 'You've just died and gone to *Heavenly*.' " She giggles. "Here's today's schedule: 'The rum-and-Coca-Cola party is in the Angel Bar, where pizza slices, sushi, and tiny meatball appetizers will be offered as you stroll. Cocktails at five, first seating for dinner at six. Second seating at eight. And gala midnight buffet every night.' "

Ida says, "Tessie should be here—nonstop eating. She'd be in heaven." She laughs. "Excuse me, heaven*ly*."

We finally find the right elevator. When it arrives we get in. A sweet-looking but plain woman in her sixties enters with us. She looks very confused.

"Can we help?" asks the always obliging Bella. "Not that we know where we're going."

The woman manages a small smile. "I was supposed to meet some friends but I can't find them. And I can't find my room, either."

"You'll run into them sometime," Evvie says.

"It certainly is bewildering. The last time I was on this cruise my husband led me around. I never paid attention. This time he didn't come along and I don't remember a thing."

"What deck are you on?" I ask.

"Celestial."

"We are, too," says Sophie. "Stick with us; we'll help you find your room."

We reach the Celestial deck and search for the even-number side. Our new buddy is four rooms down the narrow hall from us. We see her to her door. The woman thanks us profusely.

"Nice lady," Bella says as we open our own doors.

"Lady with some do-re-mi," says Sophie. "Her clothes are expensive. Dowdy, but expensive. Her room is on the ocean side, so it has sliding glass doors and a balcony."

"How do you know all that?" asks Bella, impressed.

"Well, you know what a clothes horse I am, and besides, I took a quick peek when she opened the door."

I smile. "Good detecting, Soph."

Sophie beams. "Practice makes perfect."

Our room, of course, hasn't got an outside port-hole. Sophie, with Bella clinging to her, quickly opens our interior, adjoining door, then their interior door. "Follow me," Sophie says to Bella as they enter their room.

From where Evvie, Ida, and I are standing, we can see that the winning-ticket room next to us has twin beds, a good-sized dresser, a coffee table and side chairs, and is seemingly spacious. Our room is tiny and, to our horror, what we have is a bunk bed and a small roll-away cot, and one very narrow closet. With the three of us standing in the center, there is almost no room to move around.

"Bunk beds! Are they crazy!" Ida screeches. "No way can I climb up there."

"Me, neither," says Evvie, "not with my arthritis."

And frankly, neither can I.

"And I won't sleep on the bottom, either," says Ida stubbornly. "I get claustrophobia." She looks at the blank walls. "No windows? I'm already feeling closed in."

"Don't think about it," says Evvie. "We'll only be in here to sleep."

Meanwhile the two happy campers next door are opening their suitcases and busily arranging things in their dresser, humming little show tunes as we stand like stones.

Well, I have to try something. I pick up the phone and ask for help. I tell the operator our problem. A few minutes later our appointed room steward arrives. His name tag identifies him as Herve, from Argentina. He is gorgeous. But he is at a loss—probably no one has ever made this kind of complaint before. Ida is standing with her arms crossed defensively. Evvie is tapping her foot.

Finally, I get an idea. "Can we get rid of the bunk bed and the cot and just leave the three mattresses?"

The steward, well trained, does not argue. "Yes, madam."

There is much snapping of fingers outside the doorway. Helpers arrive. Within moments the beds are gone and all three mattresses, made up with sheets, pillows, and blankets, are placed in a row against the back of the room. What with our creaking old knees bending to climb up and down from the floor level, this will be a physical challenge. Not only that, we're basically sleeping in one long bed, but it's our only solution.

Evvie hugs me. "What would we do without you, oh fearless leader?" And I think to myself, They would have done very well without me. They would have had only two beds in the room and Evvie as the perfect guide.

We hear the four o'clock signal informing us we are about to depart, and we don't want to miss the excitement on deck as the ship leaves the port.

God, how I miss Jack.

30

Run, Run, Run

We are heading back toward our staterooms to finish unpacking, grabbing the fattening little snacks being offered us along the way, when we hear an ear-piercing blast of noise. In fact, a series of seven blasts in a row. A severe-sounding voice over the loudspeakers informs us, "This is a lifeboat drill. Everyone must attend. Report directly to your rooms, collect your life jackets, and proceed immediately to the Muster Stations listed on your jackets. Do not use the elevators." The succession of seven blasts continues as the voice keeps repeating the instructions. It is deafening.

Total panic ensues.

"*Oy,*" wails Sophie. "We're only on the boat half an hour and it's sinking already?"

Bella asks, tugging at her, "What did he say? Why is he talking about mustard?"

"Calm down," I say loudly, needing to be heard above the din. "It's only a drill. A practice."

Evvie, turning her instruction pages wildly, finally finds the information. "They do this immediately after a ship takes off, so we'll know what to do if there's an emergency."

"So, how will we find our rooms again?" Ida wants to know. "I'm all turned around."

"Where are we, anyway?" Evvie asks, turning the ship's map every which way. "According to this we're at something called the Devil's Own Bar." A vicious red devil grins down at us from above.

Bella shivers. "That thing gives me the creeps."

"Follow me," I tell them, spotting a sign down the hall. "We have to take the stairs."

"How far?" asks Ida.

"Three flights," I say. "At least it's going down."

"Yeah, but then I bet we have to go back up," Evvie comments.

"Why can't we take the elevator?" Ida says. "We're old people. We shouldn't be expected to run around like this."

Evvie throws her a look of astonishment. "I never thought I'd live to hear *you* say that."

"I'm gonna faint," Sophie squeals.

"No, you're not," says Evvie, pushing her from the rear. "Move it."

The series of seven blasts keeps battering our ears. People are hurrying wildly in different directions. Sophie is pulling Bella along. Ida is pumping her short little legs as fast as she can.

We reach our staircase and hold tightly to the railing. We walk down as quickly as we can against the flow of others who are running up, jostling us as they do. It is utter pandemonium.

In our rooms, Evvie figures out where the life jackets are. We struggle into them as we go back out into the corridor and up the stairs, huffing and puffing.

"If I drop dead," Sophie says, "tell my kids to sue."

"This thing is choking me and I can't see," Bella says, struggling to lower her head over the top of the jacket, which is tied tightly under her chin. Ida grabs her arm and pulls her along.

We get to our designated lifeboat station, number three on one of the upper decks, where a large group of people are all bunched together in a sea of orange. All of them are uncomfortably peering over their chins, their heads looking as if they are not attached to their bodies. We are a panting mess.

"Are we having fun yet?" asks Bella.

Another short blast sounds and then, suddenly, silence.

"What's that?" Ida asks.

"The drill is over," says a big tough-looking guy wearing a Green Bay Packers jacket.

His wife—I assume, since she's in a matching green Packers ensemble—agrees. "You missed all the life-saving instructions."

They introduce themselves as Greg and Polly.

Sophie is incredulous. "It's over? We just got here."

People are laughing at us as they leave the lifeboat station. "You should have taken the elevator," says someone.

"Yes, you're senior citizens, you didn't need to take the stairs in a drill."

We all glower at Evvie.

She shrugs sheepishly. "I didn't get that far in the instructions. Besides, how come nobody else volunteered to be in charge of information?"

We are catching our breaths, sitting on the deck, having Mai Tais to relax us after our harrowing drill experience. We also just went through the orientation meeting in the big main theater, and our heads are still reeling from the amount of things to remember. We still have our life jackets on, but this time, opened so we can breathe. Going back to the room to drop them off seemed too exhausting. Actually, these vests are keeping us warm. It is cool and windy out here.

"We need a month to try all those activities," Sophie says happily.

"But don't forget," Evvie reminds us, "what with playing bingo and going ashore, we won't have too much time for other activities."

"I want to spend all of my free time in the casino," Ida says. "I'm feeling lucky."

"And I want to take cha-cha lessons with those

guys they hire to dance with single ladies." This from Sophie.

"Me, too," echoes Bella.

"I just want to hang around on the top deck, swim and play games, and just veg out," says Evvie. "What about you, Glad? You're so quiet."

How can I tell them all I want is to go home? "There's so much to choose from," I say lamely.

Sergeant Evvie looks at her watch. "Time for dinner. We have the early seating. And we don't dress up on the first night. Let's drop off our life jackets and just go."

We haven't stopped noshing since we boarded. Nobody's hungry, but we're not about to miss dinner. And you can bet we won't miss the midnight buffet.

Sophie grins. "I may gain ten pounds on this trip. But what a way to go."

31

First Night

The dining room is beautiful. So glittery. So glitzy. Yet elegant, with dramatic chandeliers overhead—Vegas on water. So many plates, so much silverware. So many waiters. We are escorted to our table, which seats six.

"I could get spoiled by this." Evvie sighs happily as she watches the passengers chatting with one another. "Amazing how they can handle two thousand people on this ship. Wow!"

"Who's gonna ever want to eat in our tiny little kitchens again?" says Sophie. "Wouldn't it be great to just live on one of these boats forever?"

"Great idea." Evvie is already nibbling at the huge selection of bread. "When our kids are ready to dump us in a retirement home or in assisted living, we could do this instead." Evvie does the math. "If we found a ship that cost us about five hundred dollars a week, that would be about thirty thousand dollars a year. Hey, you can hardly get a decent retirement place for that price. And they have doctors aboard, too."

Bella stares around the room, admiring it all. "It's certainly nicer than our dinky continental restaurant."

"That's for sure," agrees Evvie.

A waiter appears. I amend that. A drop-dead gorgeous waiter. His name tag tells us he is Antonio from Guatemala. "Champagne, ladies?"

Who's going to say no to him, or the champagne, though Ida barely sips at hers.

Evvie asks who is to be seated in the sixth chair. The waiter consults a chart. "No one, madam," he says.

I think to myself how wonderful it would be sharing this with Jack. Then I tell myself to snap out of it. I made my bed, now I have to lie in it. With two other women. In spite of my sadness, I have to smile at that. I make up my mind that since I'm here I have to be here, really be here. It's not fair to the girls to just keep moping.

"Do you believe the choice of entrées?" I say, taking part. "I don't know how I can choose."

"I want two of everything," Sophie says joyously, reading the menu.

"Don't be ridiculous," Evvie snaps. "You'll never be able to eat it."

"I will so."

"You'll make a fool of yourself."

"Will not."

Another dreamboat waiter takes our orders. His name tag informs us he is Gustav from Bavaria. I'm beginning to like this particular cruise-ship gimmick. Spitefully, Sophie orders two appetizers, the steamed asparagus and the lobster bisque, and two entrées, sole amandine and poached salmon. Plus, of course, the veggies that come with each.

Evvie gives her a dirty look.

"Look who's over there," says Bella, pointing.

The woman we met earlier in the elevator is seated two tables away from us. She's at a table for four. But so far, she's alone.

Bella waves and catches her eye. The woman waves back. She doesn't look happy. We are surprised to see her stand up and walk over to us.

"May I sit down for a moment?"

We chorus our agreement.

"I still can't find my bridge partners. We all planned to meet for this tournament and there's still no sign of them."

I ask, "Did you try the purser?"

"Yes, but by the time I decided to do so, his office was closed. I'll go to the bridge sign-up in the morning. If they're still not there, then I'll check with the purser."

"Why don't you join us? No sense eating alone," says Evvie.

She gratefully nods as we smile our agreement. The waiter comes back and takes her order.

"I guess we should introduce ourselves," I say.

We all do so and our new friend introduces herself as Amy Larkin from Miami Beach.

The first course arrives—appetizer or soup, though Sophie prepares to dig in to both. Evvie shakes her head in disgust.

"Oooh." A soft but intense sound comes from Ida.

We look at her and she's gone pale.

"What?" Evvie asks.

"Look," she says faintly.

"What? What are we supposed to see?" says Sophie. "All I see is tomato soup."

"It's moving!" It is a faint, strangled cry. Ida is clutching her stomach.

And yes, the soup seems to move very slowly from side to side in her bowl. Ida leaps up, covering her mouth with both hands. Now she looks green. She runs out of the dining room.

Evvie, alarmed, says, "She's getting seasick. I'll go after her." And she is off.

For a moment, we are all speechless.

Bella pokes around her salad. "Well, nothing's moving in here." She starts eating. Sophie follows with gusto.

Amy and I hesitate, but not for long. The food is delicious. Poor Ida.

Evvie reports back. "She's sick as a dog and she's got a bucket in front of her. Would you believe? One of the busboys saw her run and he brought out a bucket, a wet towel, and a bottle of club soda. What service!" She stops. "Hmm, I guess I should have tipped him. Anyway, she won't go back to the room. She wants air and I don't blame her. I wrapped her in some deck chair blankets and she said for us to have fun and come and get her when we go downstairs for the night."

"Poor Ida," says Sophie. She's already finished the salmon and is digging into her sole amandine. She's slowing down, but she doesn't want to give Evvie the satisfaction of being able to say I told you so.

Evvie watches her closely. By now Sophie is pushing the filet around her plate, pretending to eat.

Bella giggles. Evvie smirks.

We chitchat about the various choices of entertainment we'll have on the cruise, and dinner is very pleasant.

After dessert and coffee, Amy excuses herself. She's retiring for the night. She thanks us for inviting her. And we say we hope she finally finds her friends.

We, too, decide it's been an exhausting day. We find Ida, who is feeling better, and head for our rooms.

Sophie gets her door open first, and she lets out a bloodcurdling scream. "Someone's broken into our room!"

We hurry inside.

She points at something leaning against her pillow, next to a little square of chocolate. "What is it?"

I examine it carefully. To me it looks like a towel folded into the shape of a bird.

Meanwhile, Evvie has opened our door. "In here, too," she calls. We look through the adjoining door. We have three "birds" made out of our towels. But ours are attached to the bathroom door, positioned to look as if their wings were in flight.

I begin to laugh. Then Evvie joins me. "What's the joke?" demands Sophie.

"I think this is supposed to be a funny gift from the crew members who turn down our beds." I take one, amused at how cleverly they've been sculpted together.

Finally the others get it, too, and start laughing.

Evvie starts to put on her pajamas. "What a day! First we schlepp up and down the whole ship before we find our room, then we almost drop dead running up and down stairs for the fire drill, then we eat too much at dinner, and now we'll have to live on Tums—"

"And what about me?" pipes in Ida, who is lying against the far wall, a wet cloth on her forehead, and clutching a wastebasket. "I upchucked all those little meatballs and pizza bits and I'm still feeling sick."

"Then," continues Evvie, "we come back to our rooms so we can get some rest and we're scared out of our wits by towels turned into art."

As I kneel down onto my mattress, I hear Bella saying from the open door of the other stateroom, "If every day is gonna be like this, I might not survive this trip."

Ida says, "Bite your tongue."

32

Four Corners Plus Hardway

It's eight-thirty in the morning and I already feel like a wreck. Ida didn't sleep a wink, so we didn't sleep much, either. She threw up on and off all night long, including the Dramamine she took, which didn't help. If she wasn't retching into her wastebasket she was climbing off the mattress, jostling the rest of us every time, to run to the bathroom. *Oy!*

We don't want to leave her, but she insists. If she feels better later, she says, she'll come and join us. With instructions to call room service if she needs anything, we leave her curled up fetal-style, groaning.

We drag our exhausted selves up to the dining room, where we find Miss Perky and Miss Perkette, dressed adorably in matching pink capris and identical pink ruffled cardigan sweaters, under which are their bingo shirts.

They are stuffing themselves with an enormous breakfast.

"Sleep well?" Evvie asks, dripping sarcasm.

"Like on a cloud with the boat rocking us in its arms," says Sophie, waxing poetic as she mixes metaphors.

"We're supposed to play bingo at nine and we haven't even registered yet. We're definitely going to be late."

Evvie says to them, "You're done, go over to the big auditorium and pick up our stuff and get us a big table or a booth."

They look startled. "But we don't know the way," Sophie whines.

"It's where we went for the orientation meeting," I remind her.

Now Bella, whiner number two, is heard from. "Who can remember?"

Evvie points. "Walk out the door, turn left. Go to the very end, and if you fall off the boat and end up in the ocean and drown, you went too far. We'll eat something quickly and meet you there. Try to get us seats up front so we can hear and see."

Holding hands, they scamper out, looking back at us in terror.

We hurry through cold cereal and coffee and toast. Evvie doesn't want to miss the start of the tournament.

*   *   *

The auditorium is a mob scene with much pushing and shoving and shouting. Most of the crowd are women in an assortment of bingo shirts with tacky bingo slogans.

"Oh, boy," says Evvie, "we threw our girls into a lion's pit. I feel guilty."

We make our way through the crowd, and it isn't easy. There must be about five hundred people jockeying for seats. If they play bingo the way they ram and shove, we're in a lot of trouble.

"There they are." Evvie looks where I point. I can't believe it. They're actually in a front-row booth.

When we reach them we have to smile. Their hair's a mess, lipstick smeared, clothes askew. They are grinning with satisfaction. Mission accomplished.

Evvie congratulates them. "How'd you manage?"

Bella is proud. "Sophie held me around my middle and just pushed me, and I butted people out of our way. But *they* were really mean. They tried to grab our booth away from us."

Bella points at the adjoining booth where two tough-looking gals glare at us. They are in their fifties, both wearing bingo shirts and each holding a doll dressed in clothes made out of bingo cards. In front of them is a sign announcing that they are the Bingo Dolls from Tucson.

The mean-looking woman on the right sneers at us. "That's always our table," she insists.

Bella straightens to her full four foot ten, puts her hands on her hips, and says, "Oh, yeah, sez who?"

I try to make peace by introducing us to the Dolls. They tell us they are Judy, who wears a T-shirt that reads "I'm a bingo-holic," and Rose, whose shirt reads "To hell with housework, I'd rather play bingo."

Apparently, they take this cruise every year. In fact, each of them won a game last time, and they predict one of them is going to be the big winner of this one.

"Well, we'll see about that," Sophie huffs.

She and Bella turn their backs on them and the Dolls do the same to us.

Bella whispers, "I have the same T-shirt as that Judy. I'm gonna wear that one tomorrow."

"Yeah," says Sophie, "we'll show 'em."

By now one of the bingo coordinators is on-stage, standing in front of the huge lit-up bingo board. He tells a few corny jokes, reads the rules, and it's time to play. Like a football coach in the locker room, he shouts us on. "Are we ready?"

The crowd screams, "Yes!"

"Which lucky person is gonna win game one?" And of course there is a roar of "Me" from all over the huge room and a waving of lucky charms that people brought along. Naturally, our unfriendly neighbors are waving their dolls.

Sophie and Bella are wiggling up and down in the booth.

"It's every man for himself!" says the male coordinator to the roomful of mostly women. "Let's play bingo!"

Game packs are passed around; brightly colored daubers are at the ready.

Evvie and Ida (poor absent Ida must be miserable about not being here) are highly competitive and deadly serious about winning. When they don't win (which is ninety-nine percent of the time), they take it as a personal affront. Bella actually dislikes bingo as much as she dislikes playing cards, because it is much too complicated for her, but the misery is worth it as long as she can be with us.

As for me, I love puzzles and games of all kinds, but I certainly don't find bingo relaxing. And I don't expect to win with these odds. Sophie is not as emotionally involved as the others but she is very much into the fashions. She now has a collection of about twenty bingo shirts with their rather lowbrow sayings, and she feels undressed if she isn't wearing one. Today's choice has the slogan: "What does the wife say to the husband who will divorce her if she won't give up bingo? I'll miss you."

Except for Bella, the rest of us wouldn't be caught dead in them.

One minute to go—we high-five each other for luck.

Like Thoroughbreds at the gate, my pals wait

with bated breath for that first number out of the cage. And we're off!

And it's a familiar song and dance. Evvie is already bitching.

End of the Crazy Letter L game: "I was only two away."

End of the Hardway Six-pack game, she says, annoyed, to Sophie: "I was on. I needed *your* lucky number three!"

"So, it's my fault my lucky number only loves me?"

"These are the worst cards I've ever had," Evvie says.

"You think *you* have rotten cards..." Sophie answers.

"Well, I'm on, so naturally someone is going to yell—"

"Bingo!" And it's our neighbor, Rose. She smirks at us as she collects two hundred and fifty dollars.

The girls are openly jealous. Boy, do they take this game seriously.

Sophie has a different opera going on with Bella. Bella can't keep up, so this is their duet:

"Soph, what was that last number?"

"It was B-five."

"I got that one. Maybe it was the one before."

"Why don't you watch the monitor?"

"I am watching the monitor."

"Watch closer."

"What did you say? You know I don't hear good."

Sophie shouts, "*Watch the monitor!* Now you made me miss a number. Evvie, what did he just call?"

"Quiet! I'm concentrating. Don't bother me."

And the Bingo Dolls next door chime in: "Will you all shut up!"

And so it goes.

The letter Z comes and goes, as does the inside layer cake and crazy arrow, and our packs are getting very thin.

And finally it's over. Thank God. I'm exhausted. The Bingo Dolls make faces at us as they leave.

Evvie says to Sophie, "I sure hope you reserved this booth for Wednesday."

"No chance," she answers. "No reserved seats. First come, first served."

Bella blanches. "You mean we have to go through this every time?"

The girls go back to our staterooms to see how Ida is doing. I volunteer to check on what to do in Puerto Rico, our first stop tomorrow.

I am looking through the colorful brochures in the travel section of the main lobby when I see Amy Larkin pacing aimlessly near the purser's office. I make my way through the large numbers of people who are planning their first day ashore.

"Amy?" I look at her questioningly.

She shakes her head. "No sign of them."

"What did the purser tell you?"

"Well, he looked them up, and apparently one of the women canceled a few weeks ago. The other two must be no-shows. It's silly of me—I was so sure we'd all show up, I never bothered to call anyone to confirm."

"I'm so sorry, this must be a letdown for you."

"I guess people make plans and other things come up that are more important."

"But they all made their reservations," I point out. I think about what her room must have cost. "Well, I certainly hope they all got their money back."

Amy smiles. "I doubt it, but believe me, losing that money wouldn't matter to them."

"Join us for dinner again. And if you want, please come ashore with us tomorrow."

"Thanks. You and your friends are being very kind."

Tonight's dinner theme is Italian. We are dressed up for the evening, wearing long dresses we brought for the occasion. We have our hair done up, makeup, the works. I must say we haven't worn these outfits in years and it's fun.

But we are no match for the waiters, who are dazzling in their fancy costumes. In between courses—which consist of every pasta imaginable in every imaginable sauce—the waiters sing and dance, snaking their way around the room picking guests to join them.

Finally Sophie can't sit still another moment. She leaps up, and the look on her face when she's wedged between two of the handsome waiters is something wonderful to see. Bella applauds as she dances around our table.

Ida sits quietly, eating very little, mostly nibbling on tiny bits of bread, keeping her eyes averted from any soup plates passing by.

Stuffed as usual (except for Ida), we finally leave the dining room for the rest of the evening. Ida is going to try the casino. Amy wants to go to the chamber music concert in the library, and the new twins, Sophie and Bella, are going to take cha-cha lessons. With a map of the ship in hand, Sophie is feeling braver about finding her way without the rest of us. I intend to do some serious cruising along the deck to walk off the massive amount of food I shouldn't have eaten.

Tonight we find an elephant and a puppy made of towels waiting for us in our staterooms, but this time we take these little surprises in stride. All five of us get in our "jammies" and settle down on the three beds and, like girls at a sleepover, we drink another round of Mai Tais and tell of our night's adventures.

Ida tells us how she got a great slot machine and won five bucks. Of course she put in three bucks to get there, but it did last for the whole two hours and she did win. At least it took her mind off being hungry.

I tell them about all the fun games on the decks and the crowds that spent the evening swimming and hot-tubbing to a rock-and-roll band.

Bella and Sophie are ecstatic about their cha-cha lesson and the sexy hunk with curly black hair who taught them. "Señor Roberto, mmmm." Bella drools. "I want to take that green-eyed doll home with me."

"Not if I grab him first," giggles Sophie.

"In your dreams," Ida says.

"Could we take private lessons?" Sophie asks.

"Too expensive," Evvie, our treasurer, answers.

"If she does, I want to, too," says Bella. "It's nice to have a handsome guy's arm around me." She blushes.

Which makes me think about my handsome guy, left behind, and angry at me.

What am I doing on this stupid trip when I'd rather be home?

33

Going Ashore

It's early morning and already there are large crowds. Everyone is carrying cameras, sun hats, and such, eager to explore our first destination off the ship. To get our feet on land again. San Juan, Puerto Rico, here we are.

Knowing my group, I have been nagging: "Do not forget your pass. If you do, you can't go ashore. Do not lose your pass. If you do, getting back on board will be one hell of a lot of trouble." All I get for my pains is a couple of offhand *yeah, yeah*s. This is not reassuring.

Amy Larkin is with us. She'll have to wait until later to see the purser, since we're going out so early—but by now she's resigned to being alone on the cruise. And annoyed at being stood up.

Ida is glad the ship is parked right at the shore. She hates the idea of being on one of those small tenders, rocking from the ship to the shore in choppy waters. We just walk down the gangway and right into San Juan's famous Old Town.

Which doesn't look all that old: the first store I spot is a Harley-Davidson Motorcycle gift shop. Hmmm.

Evvie, the self-appointed tour guide, has suggested we get on one of the cute, colorful trolleys that passes by and ride around to get an "overview." Then we'll get off when we find someplace that catches our eye.

"So, what's our plan?" Sophie wants Evvie to lay it out. She and Bella can hardly contain their excitement.

"Touring by trolley first, then some walking and shopping, then lunch."

"May I make a suggestion?" Amy says. "I was here six weeks ago, on the ship's last bridge/bingo cruise, and my friends and I found a good authentic Puerto Rican restaurant. And afterwards, the most interesting place of all to see is the fort, El Morro."

"That sounds great to me," I say.

"The shopping part is my favorite." Sophie is already zeroing in on her favorite pastime.

"I like the lunch part," adds Bella.

Ida agrees. She intends to eat a lot on shore, in a place where soup doesn't move.

The trolley arrives and there is already a large crowd waiting. Tourists are pushing their way in. I lose sight of the girls as they head toward the rear.

I grab a seat up front with Amy. She looks pale to me. "Are you all right?"

I can see her fidgeting with her wedding ring. "No, not really. I think this whole business of not finding my bridge partners has shaken me. I'm beginning to imagine things."

"Such as?"

"Last night I couldn't fall asleep. I guess I tried to go to bed too early. Around ten o'clock, I got dressed again and went for a walk around the deck. Many people were out strolling, but I had the weirdest feeling, like someone was following me."

"Did you see anyone?"

"No. But when I went back to my stateroom, my patio door seemed different. It was as if something had pulled it slightly off its hinge."

I am getting alarmed at this. "You mean 'someone'?"

She hesitates. "No. No, of course not." But when she looks down at her thin hands, they are shaking. "I'm just being silly and overanxious."

"Maybe you have good reason. We should talk to a crew member when we get back."

Amy tries to make light of it. "What if there's a jewel thief on board? I should leave a note. 'I didn't bring any of my good jewelry with me.'"

We both chuckle at that. But as the trolley tour guide begins to announce the landmarks we are passing, I wonder if I should press Amy to tell the ship's authorities about her concerns. But then I remind myself that I'm supposed to be forgetting about these "imagined conspiracies," as Morrie calls them, while I'm on this cruise.

We ride around the town center. The buildings themselves are very old, but not the shops in them. Their names aren't familiar, J. Machini and Serenity, but they seem like very expensive Puerto Rican businesses. Many of them look like jewelry stores. And many are beautiful crafts shops, like the Butterfly People. Sophie and Bella can hardly wait to shop. Evvie insists, "Culture first." So we get on and off the trolley at various spots and Amy fills us in on the many churches, as well as the statues and plazas. We are impressed with the elegant El Convento hotel that actually was once a convent.

When we stop at the statue of Ponce de León, Evvie asks with a sigh, "Why didn't he ever tell us where that Fountain of Youth was?" That's a sentiment we all share.

Finally, with feet hurting and stomachs grumbling, we let Amy lead us down De la Cruz Street to a charming little restaurant called Spanglish.

The inside is small, two rooms, but very inviting. The owner is there with his wife and mother and his adorable children. Everyone makes us feel very comfortable, even though the Puerto Rican menu on the blackboard is intimidating. But the wonderful smells relax us.

We are sitting at our table in the front room, drinking sangria and listening to our waiter translate the food choices, when I hear someone calling, "Gladdy Gold. Can I believe my eyes? Is that you?"

All of us turn to look through the doorway into the second room, where a familiar figure in black is making her way toward us, pushing her walker ahead of her.

It can't be—but it is! Angelina Siciliano! And right behind her is the fearful Mr. Macho himself, Elio!

For a moment, we are all speechless. Then Elio laughs. "You broads still following us?"

Evvie quips back, "Maybe you're following us."

Our waiter quickly pulls up two more chairs and seats them. With that, we practically fill the entire front room.

Everyone is talking at once, trying to figure how this could be. The Sicilianos are on their second honeymoon; Angelina reminds me that she told me about it. With that she reaches over and gives Elio a sloppy, wet kiss and Elio wipes it off, embarrassed. "All because of you girls," Angelina says, almost kittenish.

"Yeah," Elio growls at us. "She never leaves me alone. I liked it better when she hated me."

"And we entered a bingo contest," Evvie explains.

"And won a cruise. On the *Heavenly,*" Ida adds.

"No!" says Angelina in surprise. "We're on the same ship."

The same ship. What a coincidence! Evvie and I exchange glances. We introduce the Sicilianos to Amy, then we chat about what sights to see, and we agree to meet them tonight for cocktails at Elio's favorite hangout on board, the Devil's Own Bar.

They take their leave of us and, for a moment, we sit, still stunned.

"How about that." Ida states what we're all thinking. "How amazing!"

But despite my best intentions, the word "coincidence" stays in my head. Is it?

Amy is right, El Morro Fort is truly magnificent. This stone edifice is compared in historical importance to the Great Wall of China and the Pyramids of Egypt. Just standing inside it awes one with its power. Amy, our history buff, states that it was built in 1540 to protect the city from sea attacks. Four hundred and sixty-five years ago and it's still standing! It has six levels, a height of 140 feet, and walls twenty feet thick—at one time it had more than 450 mounted guns.

We move from one parapet to another, looking through the large openings that used to contain cannons. The water views are gorgeous. We can even see our cruise ship waiting for us in the harbor.

But what is most awesome is the drop from these openings down to the roiling seas.

Ida won't go anywhere near the edge of any of them. The view gives her vertigo. The adventurous Bella and Sophie do so, but take turns by holding on to one another's sleeves. Evvie and I keep a respectful distance.

Bella and Sophie are impatient. We only have a little bit of time to shop.

Ida agrees. She saw a children's shop where she wants to find something for her grandchildren. No one comments that her ungrateful children won't appreciate it.

"Well," says Evvie, "there's actually a Walgreens. I need some moisturizer."

"And a Ben and Jerry's," Sophie adds eagerly.

I shrug. I might as well go to that tempting bookstore I passed earlier.

"I think I'll stay," Amy says. "I want another look around, and maybe go back to the fort's gift shop. I didn't get much time to visit last trip."

With much pointing at our individual maps, we decide to separate, and with many reminders, we agree to meet back at the ship a half hour before the time we're supposed to be there, which is three o'clock sharp.

As we head down the long hill toward the center, I tell them once more, "Do not be late!"

"Yeah, yeah!"

That doesn't encourage me. I will worry until I see every one of their silver hairs.

I wave to Amy, who also waves as she heads back into the fort.

I am the first to return to the ship, and I listen to the sounds of the charming band concert going on in the little park a few feet away. There are many palm trees, and the listeners relax in their shade while children play in the grass. So peaceful, so pretty. Passengers move past me to board the ship, smiling at the musicians as they go by. I look at my watch. Two-forty.

One by one the girls meander back with their loot. Thank God, they are all here. We start to walk inside, our shore passes in our hands.

"Wait a minute," I ask, "where's Amy?" We turn and stare back down the tree-lined pathway leading to the ship. I see a couple of stragglers hurrying.

But it turns out I was right to worry, because I don't see Amy.

34

But Not Going Aboard

Maybe you're worrying for nothing," Sophie says. "She still has four minutes."

"She would have been here on time. I just feel it in my bones that something's wrong." Despite my promise to myself, I can't ignore these instincts.

We are standing about six inches away from the gangplank and a few stragglers are hurrying past us. A large man pushes Ida aside in his hurry. She instinctively swats his back, but he doesn't stop. We also spot the MC from the huge after-dinner shows, and Greg and Polly, the couple from Green Bay, Wisconsin. I know the girls are torn. They want to get on the ship, but they don't want to leave me.

"We are pulling up in three minutes," one of the nearby sailors informs us in a tightly controlled voice.

"We have to wait," I say.

By now, other crew members have gathered. Passengers on the upper decks are looking down at us, sensing the anxiety in the air.

I look frantically in all directions for some sight of Amy, but no luck.

"We have rules—" begins the same sailor.

"I don't want to hear the rules." It's hot, with no breeze. I'm sweating. From the heat or from worry, I'm not sure.

I can see one of the crewmen on the phone speaking rapidly to someone, probably the captain.

"Madam," the mate, or whatever he's called, says, "if she does not get here on time, your friend will just have to manage on her own. She can always take a plane home."

"May I?" asks another sailor, a kinder one. "After we leave, we will call the shore police and have them look for your friend."

I do not want to hear this. "And I'm telling you there is no way she'd miss this ship unless something happened to her."

"She would never," Evvie adds, trying to help.

Ida says frantically, "Look, there are others coming."

I turn quickly, hoping.

"Hey," calls Judy, "it's the Fort Lauderdale gang. Wassup?"

I can't believe it. Here come the Bingo Dolls, strolling as if they had all the time in the world.

Judy pokes Rose. "I told you your watch was slow!"

"It's never wrong," says Rose. She looks at her watch. "It's two forty-five."

Judy pokes her again. "That's what you said fifteen minutes ago."

"It's exactly three o'clock right now," Evvie tells her.

"Oops," says Rose sheepishly.

The sailors urge them along. "This is final call, ladies. Please step up."

The Dolls walk up the gangway quickly, taking out their passes as they do. They look back at us. "Aren't you coming?"

"We're expecting a friend and she's not here yet," says Bella.

"They have to wait for her," Judy assures us. "We're paying customers."

"We tried that. They won't." Bella is near tears. "Not for one person."

"Hey, hold on! I'm coming!" yells a voice down the path. We turn again, and I hear Bella sigh, "Ooooh."

And Sophie adds, "It's dreamboat!"

"Roberto. Our cha-cha teacher!" Bella croons.

As he gets closer I can see that the object of their ardor really is gorgeous. Fortyish. Wearing a big Mexican sombrero and some sort of early western outfit. Sunglasses that make him look even sexier. A smile that dazzles. A face that could launch this ship and the proverbial other thousand. He looks at Bella and Sophie, puzzled. "Something going on, pretty ladies?"

They melt. Each of them grabs an arm. "We're waiting for our friend and she hasn't come back."

Bella adds, "They're gonna lock her out. Help us."

Sophie quickly introduces Roberto around.

Need I say all the women are agog?

I think cynically, I suppose if a man's in charge . . . But any port in a storm, I joke to myself. Let him handle it.

But even Roberto can't move immovable objects. He shrugs. "Listen, the ship doesn't actually pull out until four. You can watch from above until she arrives."

Evvie answers him. "They made it very clear, once past three they don't let anyone else on board."

"Believe me, they'll have to let her aboard. They'll be annoyed, but they will."

"Okay. That's it. We've been very patient." The sailor is losing his cool. "Now!"

Ida and Evvie scurry up the gangplank, as Sophie and Bella, still clutching Roberto, hurry behind them.

"Glad!" Evvie says. "Come on."

All of the crew is now at the top of the gangway ready to pull it in or up or whatever it is they do.

I step farther back away from the ship. I can't believe I'm actually doing this.

I cross my arms. "Then you leave with two people on shore. I am going to find her."

"Oh, my God!" says Rose. "She's jumping ship."

Nobody moves for a moment. Nobody speaks.

Then my stalwart sister, Evvie, runs back down and stands next to me, imitating my posture. "Make that three."

Ida, quick on the take, doesn't wait a second. She's out, too. "How about four?"

Sophie and Bella tug at Roberto. "Please," says Sophie, "you gotta help us."

"But I'll lose my job . . ."

"You just gotta," pleads Sophie.

"If it was *your* mother?" Bella begs.

Neither woman will let go of his arms. "How can I say no?" he says, leading them out past the startled crew. "I can never resist a pretty face, let alone *two* pretty faces."

I expect them to swoon. But at least we have someone young on our side. I'm beginning to see that as a distinct advantage. Maybe now they'll stop taking us old ladies for granted.

The Bingo Dolls look at one another. They don't need words. They're down in a flash. One of the crew tries to grab at them, but misses.

"Wait for us!" Greg and Polly, the Wisconsin couple, exchange glances and hurry down to join us. Today they're wearing green Packers tank tops and matching shorts and socks.

Now we are standing there, eight women, one male football fan, and one Roberto, whose adoring dance students grin lopsidedly up at him.

"Hot damn," says Rose. "This is more exciting than winning at bingo."

"Not quite," says Judy, who obviously lives for her game.

For once the crew is dumbfounded. This has never happened before. Old ladies not obeying their orders.

I take out the receipt I have from Spanglish and write a quick note on the back. To the astonishment of my fellow deserters, I run back and throw the piece of paper at the sailors.

As I turn, I call out, "Phone those numbers. One's my boyfriend, an ex-cop, and the other is my possible future son-in-law—he's still a cop. They'll vouch for me. Tell them the Gladdy Gold Detective Agency is on the job!"

I hear applause from the upper decks and shouts of "bravo" from the bandstand area. But it's not for the band, it's for *Los Desperados*. Or is it *Las Desperadas*? Plus *dos hombres*.

35

The Search

We are at the cab stand. There is only one taxi available and a trolley pulling up to its stop directly across from where we are standing.

I bark out orders. "Roberto, you, Sophie, Bella, and Ida, grab the cab. Get up to the fort fast. Look for Amy along the way, just in case she's trying to get back to the ship."

"OK," Roberto says. "Here's my cell phone number. We'll be able to stay in contact that way." He writes it down on a slip of paper and looks expectantly toward me.

Bella glances at me dolefully as she pokes me in the ribs. "Gladdy hates progress. We don't have a cell phone." I am dismayed and annoyed at the same time for this public betrayal. However, I do make up my mind right now what the next item is that our little business will buy.

"But I do," says Rose, as she writes down the number in lipstick and hands it to Roberto.

With that, their foursome piles into the cab.

"Let's get the show on the road," says Evvie, running across the way and climbing up into a nearly empty trolley.

"We'll meet somewhere in the fort," I call after the cab. "Don't wait for us. Start searching." I climb in the trolley after Evvie. The rest of my rescue crew is hot on my heels.

I make an announcement to driver and passengers. "This is an emergency. We need to get to the fort immediately. Please, folks, if you want to take the regular route, would you kindly wait for another trolley?"

Nobody moves. There's grumbling, but no movement.

"*Por favor,*" the driver says with a thick Spanish accent, "perhaps I say no."

Now all my girls are talking at once. Lost friend. Might be hurt. Missed the ship. Have to find her. Please help us. Matter of life and death.

A couple of the meeker passengers, sensing unwanted trouble, hurriedly jump off. A few stay, either indecisive or curious.

"No," the driver insists, "you want Calle Norzagaray."

"No," I insist back at him. "There's no other trolley and no other cab. We're here now and we need your help."

A voice behind me says, "Hey, señor, help the ladies out." It's my Packer, Greg, looking large and menacing. "Just drive straight through to that there fort."

"Yeah," agrees Polly. "We'll never tell."

Now we have a chorus of other tourists egging him on.

The driver says something under his breath, which I am thankful I can't translate, and he starts driving up a street named San Justo. If that means justice, I feel it's a good sign.

I know now that it really isn't far, it's just that it's uphill all the way.

As the trolley driver chugs along, clanging his bell to get people out of his way, we look from one side of the street to another hoping to spot Amy.

The Dolls help console our tourists by calling out places of interest so they won't miss anything.

Evvie says, after a while, "So, Dolls, how often do you win back in Tuscon?"

"A lot," Judy says.

"Yeah, she's real lucky," Rose offers.

With a heavy bump that practically knocks us off our seats, the bus jolts to a stop.

"El Morro." The driver swings open the door, eager to be rid of us.

I'm rustling around in my purse to find money for a tip, but Rose says, "Let me. After all, I won yesterday."

She offers the driver a ten-dollar bill. "*Gracias* for helping us."

The driver waves the money away. "*No es necesario, señoras. Vaya con Dios.* Find your friend in good health."

We thank him profusely and get off.

Behind us I hear Greg tell his wife, "Let's hit the road, Polly."

Obviously Roberto and the girls have alerted the guards at the entrance gate. They're expecting us. "Looking for your friend? Go right through."

Evvie and I, the Dolls, and the Packer couple hurry through the gate.

"Spread out," I say. "Yell as loud as you can if you find her. Rose, please stick with me with your phone."

And we take off, calling out Amy's name. Judy and Evvie head down the ancient steps. Rose and I climb up to the top level of the fort. Greg and Polly turn left. I see Roberto and my girls at the very far end. I am overwhelmed once again at the size and scope of this massive stone fortress. Quickly, I realize that this level is wide open and we would see Amy easily. If she were here.

As we look down from parapet to parapet, my heart is in my mouth. Where could Amy be? I can still see our cruise ship in the distance. It hasn't left port.

It's not more than ten minutes or so before I hear Ida scream, the fearful sound resonating against these walls that have seen so much pain. At the same time, Rose's phone rings.

"They found her," Rose says, her voice apprehensive.

Everyone seems to be yelling now as searchers and tourists converge from the lower areas. We run the long length of this level to where I see people peering over the gun turret ledges.

Sophie and Bella are clinging tightly to one another. Ida is leaning against a wall, her hand over her mouth. Roberto is standing, staring down toward the sea.

I run to him, my heart pounding. He says, "You don't want to see this. It's bad."

But I must. Holding tightly to the stone sides, I peer down and see Amy sprawled across patches of shrubbery, hanging about ten feet from the rocky beach below. She is not moving.

I am in shock. Roberto shakes me. "Listen. I'm running back to the ship to get help. I'm a fast runner. I'll be back soon. Do you hear me?"

Numbly, I nod and he is off.

Evvie shouts, "Forget the trolley, find a cab."

Sophie and Bella shout encouragement at him.

He throws promises back at them. "I can do it faster myself. I'll run like the wind."

I call after him. "Tell them at the gate."

Stunned at the realization of what is happening, I am filled with guilt. Why didn't I take Amy's story about being followed seriously? What happened here? Did she fall? Did she jump? I feel icy cold. Did someone push her?

Jack. Why aren't you here? I don't know what to do. I need you. I need your advice. I need your strength.

36

Rescue

There is nothing for us to do but keep out of the way while the rescuers do their job. At least it's still light and they are able to see. Has it only been an hour or so since we discovered that battered body, lying facedown, so far below us?

Men from the ship are standing by with some sort of stretcher-pulley, preparing to send it down to get Amy. The ship's doctor is waiting to examine her as soon as she's brought up. The San Juan police are here and an ambulance is outside the front gate. Everyone is breathlessly waiting to hear from the climber, a local firefighter. Armed with ropes, he is scaling his tortuous way down the sheer face of the cliff.

There is a groaning sound, a fearful one.

What is it? Evvie runs in closer to find out. I

cannot move. My legs are jelly. What's taking her so long? Finally she's back.

"He's reached the shrubbery where she is. For a moment they were afraid it wouldn't hold his weight. But it's OK."

I can't stand it. I have to get closer. I force my weak legs to move. And naturally, everyone else follows me.

I nudge one of the sailors. "What happening?"

"She's alive. She's even conscious. We couldn't tell from up here because she didn't dare move. If she had dislodged herself, she might have fallen down onto the rocks and beach."

Now the girls and I grab one another, hugging, tearful. Thank you, God. She's alive! The word spreads. The onlookers react happily. Tragedy has been avoided.

How extraordinary life is. Only yesterday this woman was unknown to me, a stranger. Today, her safety brings me to overwhelming emotion. She will forever be important to me.

If I had only been able to save him, I think. Don't go there, I tell myself. This is not the time to think about my husband.

There is much commotion. The crewmen are preparing to send down the pulley. Knowing that Amy's alive has given momentum to their actions.

The hell with being afraid of heights. We all run to the nearest openings in the wall. We can see Amy, her hands tightly clutching the roots of the shrubs. The climber whispers to her and she lets go. We watch breathlessly as he carefully shifts her.

I can't help it. I yell, "Amy! Amy!"

She actually turns her head up toward me and gives us a weak smile.

Brave lady. All this time, she must have been so frightened.

She mouths, "Thank you."

We are all a puddle of tears.

Amy insisted she was well enough to go back to the ship. Now we're standing outside the infirmary waiting to hear what the doctor has to say.

The Tucson Dolls stop by and say they're starved and are going to dinner. They ask us to wish Amy luck and tell her that if she's ever in Tucson, she should look them up. They'll teach her bingo.

We thank them profusely for their help.

"We wouldn't have missed it for the world," Rose says.

"See you at bingo tomorrow," says Judy. "You will come?"

"Yeah, tomorrow there's a one-thousand-dollar prize," Rose adds.

"And one of us intends to win it," says Judy.

"Not if we win it first," Bella retorts.

"We'll be there," Bella and Sophie say in unison.

"It all depends on how Amy is," I say.

They wave and take off for the dining room.

"Uh-oh," whispers Ida. "Look who's coming. It's the captain."

Sure enough, in his crisp white uniformed splendor, Captain Hugh Standish is marching toward us with the same two sailors who gave us such a hard time earlier.

Bella salutes nervously when they reach us. Ida pulls her arm down.

"Mrs. Gold?"

I step forward. "That's me."

"Do you have any idea how many international maritime laws you have broken?"

Bella clings to my arm and begs. "Please, Captain, don't throw her in the brig. She was just trying to save someone's life."

"Yeah," agrees my faithful sister. "She's a hero." My girls form a semicircle around me, as if to shield me from whatever is to come.

"She is a captain's nightmare, that's what she is," he replies sternly. "Do you have any idea what chaos you caused, Mrs. Gold? Ruining this very expensive pleasure trip for two thousand people? Destroying the rigid timing of this ship's schedule? And that of every other ship to follow that depends on our getting out of port on time? Not to mention the incredibly bad example you have shown by not following orders."

"I'm sorry," I whisper, "for all the trouble I caused. But I'm not sorry we went to find Amy."

"I will deal with you later. All of you."

With that, he sharply turns on his heels and marches away. His men follow after him.

"*Oy vey,*" says Sophie. "Do you think they'll put us on bread and water?"

"God forbid," says Bella.

The infirmary door opens and the doctor beckons us in.

Amy is lying in one of the two cots in the room. The color has returned to her face. She reaches out and we all take her hands in ours. "How can I ever thank you?" she says tearfully.

Dr. Fernandez introduces himself. "Mrs. Larkin has a mild concussion. And some bruising. Nothing serious. She is very lucky that it wasn't worse."

"What happened?" Evvie asks Amy.

The doctor moves toward the door. "I'll leave now so you may chat. Don't stay too long; she needs to rest. Mrs. Larkin is to remain in the infirmary overnight."

This worries me. "Wait. Please. Is there someone who will be staying with her?"

"Absolutely. The nurse is here round the clock. The doors remain locked at all times."

With that, he exits.

"I was so scared," Amy says. "I tried to yell but nobody heard me over the sound of the ocean. I was terrified that I'd be there all night if I didn't fall off the cliff first."

"That was smart you held on," says Ida as she straightens the pillows around Amy's head.

"But my hands were getting so tired. And because I was afraid to move, my whole body was getting stiff. If you hadn't come back . . ."

I shudder to think what might have been. "Do you remember when it happened?" I ask her.

"Yes, I had just looked at my watch. It was time for me to leave so I'd be on time to meet you back at the ship."

"What made you fall?" I ask nervously.

"I'm not sure. I forgot to take my blood pressure medicine this morning and I was feeling dizzy. I think someone came up behind me. He was even talking to me. I thought I knew him, but maybe I was hallucinating. Next thing I knew I was falling. I don't know. It's all a blur."

"Are you sure you didn't see him?"

"No . . . I didn't turn around."

"Was anybody else nearby?"

"I didn't see anybody."

"Amy, you mentioned you thought someone was following you last night. What if the same person followed you ashore and tried to kill you?"

She gasps and turns her head away, unwilling to face us. "It's not possible."

"Why would anyone want to do this to you?" Evvie is puzzled.

"I didn't have time to tell you," I say to the girls, "but earlier today, Amy also told me she thought someone may have tried to break into her room."

There is much consternation at this.

"You should have the captain call your husband," says Ida.

"Oh, no, don't do that. He's scuba diving in the Keys with friends. He doesn't like it if I call when he's away. I don't want to spoil his good time. I'm really all right."

Evvie adds, "But wouldn't he want to know?"

"At least we should inform the captain," I say.

"Please, there's no reason anyone would want to hurt me. I'm just a nervous kind of person. I don't do well when I'm alone. It was an accident. Don't make a fuss. Please."

Amy closes her eyes. "I think that pill he gave me is making me sleepy."

Ida fixes the blanket around her.

"We'll leave now," I say. I want to question her further, but that can wait until she's had some rest. "Is there anything else you need?"

"Just sleep."

So we tiptoe out, turning off the lights behind us.

Standing outside the infirmary, I face my girls. I am not happy about this and I tell them so. "Her husband has a right to know. And the captain, as well." I think I've begun to doubt my own judgment. Morrie. Jack. Even Casey and Barbi. Every one *proving* how wrong I am. But all my instincts are shouting out to me—why didn't I make Amy go directly to the captain? If I had felt better about myself, I might have averted this near catastrophe.

"But she said no," Sophie says.

"What kind of man wouldn't let her call just because he's scuba diving?" Ida is outraged.

"But what can he do? He can't get on the ship and she can't get off." This from Evvie. "All they can do is talk to each other."

"That would be comforting for her," Sophie adds.

"Helicopters could bring him or take her, that's what. I've seen that in a lot of movies," says Evvie.

Ida adds, "That captain already hates us. I bet he wouldn't believe us."

"Oh, no!" I stop suddenly. "I forgot, we're supposed to meet the Sicilianos for cocktails. We're so late. We'll talk about this later."

We wend our way from the infirmary to the Devil's Own Bar. That weirdo sign over it with the nasty, leering devil gives me the creeps.

I can see by the number of empty glasses in front of Elio that they've been waiting a long while. And by the tapping of his feet, he's not too happy.

"We didn't know whether to keep waiting or go have dinner." Angelina is wearing yet another of her black outfits. I wonder if she has any other colors in her wardrobe.

"We ran into a problem," I say.

"We know all about it," Elio says. "Everybody's been talking. Is your friend all right?"

Evvie answers, "Yes, thank God. It's a miracle she wasn't killed."

We all sit and order drinks. Sophie and Bella have become very fond of Mai Tais.

I'm not much of a drinker, but a tall Bloody Mary feels needed after today. Evvie dittos my call.

Ida drinks club soda. She's terrified of anything that might make her sick again.

"I still can't get over it," I say. "That we're on the same ship."

"Yeah, how come you picked this one?" Evvie asks. "I mean, like we told you, we're here because of winning that bingo cruise contest."

"I didn't pick it, it picked me," says Angelina. "I was over at my cousin Josephine's house, helping to pack away her things. All us cousins were there and also her brothers, but, of course, they left all the work to the women."

"Hah," puts in Elio, "them broads were dying to go through Jo's jewels and clothes. Her husband was very generous. He was on his way out to his country club and he told the ladies to take what they wanted to remember her by. I thought he was an idiot giving away expensive things, but then again, what did he need with women's stuff? I came over 'cause I was waiting for the fun to start when they tore each other's eyes out fighting over the loot."

Angelina humphs. "All I got was some ratty fur stole. That's all I could fit into. I don't use perfume, so who cared about that. But she did have one thing I wanted. Way in the back of her fancy lingerie drawer she had a ticket for a cruise. On the *Heavenly,* for some bridge tournament. Nobody else grabbed it, so I did. Cheapskate here hasn't taken me on a vacation in ten years. And besides, it was nonrefundable, so why should I let it go to waste? The ship gave me an argument about transferring tickets, but when I cried and told them she was dead, they said okay. Besides, now Elio bought a ticket, so they were getting extra money."

Cheapskate ignores her and puffs on his cigar, which is choking us with its fumes.

"Excuse me, I'm starving." Bella hiccups as she says this. Half a Mai Tai and she's tipsy.

"Good idea," says Elio, stubbing the smelly thing out in the ashtray. He's delighted to be rid of us.

"Good idea," I agree. The fumes are giving me a headache and so has this highly charged day. I need some food.

We are certainly not dressed for dinner, but who cares after the day we had? Though I do wish I had taken the time to wash my face and comb my hair. When we enter the dining room, the Sicilianos turn to the left for their seats, and we head right. I spot Captain Standish at the entrance, so I twist my head around to avoid being seen. The early meal service is already halfway through. We hurry toward our assigned table, trying to be inconspicuous.

Suddenly there is a drumroll. The music stops and everyone looks up.

"Ladies and gentlemen, may I have your attention." The captain is standing at a podium in the front of the room, speaking into a microphone. "Let me introduce you to the women who caused our ship to leave late." The spotlight zigzags across the room until it finds us. We all freeze, bowing our heads and trying to hide our unwashed, blushing faces. I wish the floor would open up under me.

So, this is our punishment. Public disgrace.

"These women, Gladys Gold, Evelyn Markowitz, Ida Franz, Bella Fox, and Sophie Meyerbeer, with great courage and unselfishness, this very afternoon saved the life of one of our passengers who had accidentally taken a serious fall. Let's hear it for these very special guests. The good ship *Heavenly* salutes them." Another drumroll sounds, and the band starts playing a rousing rendition of "For He's a Jolly Good Fellow." Our fellow passengers rise from their seats, singing along and applauding us with great gusto.

Now we are really blushing. But we smile and wave, pretending to be the sophisticates we are not.

The captain continues, "On behalf of the *Heavenly* home office, we wish to reward these heroic women with another *Heavenly* cruise of their choosing. First class, of course."

Well, waddaya know!

37

Sleepless in Heavenly

The room is hot. Ida has turned off the air conditioner again. Evvie waits until she thinks Ida's asleep and then turns it back on. Once the air kicks in, Ida pulls all the covers over her, including mine. I pull them back. Through our open adjoining door I can hear Sophie and Bella snoring away, their air turned on high. I am tossing; I cannot sleep. There are too many thoughts bubbling inside my head and they won't let me rest.

"You still awake, Glad?" Evvie whispers.

"Yes," I whisper back. "I thought you were asleep."

"No. I can't get over all the excitement today."

"Me, neither."

"Me, neither, too." Ida pops up. "Besides, who can sleep when it's freezing in here?"

"*Oy,*" says Evvie. "Remind me never to sleep

in the same room with you ever again. And that goes for the same bed, too."

"Fine by me."

"You girls having a party?" Sophie drags herself into our room. She is trailing her blanket and pillow behind her. "I have cookies." Under her bedding, clutched in her hand, is a pack of Oreos.

She drops down onto our mattresses. We all shift to make room for her. I get up on my knees to reach the wall switch and turn on the overhead light.

"I thought you were sleeping," I say.

"Not for a minute."

"We heard you snoring." Evvie grins, reaching for a cookie.

"I never snore."

"If you drop one cookie crumb in our bed, I'll kill you," says Ida to Evvie.

"Did I hear cookies?" Bella asks, rubbing her eyes, peering into our room.

We make room for Bella, with a lot of shifting of pillows and sheets and bodies. She contributes her stash of peanut butter cups. She also brought along her pink teddy bear, which she props up on half of my pillow.

"How can you be hungry with all we ate tonight?" asks Ida.

"It's still not too late. We can make the midnight buffet," says Sophie, leaning one leg out, ready to move in case we say yes.

There is serious thought about this for a moment.

"Nah, too much trouble," says Evvie, settling back down.

"Now if we only had milk with our cookies." Bella sighs.

"We've got milk in the minifridge." Evvie crawls across everyone's legs, ignoring our shrieks, reaches over to the fridge, and brings out a container. We take turns slurping as we pass the milk carton and cookies around, everyone enjoying the moment.

"You know what?" says Bella. "Sometimes I like being old. We can do anything we want and nobody cares."

There are contented sighs at that.

"Wasn't that something? The captain getting everyone to clap hands for us?" Sophie grins at the memory.

"Yeah, great..." is the consensus.

"Wait 'til the gang back home hears about us getting a free trip. First class!" Sophie is beaming.

We are quiet for a few minutes while we munch.

"I'm sure she didn't fall," I say abruptly.

Now the girls are all at attention.

"But maybe because she didn't take her medicine," Bella reminds me.

"Someone tried twice," I say, sure of my opinion now. My confidence is coming back. I am determined to find out who! "Let's vote." All hands shoot up except Bella's, who's still not convinced.

Evvie scrambles off the mattresses again.

"Now what?" Ida decides to get out of her

way by pulling her legs up and leaning against a side wall.

"I'm getting a pad and pen. We should take notes."

"Right," says Sophie. "The GG and A meeting now comes to order."

Bella asks, "Who?"

Sophie explains, "Gladdy Gold and Associates."

"Oh. Are we on a job?"

I say, "I think we are."

She smiles happily. "Good. But is anyone paying us?"

"I doubt it."

"Glad, what do we know so far?" Evvie asks, pen at the ready. "If we assume someone did follow Amy around and try to break in to her room, and then followed her onshore in order to kill her, who could it be?"

"But she's such a nice lady. Why?" asks Bella.

"Later," I say. "Let's get the chronology first. Amy was just about to leave the fort to join us back at the ship. That would have been just before two-thirty. I was already at the ship. The would-be killer needed about ten minutes to get back. At two-forty Evvie arrived. A number of couples got on board after her. The rest of you arrived just about that time. That's about the soonest he could have come aboard."

"I remember that first guy," Evvie says. "He was the MC of last night's show. He was sure in a hurry. Could it be him?"

"But he's so funny," Bella comments.

"What? Killers can't be funny?" Ida says. "What about that guy who shoved me?"

"Yeah. He was big," says Bella.

"About six feet," says Sophie.

"Not that tall," says Evvie. "Maybe five-eight."

"Fat."

"No, just lots of muscles." Sophie is sure.

"Did anyone see his face?"

A round of nos.

"Hair?" We all speak at once. Blond. Gray. Brown. Bald. Well, that was no help.

"We can ask the sailors," suggests Sophie. "They'll have a record of everybody who came back in."

"Then the Packers couple came along. The only time they'd think about killing is when their team doesn't win." This from Evvie.

"And then the Dolls came." Ida shrugs. "That was it."

"And Roberto," says Bella, sighing. "Thank God. What would we have done without his help?"

"We must have missed someone. Think."

No one can think of anyone else.

Sophie gets excited. "You know, in all that crowd we never saw Roberto after we sent him to get help. We have to go and thank him tomorrow."

"I got an idea," Bella pipes up. "Maybe the Dolls did it. They're mean enough."

"Only about bingo."

"Maybe the killer never came back on board. I

mean, once he thought the job was done..." Evvie says this thoughtfully.

"I would guess just the opposite," I say. "He'd feel safe, and besides, if he didn't show up he'd be the obvious suspect."

"So, with all the fuss, he has to know she's alive. I wonder what's going on in his head."

"I bet he's worried whether he can get the job done now," Ida says.

"I think Amy knows something. She's hiding it, whatever it is. She overreacted when we said she should call her husband and tell the captain. She's afraid."

"Well, she ought to be afraid if someone is trying to kill her," says Ida.

"It's more than that," I say.

"We have a place to begin," Evvie says. "Tomorrow morning, we find the sailors and get them to check their records and then we go to the purser. He promised Amy he'd check on those no-shows for her."

Sophie yawns first. Then Bella. Soon we are all yawning.

"I think I can sleep now." Bella starts to climb off our beds.

"Me, too." Ida crawls off the wall space to regain her usual spot.

Sophie gets off, too, dragging her bedding.

Bella grins. "This was fun. A regular pajama party sleepover. I feel like a kid again."

"I thought you felt old." Ida laughs.

"Same thing. Young or old, you feel free."

"Not really," Ida says. "I wouldn't ever want to go through those painful growing-up years again."

Everybody is back in place.

"Good night, Evvie."

"Good night, Ida."

"Good night, Gladdy."

"Good night, Bella."

"Good night, Sophie."

I hear Ida switch off the air. I hear Evvie switch it back on. I cover my ears. Here we go again.

38

GG&A on the Job

It's eight-fifteen and we are surprised to see Amy Larkin seated at our breakfast table, waiting for us. With just a few bruises showing, she looks all right. She chats with some of the guests who've come over to say how glad they are she was rescued.

At our arrival, the attention once again shifts to us for saving her.

"How are you?" Evvie asks, once the other passengers have left.

Amy smiles wryly. "Aside from every bone in my body aching, I'm fine. These painkillers are keeping me going."

I am upset. "I wish they hadn't let you leave the infirmary by yourself."

"That's all right. Lots of people were around."

"Well, you better stick close to us until we find out what really happened," Evvie insists.

The girls rush through breakfast. Sophie suggests Amy join the bingo game and watch us win a thousand bucks today.

"Yeah, sure," says Ida. "That'll be the day."

Bella is already standing. "We gotta go or we'll never get good seats."

Everyone manages to gobble down a last few bites. They all get up except for me.

"Glad, come on," Evvie says.

"I'm going to the purser with Amy to see what we can find out. We'll join you in a little while."

I glance at Amy to make sure it's all right with her. She nods.

The girls grab their bingo bags and tell us to hurry.

After a more leisurely breakfast, Amy and I head back down to the main lobby, which, as usual, is bustling with activities. Our next stop, tomorrow, is St. Thomas, and people are gathering information and signing up for shore trips.

The purser, Dennis, is a sweet young man with a lot of freckles and a friendly smile. He's obviously heard about what happened and he tells Amy how glad he is that she's all right. She thanks him.

"What about my friends?" Amy asks. "Were you able to find out anything?"

He scrambles around his busy desk looking for his notes until he finds them. "I couldn't reach the Martinsons," he says, "but I did hear from the

Johnson family. I'm sorry to have to tell you that Mrs. Johnson passed away last week."

Amy is shocked. She holds on to the wall, as if her legs won't support her. "I can't believe it." Her eyes tear up.

I put my arm around her.

Dennis pauses, then speaks quietly. "Here's something. One of the tickets was used. But under a different name. If you want, I could check that out for you."

"Please do," she says, her voice quivering.

"May I ask you something, too?" I ask.

"Of course," he answers.

I want to know if he can find out for me who the last people to board were yesterday afternoon. He tells us all passes are electronically swiped. Only the captain would have access to this information. It's considered classified and not available to anyone.

That takes care of that.

"That's a shame about your friend," I say to Amy when we leave his office.

"Yes," she says. "I didn't know her that well, but she was such a lively woman, it's hard to believe."

"Do you need to lie down and rest? I could stay with you."

"No. I think I'd rather be up and around. All I'll do is dwell on what almost happened yesterday." She shivers. "You really think someone pushed me, don't you?"

"Yes, Amy, I do."

"He's around here somewhere, isn't he?"

"I think so, yes."

"Do you think he'll try again?"

"Not if you're never alone. Let's go and talk to the captain now."

"No, please. Not yet. I can't deal with it. I just can't."

"But Amy, you're in danger."

"Please. Soon, maybe later."

I want to insist, but she seems so fragile. "Do you want to play bridge to distract you? Maybe we can find you some players?"

She shakes her head. "By now, all the tables are set. Let me stay with you and watch the bingo game."

As we walk toward the bingo hall something is niggling at me, but darn these old brain cells, always failing me when I need them the most.

I'm surprised to see the girls seated in the same booth as on the first bingo day. They are busily daubing numbers being called and shown on the big board.

Sophie, as she makes a quick daub, tells us, "The Dolls saved it for us. Isn't that sweet?"

At that, Rose and Judy wave at us. I wave back.

I slide into the booth, and Amy moves in after me. I wait for the next game and try to get into it.

"Glad," Evvie shakes me. "You're not paying attention. You missed a number, B-three."

I mark it, but hard as I try, I can't concentrate.

So many thoughts are jumping around in my head. I'm missing an important fact and my mind won't let me pull it up.

"Glad, what's wrong with you? Where are you?" Evvie asks.

"I have to remember something I just heard," I tell her.

"What is it?"

"If I knew I'd tell you." My rotten short-term memory.

I deal out my stack of packets to Evvie and the others. They are horrified.

"What are you doing?" Evvie asks.

"Play for me. I need to think."

"Think later," Ida says. "Play now."

"I can't."

"And I can't handle so many papers," Bella says, near tears.

Ida pulls them away from her. "Well, I can."

"Thanks," she says gratefully.

"I'm on," whispers Evvie. Everyone is on alert.

"Waddaya need?" asks Sophie.

"I-seventeen."

"Oh, no," says Bella, "our most unlucky number."

The girls hold their collective breaths as the next numbers come and go. O-70. B-6. O-66.

I hear their little groans of misery. We all believe the more numbers called, the less chance of getting the one you need.

And finally, B-13 and someone screams "Bingo!"

And so do I. "Bingo!" The girls look at me as if I were loony. "I remember it!"

I tell Amy to slide back out of the booth. "Come on, girls, let's go!" Now the Bingo Dolls are looking our way, wondering at the commotion.

"Are you crazy?" Evvie shrieks.

"Now. Up. Up. Come on." Amy is standing alongside the booth. I slide out after her and stand up, too.

The numbers are checked and the winner wins five hundred dollars to a roomful of applause.

I feel like such an idiot. Those names. Of course!

"I'm not going," Sophie says.

"This is really necessary," I insist.

"Why?" says Ida, arms crossed.

"I'll tell you outside."

The next game starts. The girls automatically look at their numbers. I hurry Amy to the back.

The girls are torn. Finally Evvie acts. She grabs all the bingo packets out of the girls' hands and leans over into the Dolls' booth. She shoves all the packets at them.

"Play for us," she says. "If we win the big money, let us know and we'll split it fifty-fifty."

Evvie starts up the aisle. After a moment, the others follow her. The Bingo Dolls look after us in total disbelief.

39

Bingo

We stand outside the main theater, where the bingo games continue playing. The caller's voice can be heard through the closed doors.

Four faces glare at me. Four people who do not intend to move from this spot.

"How could you do this to us?" That's Evvie.

"We were practically about to win!" Now Sophie.

"Yeah," echoes Bella. "I was already on twice." She leans her ear against the door, trying to hear.

Ida folds her arms. "What's so important it can't wait?"

Sophie puts her hand on the doorknob. "Give us a report later."

Bella moves closer to her side. "My winning ticket got us a bingo cruise and we're cruising now and I don't want to miss anything. That's *my* report."

Sophie elbows her. "*My* winning ticket."

"Ouch."

Amy is as puzzled as the others. "Is this about me?"

I nod at her and turn to face my gang. "All right, my impatient ones, I will do this alone. Brace yourselves. I know why Amy's three friends aren't on board. They are *all dead*!"

There is a collective gasp.

Amy instinctively touches her fluttering heart. "But I don't understand—the purser only told me about Beth. How can you know about the others?"

"Soon you'll understand." I take her by the hand and start toward the deck.

Evvie rushes after me and grabs my arm. "Oh, no. You don't get to throw that bombshell at us and then walk away."

My captive audience is all ears now.

"Listen, I'll tell you everything, but first help me find the Sicilianos." My gang follows as quickly as they can with those arthritic knees. Amy, stunned by what I've said, keeps up. Her mind must be in turmoil.

"Where are we going?" Evvie pulls at my arm again.

"We need to have Amy meet Angelina."

"How will we find them? On board this ship? Impossible." Evvie is incredulous.

"Thousands of people. A hundred different activities. They could be anywhere." Ida is equally negative at the possibility.

"We'll have them paged." I'm heading for the purser again.

"I never heard any names paged," says Ida.

"Only messages from the captain," Bella agrees.

"They never had ten people jump ship before, either," I remind them. "There's always a first time for everything."

"Hello, again," Dennis says, smiling, when we reach his desk. "What is it you need now?"

"Actually, we need to find two people as soon as possible. We need to have them paged."

The smile fades. "We don't do that."

"But this is important."

"There are two thousand people on board this ship. If we let everybody call their pals, can you imagine how noisy it would be?"

"This is very important."

"Sorry. Only if it is an emergency."

"Well, it is, to us," I say.

He turns his back on us, pretending to be busy. Amy and the girls look to me. Now what?

"Please call the captain."

He turns again, startled. "I beg your pardon?"

"Captain Standish, if you please," I say, pointing to his phone. "Tell him Gladdy Gold needs to make a very brief announcement."

He looks at me as if I'm crazy. I just wait him out.

Finally Dennis turns away again and a moment

later I hear him whispering. Then I hear him say, "Yes, sir."

The purser hands me a mike. He is surprised, but he knows how to follow orders. "Make it fast."

I've got clout on this here ship now.

We find the Sicilianos waiting for us on the top deck in the Jacuzzi adjoining the pool. Kids are screeching with glee as they tumble down the water slide. The deck is mobbed with people. A rock band is playing. Couples in bathing suits are dancing. The lounge chairs are filled with sunbathers.

Angelina is still deep in the tub, surrounded by bubbles. Need I say her bathing suit is black? Elio is seated on the ledge. He smiles, but it's more like a sneer.

"You just can't get enough of me, hey, babe?"

"Shut your face, *putz*." Angelina punches him in the knees. She grins, having learned that word from us. "What can I do for you, Mrs. Gold?"

"We need to talk. It's very important."

"All right." She pokes Elio again. "Pass me the towel and help me out." Elio obeys instantly. Looks like Angelina's reheated love doesn't stop her from being the boss.

Our group settles at an outdoor table as far away from the deck action as possible. I make sure no one is within hearing distance.

After the drinks we've ordered have arrived, all look to me to tell them what this is about. Except for Elio, who stands up, taking his drink with him. "I guess I'll just leave you ladies to your hen party and go find myself a poker game."

I say, "Mr. Siciliano, you're going to want to hear this."

Before he can argue, Angelina pulls him back down into his seat. He glares at me, arms crossed. "Can I smoke a cigar, at least?"

There are seven loud "nos" at that. He finally gives up trying to annoy us. He's trapped.

"And enough with the Mr. and Mrs. How about Angelina and Elio?" Angelina offers up to me.

"Yes, thanks, Angelina."

Angelina looks at Amy. "How are you today?" she says with concern.

"All right," Amy replies.

I take a deep breath.

"What I'm about to say to you will sound incredible. I can hardly believe it myself. In my wildest imagination I could never envision such a thing happening. I've figured most of it out, but I need both Angelina and Amy to put the final pieces together for me."

My girls lean in closer. Amy and Angelina look at one another curiously. I am sure they're unable to think of any way in which they could possibly be connected.

Bella slurps her drink, then giggles in embarrassment. "Sorry."

I continue. "All of this started for me over a month ago when I was trying to show off in front of my boyfriend and his son. Both policemen."

I stop. My girls look surprised. I never got around to telling them about Jack being a cop, as well. Only Evvie knew.

"Then Sophie won a free cruise and we turned up on the *Heavenly*." Sophie smiles at being referred to.

"I better stay in the present and work backward. On the ship we accidentally meet Amy, who is lost and puzzled because she can't find the three women she was supposed to meet for the bridge tournament. I need you, Amy, to tell everyone, were these women close friends of yours?"

"No," she answers. "As a matter of fact, I only met them six weeks ago at the last bridge tournament on this very ship. We got along so well we all agreed to meet again for the next one. This one."

I smile. "Aha, I thought so."

"What's with the 'aha'?" Sophie wants to know.

"First things first. Amy is told at the purser's office that one ticket was canceled. Two were no-shows."

I take a long sip of my drink.

"I went with Amy to see the purser again today. He informed us that Mrs. Johnson had died. It further seems that one of the tickets belonging to another of the women is being used by someone else. Two names are mentioned: Johnson and Martinson. I don't react because these are fairly common names. And because I have a senior moment and my mind doesn't make the connection—until I am in the bingo hall this morning and it hits me like a hurricane. I know these names."

Angie startles. "*I* know one of those names. My cousin, Josephine Martinson."

Amy looks at her, mystified. "Jo Martinson is your cousin, and you're on this ship and she isn't?"

"Josephine died a few weeks ago. I used her ticket. Elio bought another one and here we are."

"Oh, no," Amy says, looking at me finally having to believe what I told her earlier.

Now my girls are about to jump out of their skins.

"The one who died and lost her diamond ring in the cave? Elizabeth Johnson? I was in that cave. I found her ring!" Sophie is nearly leaping out of her seat.

"Don't tell me the third woman was Margaret Sampson?" Evvie says incredulously.

Amy nods yes.

"She died of a heart attack playing golf," Ida adds. "We saw it in the newspaper."

Amy is stunned.

I look pointedly at Evvie. "All three of the women Amy is supposed to meet. What a coincidence."

"You ought to know, Gladdy doesn't believe in coincidences," Evvie informs the group.

"Let me go back again for a moment. At that dinner with my boyfriend and his son, Morrie, the young policeman was talking about his cases. I was telling him about mine."

Evvie interrupts to tell Amy, "Gladdy and us girls are detectives."

"That's how we met," says Angie. Elio glares at her. "I had a small problem they solved," she adds, smiling sweetly at her problem.

Amy is still dumbfounded as Ida hands her one of our cards.

"So, I tell my boyfriend and his son, I can't believe these coincidences. At this point it was Margaret Sampson and Josephine Martinson who had died within less than a week of each other. They dismiss my theory. I decide to check it out and do a little investigating with my sister, Evvie."

"So that's what you were doing at Jo's funeral, detecting?" Angie says to me.

Evvie says, "We were sure surprised to see you there. We didn't know you were Josephina's relative."

"You saw them at the funeral? How come I didn't see them?" Elio is annoyed at not being in the know.

She gives him a playful pinch on the cheek. "Because you're half blind, *rospo*. Besides, I didn't want you to."

"How come you never told us about the funeral?" Ida asks me indignantly.

"Yeah," Bella says petulantly. "Only Evvie gets to know everything."

I sigh. "It's a long story. I'll tell you later."

I turn back to Angie. "Believe me, we were just as surprised to see you there as you were to see us."

She looks at Elio. "I caught them lying when

they tried to tell me they have a Chinese Catholic uncle."

Evvie says, "You caught us spying and we needed an excuse."

Bella is confused. "Who has a Chinese Catholic uncle?"

Evvie pats her on the back. "No one, sweetie."

"Then Elizabeth Johnson died. Three heiresses in less than three weeks."

Amy's voice is tremulous. "You're saying all the women I was supposed to meet died in the same month?"

"Let me put it this way: They all died *after* you were on that first cruise together."

I give everyone a few moments to think about this. Then I say to Amy, "You mentioned that your husband was also on that cruise. Were any of your new friends' husbands along?"

Amy says slowly, nervously, "All of their husbands were on board. While we played bridge, they hung out together and gambled in the casino."

"I was informed that all three of these women died of natural causes. In fact, I was made to feel that I was a failure for going against all the 'facts.' That the husbands had perfect alibis. In fact, there was no motive for these so-called individual crimes. There was no connection whatsoever between these three deaths.

"Well. Now we have the connection. All four couples did meet. Logic then tells us that since someone has been trying to kill Amy, then the other three women had to have been murdered, as well, and you were to be the fourth victim."

With that, Amy faints. Angelina screams. Elio is on his feet, cursing. And my girls are just plain flummoxed.

40

Amy Tells All

We all fan Amy with napkins. She slowly comes to.

Evvie asks, "Are you all right?"

She nods but just barely.

Angelina is clutching Elio. The girls are in shock. I feel terrible, but what else could I do? We have to get to the bottom of this. A murderer is loose on this ship.

Elio suggests we go to their stateroom.

Somberly we follow the Sicilianos. Sophie and Ida are supporting Amy. The winds are picking up. We hold on to our sun hats so they won't blow away.

I notice a couple of things as we enter the Sicilianos' stateroom. The room is enormous. It's actually a suite with a French door that opens onto a private balcony. Probably cost a fortune. The other is Amy's visceral response. I see her clutch at her stomach. Has she been in this room before?

We settle her down in an easy chair. She does not want to lie on the bed. We all take seats except for Elio, who paces. No one is saying a word, but they steal glances at me.

"Do you need anything?" I ask Amy. "Water? Tea? Should we call the doctor?"

"No." Her voice wavers and is very low. Her hands are trembling. I take a small blanket from the bed and place it across her knees.

"I'm so sorry," I say.

Evvie says to me, "Maybe we should wait until later."

"No," Amy says again. "I need this over with."

Elio demands to know "What did you mean, they had no motive? They had millions of motives."

"Wait," I tell him. "I'll get to that."

I ask Amy, "How did you meet Margaret and Josephine and Elizabeth?"

"At the bridge sign-up. We were placed at the same table. We instantly connected. We were familiar with one another since we all came from Florida and were involved in similar charities. We knew people in common at our country clubs."

"You were all rich," says Sophie, never known for her subtlety. Evvie throws her a dirty look.

"Yes. And we were great bridge players. We won games easily and there was an instant camaraderie. There was something about being on the ship...I guess a determination to have a good time." She pauses.

"Your husbands," I prompt her.

"We didn't all meet right away. Harry and I met Tom and Elizabeth at dinner the first night. We were seated at the same table. She and I smiled at one another, as if sharing a delightful secret. Both our husbands were younger and very handsome."

"Yes!" whispers Evvie victoriously. She glances at me knowingly.

I shake my head to silence her.

"The four of us met Jo and Bob in the gambling casino. We looked at one another and grinned. How funny. How perfectly marvelous."

"He was young and gorgeous, too!" Bella can't resist.

"Yes," says Amy sadly.

"Don't tell me!" Ida exclaims. "So were the last couple!"

"Yes. Margaret and Dick. We had all married younger men. Poor younger men."

"Talk about your coincidences," Elio echos my comment.

"*Tom, Dick and Harry,*" says Evvie, who can't resist. "Great forties movie with Ginger Rogers." She grins.

"And 'Bob'? Where'd he come from?"

Amy continues. "That's what we said. What were the odds on all of us finding one another? The guys thought it was a great big joke, and soon they were telling stories about what they had been doing before we women rescued them from nothingness.

"And everything seemed funnier. The men instantly took to one another. They hung out together when we were playing bridge. And then all eight of us became inseparable the rest of the trip."

She stops. "May I have water?"

Elio instantly brings a pitcher and a glass and puts them on the small table beside her. He looks at his wife, who sits scrunched down deep on the couch, seemingly dazed. He sits down beside Angelina and reaches for her hand.

We wait expectantly.

"I don't know if I can go on," Amy says. "I'm so ashamed."

"Please," Angelina says. "I need to know."

She calms herself and begins again. "Then suddenly, things got wild. The men started drinking more while we played, and then they wanted us to join them and catch up. Every night we partied in each other's rooms."

I look around and realize that Jo Martinson must have reserved this same room on her last trip. It was creepy imagining these things happening where we now sat.

"One of the men brought drugs. Ecstasy, cocaine, who knows what." Amy pauses. "The parties escalated. Beth and Meg were gung-ho for it all. They were flirting with our husbands. Jo and I were uncomfortable. Then, the last night on board, things got ugly."

Amy rises and opens the door and walks out onto the balcony, keeping her back to us. We can see her lean over the railing with her head hanging down. The wind is blowing her hair.

Evvie starts to get up. I touch her arm to keep her down. Sophie and Bella are now whispering to Ida.

Amy remains outside. There is a rustle of movement in the room, but we stay where we are.

I look at Angelina, still huddled down in the couch. What must she be thinking?

Finally Amy comes back in and sits down again. "Money does funny things to you. I wasn't born rich like Elizabeth or Margaret. Jo and I talked about it the few times we were alone. We grew up middle-class. But as we watched the other two, we realized that we had become like them. We felt privileged. We had come to expect people to cater to our every want. We were above everyone else. Special. Worldly. It didn't always come easily, but that's what Jo and I had learned in order to belong.

"My family was horrified when I married Harry. My first husband died and left me very wealthy. I was alone for a long time. Finally, watching my rich friends, I decided I could buy a man like I would a new Rolls or a second home in Europe. I met Harry at the vet where I brought my show dog, my *bichon frise,* to be cared for. He was an assistant—you know, cleaning cages, feeding the animals. But I took one look at him and I knew I could have him. Harry grabbed at the chance. He didn't pretend to love me, but he knew the rules. Be my companion, in bed and out. Behave lovingly to me in public. I gave him a long leash." Amy laughs. "He lived a separate life. I didn't care what he did as long as he didn't embarrass me."

She sits there, lost in her troubled thoughts.

Finally I remind her, "The last night?"

"Everything seemed . . . surreal. We were drunk and drugged. The men were mean. Their jokes were about us, and cutting. As if safety in numbers made them brave enough to say what they really thought of these silly women who had bought them. I tried to tell Jo, but she was numb."

Amy gets up again. "I can't stand it," she says, and bursts into tears. She paces, now speaking quickly as if to get it over with. We follow her with our eyes.

"We met them in that bar they liked so much with that leering devil's face. They looked guilty about something. And also excited. Yes, very excited. They had just dumped the room key cards on the bar and were picking them up again . . . not picking up their own keys. No, not their own."

" 'Last night on board and the ultimate game.' I remember it was Tom Johnson who announced it. He walked—more like wobbled—toward Margaret and put his arm about her, nuzzled her neck, and waved her room key at her. 'Shall we?' She got it right away and nuzzled back. Margaret was giggling and winking at us as they walked away."

Now Amy stops moving. Her voice seems strangled.

"Then Dick Sampson went over to Jo. She was so far gone, I don't think she even knew what was happening. And my Harry snuggled up with Elizabeth. I saw a look in his eyes that made me shiver. There was cruelty. Like the vet's assistant he was, about to put a pit bull down." Amy's voice becomes a whisper. "Bob Martinson took me. I didn't want to go with him. I tried to get away but his hand holding my arm was like steel."

Elio mumbles an angry Italian curse word. Angelina seems devastated. She moves even closer to him for comfort.

Amy looks at me. "I wasn't honest with you. I thought about calling the women, but I was ashamed. And I thought they might be, too. I was so sure that we would meet again on this trip—without the men—and maybe be able to talk about what went wrong."

She sinks back down in her chair, eyes closed, utterly exhausted. Angelina gets up and, with her walker, moves over to her and touches her hand gently.

It is very quiet in the room. We can hear the band playing on the deck right above us and people laughing.

"Those sons of bitches!" snarls Elio, nearly leaping out of his seat.

Angelina grabs his arm to restrain him. "What's to figure out? They killed their wives. They were after the money."

"They all had alibis," I say.

"Then they hired a killer. That's what rich people can do," Angelina adds.

Here goes nothing. I'm going to ask, but I know

the answer. "Amy, I was informed that the other women had prenuptial agreements. Did you?"

"Of course. Harry knew up front. I had a settlement drawn up for him. A very generous one. My house to live in for his lifetime. A large monthly allowance. Stocks and bonds. He was very satisfied with that."

"Then, what changed?" I ask. "Why would four strangers suddenly decide to kill all their wives?"

41

Boy Toys

SIX WEEKS EARLIER

They were sitting at the Devil's Own Bar. The glittering neon sign above them showed a sneering, cartoonish red devil with its menacing tail wound about an animated sign that read "Three Sins—Drink, Women, and Money."

Since this was the last night on board—Captain's Dinner night on the world-famous cruise ship Heavenly—*the four young, handsome men were elegantly dressed in tuxedos. They were deep in intense conversation.*

They were diligently drinking, as well, four empty martini glasses lined up in front of each. One newly filled. It was time for a toast.

Totally unmindful of the activities around them, they ignored not only the posh couples parading past them along the walk-through corridor, but also the Angels' Strolling Choir serenading the guests with suitably chosen songs for the cocktail hour. Right now they were singing "Pennies from Heaven."

Yet the men noticed nothing. They lifted their glasses.

"The game's over. It's our game now."

"It was all about trust."

"No promises broken."

"No backing out."

"Agreed."

"All for one and one for all."

They clinked their glasses with shared smiles.

The woman was pushing fifty, pretending to be forty, overdressed, overly made-up, desperation hidden by her idea of witty repartee. She elbowed up alongside them.

"Can I believe my eyes? Four dashing guys drinking alone without pretty women draped around their shoulders?"

She ran her fingers through the blond hair of the man seated closest to her. He removed her hand.

"Sorry, old girl, take your business elsewhere."

"Yeah. We're happily married guys," said the next one. But there was ice in his voice belying his words.

Rebuffed, she tried for an exit line. "I never met a happily married guy, let alone four of them. Maybe they should put you in a wax museum or something." With that she backed off.

It was as if there had been no interruption. The men removed their room key cards from their pockets and tossed them onto the bar. Each man chose a key card other than his own.

"They thought we wouldn't find out?"

"They're in for a big surprise."

"Hot time in the old town tonight."

"What I like best about it . . ."

"Yeah?"

"No one, and I mean no one, will ever figure it out."

42

Strangers on a Ship

It's two o'clock in the morning and I'm pacing. Not easy to do in a room the size of a postage stamp. The girls fell asleep early. No wonder, they were exhausted. I am, too, but my mind won't shut off.

"Glad?" I hear Evvie whisper. "You can't sleep?"

"No. I'm sorry, did I wake you?" I whisper, too, so that we don't wake Ida.

"I have to get up to go to the bathroom anyway." With that she walks past me into our tiny commode.

"Don't forget, don't flush," I say.

"I know," she answers.

The mechanism that makes the toilet flush is so loud it could wake the dead. The first time we heard it, we nearly jumped out of our skins. Then we started to laugh and decided never to flush at night.

Evvie comes back out and sits down on our lone chair. "What a day!"

"That's for sure." Amy has moved in with the Sicilianos, sharing their large suite. Elio swears he will guard her with his life. She will be safe with them. He is all for going to the captain tomorrow morning and telling him what we know. But I can guess what Captain Standish will say. What makes us so sure? What's our proof? How would he find a killer among thousands of people? A nameless hired assassin.

"What's bothering you?" Evvie asks.

"It's the motive. If I could only make that connection between those men." I sit down on the edge of my mattress and cross my legs yoga-style.

"They talked it over and decided they wanted the money now."

"But why? They had plenty of money and plenty more coming later. They had a sweet setup. Why take a chance on maybe getting caught, ending up in jail and getting nothing?"

"Sometimes when people get in a group, someone starts to give the others the idea."

"Maybe, but it would have to be strong for them to chance losing what they already had."

"You want to watch the late movie? Maybe it'll put you to sleep." Our ship makes sure we're entertained twenty-four hours every day.

"I hope so. If it's an oldie in black and white, that'll get me to nod off."

We both climb back down onto our mattresses. Evvie turns on our TV and keeps the sound low. We scrunch into our pillows to get comfortable and pull the covers around our necks.

Evvie punches my arm in excitement. "Look! Look what's on. It's one of my favorite movies."

In a matter of moments I recognize *Strangers on a Train*.

"Aw, shucks," Evvie complains. "We missed the part when Robert Walker tells Farley Granger about killing one another's wives. Ooh, I love this movie."

"And I love to sleep!" Ida opens one eye, pulling her pillow over her head.

"Go ahead, who's stopping you?" Evvie answers.

"What are you watching?" Ida asks, her voice now muffled.

"*Strangers on a Train*."

"I hate that movie. It's stupid. Who'd believe that plot?" And Ida is snoring again.

Evvie jumps up and down. "*I* believe that plot! That's what these guys did. There was no hired killer. They exchanged wives. Strangers on a Ship!"

I'm right with her. "That's what the key cards were really for. That's how they picked their target!"

"We solved it!"

"Not yet. There's a piece missing. I have to call Amy."

I get up and head for the phone.

"You can't." Evvie puts her hand on my arm. "It's the middle of the night."

I stop in my tracks. What was I thinking? "You're right. I'll ask her tomorrow morning. She doesn't know it, but she holds the key to the motives of those evil boy toys."

I'll never be able to fall asleep now. But who cares?

I smile. Gladdy Gold is back on track.

43

Breakfast at Heavenly's

The ship is fairly deserted by now. Everyone's gone sightseeing in St. Thomas, though the sky outside seems to be threatening rain. We're practically alone in the dining room. The Sicilianos. Amy Larkin. Me and my girls. Only Sophie and Bella are scarfing down goodies from the wonderful spread in front of us. Ida still eats carefully. Evvie nibbles. But Angelina, Amy, and Elio aren't interested in food; they only want to know why I called them together so early this morning. None of them look like they slept much last night, either.

I'm drinking too much coffee, trying to keep myself alert after my own sleepless night.

"When should we go to the captain?" Elio asks.

"Maybe after this," I say.

I've already filled them in on what Evvie and I discussed last night. Ida is still incredulous that we actually figured it out by watching *Strangers on a Train*.

"Bob Martinson," Amy murmurs. "Now it comes back to me. It was his voice I heard behind me before I fell. He pushed me."

Angelina and Elio are stunned. Jo's husband is on this ship!

Elio says angrily, "If he's here, I'll find him."

Evvie says, "I already checked the entire passenger list. He isn't on it."

"Maybe he's a waiter," Bella says, looking furtively at the staff now setting up for the first lunch seating.

"I doubt it," says Ida. "He wouldn't take a chance on being spotted by Amy. And if he knew Angelina and Elio were on board, he'd be twice as cautious."

"A sailor," Ida suggests. "No, forget it, that's too complicated. He couldn't just get on board whatever ship he wanted."

I say it. "An entertainer. Using a stage name."

"The MC?" Ida asks. "He was one of the last guys on board."

Angelina says in a strangled voice, "Jo's husband, Bob, taught Latin dancing."

"You mean like the cha-cha?" Bella says timidly.

Now it hits. "Roberto?" moans Sophie. "Our gorgeous Roberto?"

Sophie and Bella look at one another in despair.

"How dumb we didn't get it right away," Evvie says, smacking at her head. "We were so impressed with his helpfulness, we never paid attention to the fact that *he* was the last man back at the ship."

"And he didn't want to go on the search with us, but Sophie and Bella forced his hand." Ida sips at her now-cold coffee.

"But he must have figured that way he could make sure Amy was dead. I'll bet when he saw that she was still alive, he panicked. No wonder he volunteered to run for help. He wanted to get away. He didn't want Amy to see him," I say.

Elio is on his feet. "Where is that slimeball's classroom? Let me at him."

"Wait," I tell him. "We can't do anything until we talk to the captain. He's dangerous. We don't want anyone hurt." I look at Amy.

"You had a question?" Amy tears up little bits of her blueberry muffin. She's picking at her food but not eating.

"I do. Something must have happened before you went on that trip or during. Something that you've forgotten?"

"I can't imagine what."

"Think, Amy," Evvie prods her.

The waiter comes by carrying coffeepots. Elio waves him away.

"The only thing that comes to mind is that I almost didn't go on the first cruise at all. But that can't mean anything."

"Why not?" Sophie can't stand the suspense. She wants to move this along.

"My dog died. My beloved Poopsie."

"Poopsie?" says Bella, laughing.

Sophie nudges her, laughing along with her.

"I loved that dog! She was my angel. I had her for fifteen years. Nobody loved me more than that doggie did!"

Bella and Sophie quickly wipe the smiles off their faces.

"Harry had no sympathy at all. He, who worked with animals, said I was being a sentimental fool. Besides, he was a cheapskate. With my money. We'd already paid for the cruise so we should go. I was so angry at him."

Sophie and Bella now murmur sympathetic sounds.

"That's all I could think of. What could I do to honor Poopsie's special memory? So I decided to leave the majority of my money to the SPCA, the Society for the Prevention of Cruelty to Animals. I made up my mind to change my will."

She sobs quietly into her napkin. "Poopsie... Poopsie..."

"Oh, my God," I say. Slowly some of the others are getting it, too. "You didn't happen to take that will along with you on the ship, by any chance?"

"Of course I did. I needed to write it all up the right way..." She breaks off. "Oh, no."

"Harry found it," I say.

Evvie is right with me. "And told the other guys."

"No, it can't be..." Her eyes are wide with fright.

"Lot of booze, drugs," I continue. "The guys

were worried. More than worried. Suddenly this was a warning. A threat to their security. And they decided if one wife didn't keep to her part of the bargain, would the other men be safe? What whim might cause any of *their* wives to change their wills?"

This time Ida picks up the ball. "They weren't going to take any more chances. They were going to collect all their money now."

"And there's your motive," Elio announces.

Everyone stares at Amy. She leaps up, overturning her chair. Her eyes are wild and frenzied. "I didn't mean . . . I wasn't thinking . . ."

She starts to back away. "I didn't think how Harry . . . I was in mourning, for God's sakes!"

She's running now. "I killed them! They all died because of me!"

She races out of the room. Everyone is speechless.

Except for Bella. Mulling over the meaning of it all. "It's all Poopsie's doing. Getting revenge for that stupid name."

44

Cha-Cha-Cha

We race after Amy down the hallway. But there is no consoling her. We all try. She is in a state of hysteria, flailing her arms, hitting her body against the wall. She is taking the blame and holding it tightly to her being.

It's heartbreaking to see her this way. I feel my own sense of guilt for having brought her to this state.

Finally Angelina suggests we take her to the infirmary. There she is given a sedative.

We leave her under a nurse's care with the warning that no one is allowed in except us.

I'm at the door when, in a quivering voice, Amy calls my name.

I turn and look at her. Her face is pale. Her hands are shaking.

"God forgive me," she says, and turns her face to the wall.

On the way back to our stateroom I pick up a wall phone. I call the captain and tell him I must see him at once. It's a matter of life and death.

"Yes, well, that's not possible right now," he says. "Don't you feel the ship rocking? We have a storm situation brewing, Mrs. Gold."

"You have to batten down the hatches and all that stuff," I say.

"Precisely. All that stuff."

He's about to hang up. "But when?" I demand to know.

"All right. Come up at five. The conference room, upper deck. By then we'll be well out to sea. If I have to change our appointment I will call you."

Before he can hang up again, I tell him, "I'm bringing seven people, maybe eight, so be prepared."

"Seven? Why not twenty-five? Shall I serve cocktails?"

Boy, does he know how to do sarcasm. I thought a captain needed people skills. "That won't be necessary, sir."

"Why am I not surprised at anything you say or do, Mrs. Gold?" is his droll retort. "Is it all right if I hang up now so I can save the ship from sinking?"

"Yes, sir," I say smartly.

* * *

We stay in our stateroom all day, trying to keep a low profile until we can meet with the captain. We play cards, rest a little, and try not to worry about Amy.

Now I look at Bella and Sophie. "What is 'Roberto' teaching today after everyone gets back from touring?" I ask the totally demoralized duo.

"Salsa," they answer in tandem.

"And we have a lesson at four," says Bella, "which, of course, we're not keeping."

"Maybe you should," I say. "Look, you'll have just enough time before we're due at the captain's. It's better than just waiting and pacing."

Sophie and Bella cling to one another.

"No, you can't make me go." Bella is actually stamping her foot.

"I'd faint. I'd stutter. I couldn't look him in the eye." Sophie is equally adamant.

Evvie gets into it. "You have to. Robert already knows the two of you. He'll believe you if you tell him that all Amy remembers is that she tripped and fell."

"I'm too scared. I'll start to cry," Bella adds.

"If you don't show up for that lesson, he'll get suspicious," I say. "Listen, I'm not sure we're right to do this. Either way is a risk."

Ida, who is sprawled across all three of our mattresses, eating macadamia nuts, now scrambles into a sitting position. "What a pair of wusses! I'll go. I can look that viper right in the eye and lie through my teeth."

"You're hired," I say.

Bella is curious. "Ida, you know how to dance?"

"I got feet, don't I? So I'll dance."

"I'd go," says Evvie, "but I don't want to leave Amy alone for too long."

"What are we, chopped liver?" Sophie says, annoyed. "Can't we watch her?"

"We'll all three stay with her in the infirmary, together," says Evvie.

"All right," Sophie answers, only slightly mollified.

We'd left Angelina and Elio in their stateroom. I'm sure they needed to be alone after our shattering meeting. What a terrible shock for her to know her cousin had been murdered. By her own husband, trading her off to be killed by another man. Elio, to my surprise, is turning out to be some *mensch,* gentle with Angelina and very grateful to us.

Even though I'd seen Bob Martinson's photo at Gossip, and seen him at the Boca funeral, I didn't recognize him on the dock. The sombrero was distracting. Maybe on purpose. But then again, at that time I wasn't looking for Bob. I only saw "Roberto."

"But Angelina said Bob Martinson is blond with green eyes," says Bella, confused. "Roberto has black hair and brown eyes."

Sophie looks at her balefully. "Haven't you

ever heard of hair dye?" She pats down her Wild
Strawberry Blonde coif. "And what about contact
lenses?"

Meanwhile we are noshing on whatever goodies we have stashed in our room, since some of us
hardly ate breakfast and we all missed lunch. I
watch the clock. The dance class will start in about
twenty minutes.

What a day so far! I desperately need a nap, but
I'm too revved up to sleep. I guess I'm going out
dancing.

We join five eager women of indeterminate age
waiting for Roberto to arrive at the dance studio to
give his lesson. The room is smaller than I expected, but plush. One whole wall is floor-to-
ceiling mirrors.

Ida and I have gussied up a bit, with flared
skirts and colorful blouses. Since none of us wears
high heels anymore, except for impractical Sophie,
we wear low-heeled sandals. Ida whispers good
luck to me. I suggest we imitate Bella and Sophie
and try to gush. We both giggle at that.

Roberto enters wearing tight black pants, a
frilly white shirt, and soft black leather dancing
shoes. His dyed black hair gleams. He smiles that
radiant smile at all of us. I might gush after all. I
look more closely at him now. Now I can see
through the disguise. Now I see Bob.

He addresses the other women by name.

Regulars. He recognizes us and there is the tiniest of flickering in those fake brown eyes.

I speak up quickly. "You remember us, Roberto. We all jumped ship together." I manage a large phony smile.

"How could I forget?" He looks deep into my eyes. I pray I won't flinch.

Ida speaks up right on cue. She tosses a friendly wave at him. "We never had a chance to thank you for helping us save Mrs. Larkin."

"And how is...Mrs. Larkin?" Now Ida gets the questioning look in the eye. She doesn't flinch, either. I congratulate him silently on how well he pretends not to know Amy's name.

Ida remembers her speech. "She's shaken, but all right. Poor thing forgot to take her medicine that morning. She got dizzy and fell."

I can see him pause, waiting to be sure we aren't lying, and then he relaxes.

If he really knew what we know now, it would shake that arrogance right out of him.

"I can't tell you how happy that makes me. Oh, and by the way, where are the delightful Miss Sophie and Miss Bella?"

I'm just about to speak, but Ida does an impromptu on me. "Food poisoning," she blurts. "They both had the lobster thermidor for lunch." She shakes her head sadly. "Spoiled fish."

I send her a look. I guess she didn't think "tired" was a good enough excuse.

Roberto whirls around gracefully, his frilly shirt fluttering as he does. "Time to salsa!" He goes to the small CD player and turns it on, loud. Immediately the other women are starting to gyrate to the catchy Latin beat. I imitate them and Ida imitates me.

"But first, costumes. To get into the Latin mood." He points to a large carton on a table.

"Oh, my," I say, worried. Is he going to dress us up like Carmen Miranda with bananas on our heads?

The regulars hurry over and gleefully pull out an assortment of items of riotous colors. I settle for a large fringed red shawl that reminds me of what people used to put on top of their pianos. I tie it around my waist. Ida pulls out some kind of long skirt thing with a lot of added extra layers of brightly colored zigzaggy material and pulls it on over her own skirt. She actually winks at me. This is an Ida I don't recognize.

Roberto claps his hands at us. "OK, ladies, get in a line and try to follow what I do."

He turns his back on us and faces the full-length mirror. And we get to stare at the back of him. I have to admit, that is one sexy tush he has undulating at us.

The music is very fast and hot. And so is Roberto.

"Step forward with the right leg and bring it back to center. Step forward with the left and do the same. Keep repeating. Quick, quick, slow, quick, quick, slow."

I watch him watching us. Is he mocking us? He

smiles widely at me. I smile back just as wide. It makes my teeth ache.

"Ladies, now add those hips to it, let those hips rip."

I'm ripping as fast as I can, but I can't keep up with him. I look toward Ida. She is biting her lip, apparently concentrating hard on following.

"Now let's try it to the side. Step to the right. One-two-three-hold, now step to the left and one-two-three-hold, now cross over and do it again."

I'm tripping over my feet. I haven't a clue what to do or where to do it.

This seems to go on endlessly. Whatever he's doing, I'm not. Finally, thankfully, he stops.

The women are all puffing. That was a workout.

"Very good," says Roberto. "Now I need a volunteer. After all, this is the second most important thing you'll ever do with a partner." He smirks, letting us guess what the first might be. Ha-ha.

He walks directly to Ida and me. He grins at me and I grin back. I feel like my face will crack from all this smiling and grinning.

I slouch like a little kid in class who doesn't know the answers and doesn't want to be called on.

He reaches out for Ida's hand.

And there they go, our Ida quick-quick-slowing with him every step of the way. Ida, gracefully letting her swirly skirt swirl.

Ida, dipping and bending when he dips and

bends. Her head snapping back when he snaps. I wish I had a camera. She's adorable. Who knew?

We're about to leave, when Roberto calls me back. He'd like to give me a few personal pointers. Ida and I look at one another. I shrug. She nods and leaves with the other women.

Roberto puts on another tape. This is a slow rumba. He pulls me to him.

"I'm really not good at this," I say.

"Don't worry. I'll lead you."

And he is a very good leader.

He pulls me even tighter to him. This is not good. His aftershave is overwhelming. It's making me want to sneeze. Why did I let Ida leave?

He whispers. His mouth is so close to my ear, I can feel his breath, and I shiver. "I've been watching you, Mrs. Gold. You are a very smart lady."

"Thanks." I am desperately trying to create space between our two bodies, listen to what he is saying and hear what he really means, and think fast, all at the same time.

"But it's not a good idea to get involved in other people's business." His fingers dig a little too deeply into my neck as his other arm tightens even more around my lower back. I am feeling body parts I haven't felt in a very long time. His. Not mine.

I giggle nervously. "My mother used to tell me the same thing." He twirls me around. I nearly fall on him as he spins me back. "But I never listened."

"Listen now. A ship can be a dangerous place for an elderly woman like yourself. Accidents can happen. A slippery deck. A broken railing. Steep metal steps."

Oh, how I'm dying to tell him, he doesn't need to kill Amy or even me anymore. The jig's up.

Enough. Time for an accident of my own. I "accidentally" step hard on his right foot and, at the same time, my allergy to his aftershave makes me sneeze hard, right into his face.

"Clumsy..." He pulls away, wiping his face in disgust.

I move to the door, fast. "I can't agree with you more. An old person better be careful. Thanks for the lesson."

And I am running down the hallway. I don't know if I'm running for my life or for my shower. For a very cold shower.

Whoa! Talk about sex and violence.

And cheap thrills.

45

The Captain, the Killer,
and the Private Eye

We arrive at the captain's office promptly at five. The Sicilianos are already there. "Don't ask," I told the girls when they asked about my dance with Roberto. "You don't want to know."

Angelina asks about Amy. I checked with the infirmary. She was still asleep.

The door opens and we are invited in. It is your ordinary conference room. A large gray table with matching chairs around it. Even the walls are gray. We all take seats. My group looks to me.

I introduce everyone to the captain and he introduces us to his three top men.

"Speak," says Captain Standish.

I jump right in. "We have a murderer on board. His name is Robert Martinson, aka Roberto, who teaches your Latin dance class, and you should grab him fast."

"Start from the beginning, Mrs. Gold, and then I shall determine what course of action I shall take."

Okay, we know who's in control here, don't we?

I start. Nonstop. With no interruption.

I don't know how long I've been talking, but my voice feels raspy and I don't dare sneak a look at my watch.

I am aware of an occasional squeak of chairs, a cough now and then, and an intermittent need to hold on to the table since the ship is rocking quite a bit.

And once or twice I can see Angelina, clutching at a handkerchief and crying.

I can also tell my girls are dying to jump in and contribute but are awed into silence by the very intimidating captain.

Finally I wind down. "So, Captain Standish, what do we do now?" Notice the "we"—he's my partner now.

We tell him where Amy is and her condition. For a moment there is silence. He addresses the Sicilianos. "I can only guess how difficult this situation is for you. Please know I shall do whatever I can to help you. I will, of course, inform all the necessary authorities. And until we can take Mr. Martinson into custody, you will be accompanied at all times by my men, and a guard will be posted outside the infirmary."

"Gladdy was threatened, too," Sophie pipes, then quickly shuts up.

He nods to his second-in-command, who goes to the wall phone and speaks softly and quickly.

The first mate hangs up the phone. "They're searching for him right now. I told them not to do anything other than to locate him."

"Good," says the captain.

Captain Standish looks at me. I wish I could know what he's thinking. What does that glint in his eye mean? Then he says, "I might mention that at your suggestion, Mrs. Gold, I contacted Detective Morgan Langford and retired detective Jack Langford. I was warned by them that you were a force unto yourself. And I should take you very seriously."

I smile. There is a muttering of agreement among my group.

I say nervously, "I made a big mistake trying to outsmart Martinson by going to his dance class. There's no doubt he's on to us."

Our group gets up, ready to leave, when the phone rings again. The first mate answers, listens, hangs up.

"They haven't been able to locate him as of now, sir. He missed his four-thirty class."

My heart sinks. I think of slippery steps and broken railings.

The captain turns to his men. "Find him. Be as inconspicuous as you can. I don't want to alarm the passengers."

Bella can't stand it anymore. She blurts, "But what if he has a gun?"

Sophie joins in. "What if he runs for it?"

Evvie can't resist a famous movie line: " 'He can run, but he can't hide.' "

There is a smattering of nervous laughter.

"We're out on the ocean, ladies," the captain reassures us. "He can't go far."

"I want to have a turn at him when you catch him," growls Elio.

"What if he grabs a hostage?" Ida adds.

The captain dryly asks us if we watch a lot of movies.

Yes, and a good thing, too. I want to say it but I resist the temptation.

He walks us to the door.

I stop. "Captain, sir, may I make a suggestion?"

"Can I stop you?"

"I think I have an idea of how to search for him while keeping the passengers out of harm's way."

"I'm listening," he says. Boy, is he scary. This is the second time today I feel like a child. Afraid of this very big teacher standing there with a very large ruler in his hand.

Here goes nothing. "Maybe you should call a fire drill. Then everybody will be gathered together in controlled areas, and with the ship emptied out, he should be easier to spot."

For a long moment the captain stares at me. Then he shakes his head as if in disbelief. And there's that twinkle in his eye again.

"Mrs. Gold," he says, "who *are* you?"

I could tell him I'm from the planet *Meshugeneh*, but I think I've overstayed my welcome.

To his men he says, "Prepare to sound the alarm."

46

Who's Rockin' the Boat?

It's six-thirty P.M. and here comes the captain's
promised run-for-your-life-jackets mambo. If the
runners and dashers passing us knew that I'm the
one who's interrupted French Gourmet Night in
the dining room, I'd be skewered on a rotisserie
for sure.

The ship is rocking from side to side. Then up
and down. Then round and round. At least it feels
like that. Winds are gusting hard and we are holding on to the outside rails as tightly as we can as we
reach our Muster Station on the upper Starlight
deck. Wearing that clumsy orange life jacket
doesn't help. I feel like I'm choking, and I can
hardly see over the top of it as we run.

The girls are mad at me. Even Evvie, who is
usually my steadfast ally, screams over the deafening alarm blasts, "You and your big ideas. You had

to give the captain the suggestion to call a fire drill at dinnertime?"

"But—I didn't say when—"

"Yeah," says Bella, cutting me off. "We hardly had breakfast and didn't eat more than a crumb after."

Sophie gets on the bandwagon. "And we missed lunch because you made us hide in the room."

Ida's turn. "You think those stale peanuts satisfied anybody?"

Evvie's big finish: "And now we're missing pâté de foie gras! I'll bet we're the first people who ever starved on a cruise ship."

What a bunch of ingrates! If I ever started getting a swelled head for my efforts, this group would know how to deflate it.

We weave from side to side, grabbing at whatever we can for handholds, at our station. Many other passengers are already there holding on to poles and guardrails and anything else bolted down that will keep them steady. The wind is whipping even stronger now. As frightening as the gusts are, the noise they make is worse. The ear-splitting blasts add to the feeling of chaos and discomfort.

I wonder where the Sicilianos are. And I hope Amy isn't frightened. Last I saw of Angelina and Elio, they were being accompanied by armed guards.

A nervous woman calls shrilly, "Is this for real? Are we in a hurricane?"

I want to reassure her, Hey, this is a false alarm. But is it anymore?

The ship's getting even rockier. So much for stabilizers. The waves look ominous and high. My girls are wide-eyed and I'm beginning to really worry.

"Oh, no!" Evvie lets go of my arm and stumbles to the outer rail, hanging on for dear life, and throws up. Thank goodness the wind is blowing away from us. She leans her head weakly on one of the lifeboats latched to the outer rail.

Seeing Evvie is all it takes for Sophie to have her turn zigzagging her way to the rail and tossing what's left in her stomach over the side.

And Bella, moaning, follows right after her. I am barely able to keep from being sick myself. I look at Ida, standing next to me, her head high, arms stretched out wide, letting the breeze caress her face. Her eyes are closed. Her smile is beatific.

I can't believe it. This is the real thing, not just sloshing soup! "Ida. Are you feeling all right?"

She opens her eyes. "What?"

"Everybody's seasick."

Ida looks at our gang hanging their heads over the rail. "Not me. I guess I finally got my sea legs." She closes her eyes blissfully.

I hear Evvie at the rail say, "Now I'm glad we didn't get much to eat today."

Just then the ship tips and people start to topple into each other. Someone is yelling, "Oh, my God. Look at that!" So I do, and I see a fearful sight. A massive wave. Coming right at us. Huge. Terrifying.

Someone yells, "Hang on!" as the boat tilts the other way, like something is pulling the sea right out from under us. There's no way we can make it to the inside and away from it.

Panic hits. People grip each other, stricken, whimpering or screaming. I hear a woman shout plaintively, "Murray! We'll never see the grandchildren again."

Her husband, I assume, answers her, "Shirley. They're a pain in the neck and they treat you like dirt."

I hear Bella, still at the rail, moaning, "We're gonna die, we're gonna die."

I keep waiting for my life to pass before my eyes, but it doesn't. I think of death and I think of my Jack's death. Am I now going to join him? I think of my Emily and my beautiful grandchildren. And the thought that I may never see them again. All I can do is stare at that black mass relentlessly coming toward us. It's like a tsunami. Larger than life. Mother Nature at her worst. I close my eyes.

The wave crashes. The ship creaks ominously, but holds, as the wave hits hard against the hull below us. Thank God. We didn't drown, but we sure got soaked.

There is silence as everyone stands unmoving, unsure of what might happen next. The winds have lessened.

Evvie, Sophie, and Bella stagger their way back to where Ida and I are still hanging on to our rails.

"Wasn't that invigorating?" says Ida.

We look at her as if she's crazy.

We all hug, glad we're still alive.

Evvie says, "I have such a headache. When I was leaning against that lifeboat, something moving inside kept knocking against the side and kept hitting my head."

"Maybe the anchor," says Ida.

The seven blasts haven't stopped. That means they still haven't found Bob Martinson. I turn and look at that lifeboat. "Maybe not an anchor?" I look at Evvie.

"Maybe not," she says, reading my mind.

Evvie and I make our tortuous way toward the boat. The other girls, surprised, follow carefully after us. I put my ear against its side, listening.

Suddenly, the cover is kicked off and there, disheveled and disoriented, is Bob Martinson, tearing himself out from under the canvas. He sees us. We see him. For a moment we are like some frozen tableau, no one moving.

Then Bob looks behind him, seeing nothing but a great fall down to the ocean. Looks back at us again.

Bella says, amazed, "Just like in the movies. They always hide in the lifeboats."

I yell to the passengers, "Someone call the captain!"

Ida can't resist. "Get out, *putz*. Women and children first."

Bob makes his decision between the deep blue sea and us "devils." He jumps out of the lifeboat and onto the deck, knocking us aside like a row of bowling pins.

He runs through the crowd. We run after him. "Stop him! He's a murderer!"

People are confused. Some move out of his path. Some grab for him and miss.

Amazingly, Ida manages to take hold of his fancy dance jacket and now he is pulling her along.

"Hold on!" I yell.

"Cha-cha-cha," Ida yells back gleefully.

Meanwhile the girls are looking for weapons. Sophie grabs at a shuffleboard stick hanging on its hook. Bella seizes a life preserver off the wall.

"Make way!" I shout. Some people let us through, others get in our way.

I can still see Ida hanging on for all she's worth, while he keeps trying to shake her off. Now she's down almost on her knees and she makes a grab with both arms for one of his legs. He drags her along and now she's nearly flat on the ground, the toes of her shoes scraping the deck.

Sophie is almost up to him and she flails her shuffleboard stick out, trying to hit him.

"Ouch," says one of the passengers near her.

"Sorry," says Sophie.

Bella takes her best shot and skims the life preserver like a Frisbee into a perfect ring toss. Only it's landed on the head of a befuddled little old man in a wheelchair.

"Oops," Bella says as she pulls it off.

Other passengers seize upon the excitement and join the chase. All of us are still wobbling from side to side, slipping and sliding. Some are hitting the deck. Literally. The girls are chanting, "Stop him! Stop him!"

With elbows flailing, Robert plows through the crowd, shoving people out of his way.

And finally he has shaken loose of Ida, who lands flat on her face. I catch up to her and help her up.

I hear a familiar voice ahead of us. Who could forget that midwestern twang? It's the Green Bay Packers guy, Greg. "Don't worry, ladies," he shouts. "He ain't gonna make that first down."

With that, we see him dive for Robert. He tackles him, and the two of them go flying. Three other men jump into the scrimmage and grab on, too. From under the resulting pile, I hear Greg gleefully say, "Brett Favre, how do you like them cheese curds!"

And here comes the cavalry—oops, I mean the captain—and his gang for the coup de grâce. Roberto is toast.

And, when he gets up, we girls hug Greg in another kind of scrimmage.

We never do get to eat. Due to the storm, the French Gourmet Night and the midnight buffet are canceled. It doesn't matter because we wouldn't have made it anyway. Terror and excitement wore us out. When we get to our room, we notice our message button on the phone is blinking, but we're too tired to check. We are asleep as fast as we can drop out of our sopping wet clothes, shower, get into our jammies, and fall into our beds.

47

Two Jacks

I wake up from my dream, smiling. At eight A.M., waddaya know. A dream ending at a decent hour. Or maybe it was Evvie's leg heavily thrown over mine that woke me.

I sit up. Both girls are still asleep. Ditto the two in the next room. No surprise after the exhausting day and night we had. I hope the sun is shining after that horrific storm. Too bad we have no porthole.

The dream. What a dream! I relish the quiet so I can savor it.

New York City. In front of the main branch of the public library on Fifth Avenue and Forty-second Street. The place where I worked. Jack is going up the stairs. My husband, Jack, wearing the de rigueur outfit for the fifties' college professor, a tweed jacket with leather patches, cords, black horn-rimmed glasses, and a pipe in his mouth. Usually unlit.

"Where did you leave it?" he asks me.

"In my desk, right-hand drawer," I tell him.

"What's the name of it?"

"Paradise Lost," I remind my absentminded professor yet again.

He gives me one of his dazzling smiles, waves, and goes inside.

I wait, happily basking in the bright sunlight.

The two famous, originally pink, now gray, marble lions that guard the stately front doors turn to me. "You must have patience," says the one whose name is Patience. "You must have fortitude," says the one named Fortitude.

I giggle. This is delicious. Originally the lions were named after their benefactors, Lord Astor and Lady Lennox, but our famous mayor, Fiorello La Guardia, renamed them to inspire people to persevere during the economic depression of the thirties.

One of the front doors opens again. It's Jack, grinning and waving a book at me.

But it's Jack Langford. Dressed in a suit and tie and an open trench coat, with a shiny brass NYPD police badge attached to his lapel.

"Jack?" I say in the dream, surprised.

"The book you wanted was gone, but this one was there in its place."

He hands me *All This, and Heaven Too.*

How perfect. A real soppy soap opera of a book now given to me on a ship called *Heavenly.*

I laugh. And then I cry.

48

All's Well That Ends

People breakfasting in the dining room are all abuzz. Everyone is talking about last night's storm and the great chase on the Starlight deck. And sure enough, this morning, the weather is gorgeous, as if nothing had ever happened.

As we dip into our oatmeal, the Bingo Dolls barrel toward us. "Where were you?" Judy snaps at us. "We've been looking all over."

Rose says, "Don't you girls ever pick up your phone messages?"

We apologize. "Hey, the storm—" begins Ida.

"Storm, shmorm," says Judy. "Who cares. What matters is you won the big prize." With that, Judy opens her ample bingo bag and spills a thousand dollars in cash onto the table.

We are dumbfounded.

Sophie asks excitedly, "Whose packet won it?"

"Who knows?" says Rose. "You ran off so fast you never marked your names on them."

The girls paw the money happily as the Bingo Dolls watch us with great satisfaction. "You won it on the last coverall."

Evvie smiles. "So how come you told us? You could have kept it all for yourselves."

Rose is insulted. "That would be stealing."

"Just teasing," Evvie says, grinning. "So take your half. That was our deal."

Sophie sputters, wanting to object, but Evvie gives her a dirty look. We all know Sophie will say *she* never made that deal.

The Dolls hesitate. "Take it," Ida insists.

They happily count out their half as Sophie turns away, unable to bear the sight of money being given away. Evvie puts the rest of the bills in her purse.

"So how come you ran off so fast?"

"We had to catch a killer," Bella says brightly.

"Yeah, yeah," says Judy scornfully. "Can't you think of a better excuse?"

"Well, we're off," says Rose. "Aren't you going ashore to see Antigua?"

We look at one another. What with all yesterday's excitement, we never got around to discussing that.

"Probably," says Evvie. "A little later."

"See ya," the Dolls say as they head out. We can hear Rose comment, "I told you they'd share."

Our oatmeal is cold, so we are glad when our

warm scrambled eggs arrive. Just as we're about to dig in, we hear:

"Hey, detectives. How are ya?" Elio and Angelina are hurrying toward us. What's this? Angelina is wearing a yellow pantsuit?

"How are you?" I ask her gently.

She manages a small smile. "Life goes on. Elio went ashore early and bought me this."

"I like color," he says shyly. "And this is for you." Elio whips out a check already filled out. Sophie grabs it, attempts a whistle. It comes out a whoosh. "That's a lot of money."

"You don't owe us anything," I say. I hear Bella and Sophie groan.

"Yes, we do," says Angelina firmly. "If it weren't for you we never would have learned the truth, and he would have gotten away with killing my cousin." She quickly wipes away tears.

"We have news," I say. "The captain called this morning to tell us Bob sang like a canary as soon as they grabbed him. He wants to make a deal, dumping all the others."

"Always thought he was a coward," Elio comments. "Never could figure out what she saw in him. Always dancing around on tippy-toes. What kind of man is that?"

"We're leaving the ship," Angelina adds. "We're taking Amy with us. We need to get home and be with our families."

We get up and take turns hugging the Sicilianos.

"Please stay in touch," I tell them. "I mean it."

"If we don't see you sooner, we'll expect you

for Christmas Day dinner," Elio says. "We throw a hell of a party. And if you play your cards right, there might be a little something under the tree for each of you."

They wave and head out.

We brush away tears. Poor Amy. I wonder if she'll ever get over this trauma. All of it such a sad misunderstanding.

Our eggs are cold.

"I like this," Bella says.

"What? Cold eggs?" Ida asks.

"People coming over and throwing money at us."

Hugo, our gorgeous waiter from Stuttgart, brings us coffee and an assortment of luscious-looking pastries. The girls dig in fast before anyone else can come over to distract us.

"All right," I say. "Thanks to Robert telling the captain all, we finally have the last piece of the puzzle."

Evvie takes a notepad and pen from her purse. "OK, let's get it down." She writes names and draws lines along the names. "Margaret is killed by Tom, Elizabeth's husband. He was a male nurse and knew how to cause a heart attack with a hypo-dermic needle."

"Causing a bubble of air forcing an em-bolism," I add. "Her husband, Dick, gave Tom her golf schedule."

"Okay," says Evvie, making a check mark next to Margaret's name. "Let's call this one Death by Hypo Needle."

Taking another bite of her bear claw, she goes on. "Josephine is killed in her spa by Dick, Margaret's husband, who used to be a plumber."

"Right," I say. "Dick snuck in and rigged the temperature, making the steam so hot it would boil the poor woman. Death by Steam."

Evvie writes. "Elizabeth has an asthma attack brought on by a parrot, urged on by Harry, former veterinary employee and Amy's husband. Obviously her husband, Tom, informed him of Beth's phobia. Death by Parrot."

"And Amy would have been killed in 'an accident' by Bob 'Roberto' Martinson, who knew in advance that she was going on this cruise and got a job as a Latin dance teacher, his former occupation."

Evvie adds, "She would have been Death by Falling off a Cliff."

"Oy," says Bella, "I have such a headache from all this *meshugas*."

"They all used their former talents to do the job," I say. "That's pretty diabolical."

"Yeah. *Strangers on a Train* with special skills." Evvie looks me straight in the eye and says, "It was not about heart attacks, after all."

I know she's referring to our talk about my being obsessed by murder. "Ironic, though. I wouldn't have paid attention if I'd heard they were 'accidents.'" And I think to myself how close I came to not coming along on this trip at all.

"Got it?" Evvie asks the girls.

"No," say Sophie and Bella together.

"So," Ida says to me, ignoring them. "And what about all those coincidences you say you never believe in? Like coming aboard this ship and meeting Amy?"

Says Bella, "And you going to a funeral for a rich dead lady and finding out she's Angelina's cousin?"

"Yeah, and then meeting the Sicilianos in the restaurant in Puerto Rico. We could have been on board the whole trip and never run into them." This from Evvie.

"And then finding out we're all on the same ship," says Ida.

"And us meeting Roberto 'cause we took dance lessons," says Bella. She sighs. "How could such a dreamboat be a killer?"

"And," says Sophie, "my winning a cruise in the first place and the ship turns out to be *this* one."

They all look to me to hear what I say about that. I take a slow bite of my prune Danish. Then a sip of my coffee. "I don't consider any of these coincidences," I say grandly.

"What!" Evvie says in disbelief.

"What!" echo the others.

I wait for a few moments and I smile. "It was all *beshert*."

I don't have to translate for them that "*beshert*" means "meant to be."

Yes, it was definitely meant to be.

Epilogue

Lovers Take Flight

We are in the atrium, with sun hats and cameras, ready to go ashore to visit Antigua. As we glance through colorful brochures, we hear the PA system announce: "Mrs. Gladys Gold and companions, please report to the captain's conference room."

"Now what did we do?" Evvie asks sarcastically.

"Maybe he just wants to have more fun at our expense," I say. I wonder if he's married. Nah! What woman would put up with him? On the other hand, he's got a sense of humor. Weird, but funny.

Bella suggests, "Maybe he has money for us. Everybody else does."

A man in a Dolphins cap hurries to where a small group of passengers are getting checks cashed. "Hey," he says to his friends excitedly, "you gotta see this. There're cops outside."

In a flash, we hurry out after the curious passengers, onto the nearest deck. Sure enough, we are just in time to see Robert Martinson being led into a police car.

The Sicilianos are also there. I can see Elio, being restrained by a policeman, as he shakes his fists and shouts at Bob, but I'm unable to make out his words. I can guess, though.

"Should we go down there?" Evvie asks.

I am torn. I'd like to force pretty-boy "Roberto" into taking another look at the women who brought him down. Gloating would be such fun. But the captain is waiting for us.

"You're not such a great dancer!" Bella yells down at her Roberto. I hope that sad shout eases her disappointment in her idol. Sophie can only turn away.

"Come on, girls. Let's see what new surprise the captain has for us."

There is a surprise. And what a wonderful, unexpected surprise it is. Chatting with Captain Standish are Morrie and Jack. *My* Morrie and Jack! Amy is there, as well, and also the first mate.

Jack and I take one look at one another and ignore our usual caution. We run into each other's arms.

"What are you doing here?" I ask breathlessly.

"I came to keep you from getting into more trouble." His smile could light up the room.

"I'm so sorry I left without calling." I want to run my hands through his hair. I want to touch every part of his face. And more . . . but I don't dare.

"No, I'm the one to be sorry for being so stubborn." He is also restraining himself in front of this group, all of whom watch with great interest. Except for the captain, whose demeanor says he's seen it all.

"No, it's my fault, not yours."

"Kiss him already," says Bella delightedly, "so we can find out what's going on."

And I do. And for once I'm not concerned what my girls might be thinking. And neither is he.

We get a smattering of applause.

"How did you get here?" Evvie wants to know.

"A private plane," says Morrie, "compliments of the Boca Raton police department. They sent us to make sure Martinson gets extradited back to them."

"See, and you guys never believed me." I am quite smug now.

Morrie says, "That's because you're senile and we never listen to old people, let alone women." He grins.

Bella reaches over and gives him a gentle swat on the tush. "Behave yourself." Bella, old family friend of the Langfords, feels she can take this liberty.

Jack chimes in. "Come on, you never believed it yourself at the beginning. In fact, you made the whole thing up just to get attention." He reaches around my waist and holds me tightly. I hope he never lets go.

Morrie says, "I thought you gals would like to know, right now the police in West Palm Beach, Sarasota Springs, and Miami Beach are picking up the husbands of Elizabeth Johnson, Margaret Sampson, and Amy Larkin."

"Is there a reward," Bella asks brightly, "for catching these killers?"

Everyone laughs at this. Except me. I stare at her in sharp reproach. Enough already, Bella.

Morrie takes a check out of his wallet. "As a matter of fact, I've been holding this for you until you got home from your cruise. This is for finding Mrs. Johnson's diamond ring."

"How much?" Both Sophie and Bella chime in on that. Bella's hand shoots out to take the check. She shrugs and grins at me. She's on a roll. Money just keeps pouring in.

"Just one moment," I say coolly. "Who paid this reward?"

"Thomas Johnson, her husband."

"The same Thomas Johnson who murdered Margaret Sampson and arranged for his own wife, Elizabeth, to be killed by Harry Larkin? No, thank you. I call that blood money."

"Spoilsport," Bella whines.

"Give it to charity," Sophie says, mimicking me.

"We were right!" Evvie says excitedly, practically jumping up and down. "The initials on the treasure chest! HL! Harry Larkin."

With that, I dig my elbow into Morrie's stomach. "I told you so!"

"Ouch," says Morrie.

"Next time listen to the old broad."

"Well," says Captain Standish, looking at each of us in turn, "I might thank you for giving us such an exhilarating voyage. Then again I might not." Here goes droll again.

"You'll probably be seeing us on the next bingo cruise," Evvie informs him.

"I can hardly wait." With that he turns and leaves with his first mate. His first mate winks at us behind the captain's back.

There is silence in the room.

"Well," says Ida, "time to go sightseeing." Our man-hater hasn't even peeked at Jack this whole time.

The girls head eagerly for the door. Then they glance back at me. I haven't moved and Jack hasn't let go of me.

Here goes nothing. I take a deep breath. "Would you mind if I left the cruise and went back with Jack? And Morrie?" As if Morrie is supposed to be a chaperone. No one's fooled.

More silence. I almost wish stony Standish was back again to pep things up.

Sophie takes a wild shot. "You'll miss the last bingo day. The big prize is five thousand dollars."

"Go for it," I tell them. "With your winning streak, you're bound to win it. Just remember," I say, staring directly at Sophie, "I'm still your partner."

The girls now look to Evvie. Last chance.

She and I exchange a sisterly look. Time to let go, Ev, is the message I'm sending. She nods. She got it.

"You go on, Glad. You never liked bingo anyway."

"Will you be okay?" This is me to all the girls.

"You think we're kids or something?" Bella says, insulted. "We got maps." She giggles. "And lots of money to spend."

"Yeah," adds Sophie, "we can take care of ourselves."

"Evvie can take your place," says Ida spitefully. Then she smiles a truly loving smile.

"Hey, girls," I say, "one more thing." I speak with great assurance now. "I know how to find out who the Peeping Tom back home is."

"Oh, yeah," says Ida. "How?"

"Remember all the poems crazy Greta Kronk wrote? And her apartment, where we found those drawings of our neighbors that matched the poems on her wall?"

"I remember," says Sophie. " 'Tessie is fat, that's that.' I loved that one."

"So?" Ida is waiting.

"She had one on the wall about someone who was a 'sneaky, peeky.' Anybody remember that?"

A shaking of heads.

"I do, but with my memory, I can't think of who she meant. Good thing we saved all those drawings."

We all hug. They say good-byes to the guys.

And leave. Not even a last look back. They're out of here. And on their own.

Morrie announces tactfully that he'll wait for us downstairs. Then he grins at me.

Finally. "Alone at last," I whisper to Jack.

"Not an easy place to get to."

Another big kiss. When I come up for air, I say, "We better leave before they change their minds. Let's go to my cabin and I'll get my things."

As we head down the corridor to the elevator, Jack says, "I've never seen Antigua. Want to find a place here?"

"No way. Pick somewhere else. Anywhere in the world but here."

Jack is puzzled. "Why?"

"Because they'll find us. I promise you they will. As Evvie likes to say, 'You can run, but you can't hide.'"

As we get into the elevator, I say, "I have something important to tell you."

"I know," he says.

He holds me tightly. I feel the ice around my heart finally begin to melt.

Acknowledgments

Camille Minichino, Jonnie Jacobs, Margaret Lucke, my mystery-writer pals. Thanks for all our "kitchen klatch" sessions, so much fun and so helpful.

Caitlin Alexander for being the perfect editor. Always right on!

Josh Jason and Sharon Propson for guiding me through the perils of PR.

Dick Katz for great last-minute insights.

The Women Who Walk on Water in Wisconsin for being first readers. And to Margaret Sampson, who "gave her life" to Chapter One.

And yes, Judy and Rose again, the bingo *mavens*.

And to the Bingo Dolls, who couldn't come aboard.

And again for all my friends and supporters. You know who you are.

About the Author

Fate (aka, marriage) took Rita Lakin from New York to Los Angeles, where she was seduced by palm trees and movie studios. Over the next twenty years she wrote for television and had every possible job from freelance writer to story editor to staff writer and, finally, producer. She worked on shows such as *Dr. Kildare*, *Peyton Place*, *Mod Squad*, and *Dynasty*, and created her own shows, including *The Rookies*, *Flamingo Road*, and *Nightingales*. She wrote many movies-of-the-week and miniseries, such as *Death Takes a Holiday*, *Women in Chains*, *Strong Medicine*, and *Voices of the Heart*. She has also written the theatrical play *No Language but a Cry* and is the co-author of *Saturday Night at Grossinger's*, both of which are still being produced across the country. Rita has won awards from the Writers Guild of America, as well as the Mystery Writers of America's Edgar Allan Poe Award and the coveted Avery Hopwood Award from the University of Michigan. She lives in Marin County, California. Visit her on the Web at www.ritalakin.com or e-mail her at ritalakin@aol.com.

If you enjoyed
GETTING OLD IS THE
BEST REVENGE,
you won't want to miss
Gladdy Gold's return in

Getting Old Is
Criminal

by

Rita Lakin

Available now from Dell Books

Pick up your copy at your
favorite bookseller.